THE SUGARED GAME

KJ CHARLES

The Sugared Game

Published by KJC Books

Copyright © 2020 by KJ Charles

Edited by Veronica Vega

Cover design by Tiferet Design

ISBN 978-1-912688-17-3

READER ADVISORY

This book contains references to self-harm and miscarriage.

A full list of content warnings is available at my website,
http://kjcharleswriter.com/content-warnings/

For Mum, with thanks for the emergency book surgery!

ONE

W ill Darling was going dancing, and he felt pretty good about it.

With the legal machinery of probate finally ground through, he was the official owner of his deceased uncle's savings as well as his antiquarian and second-hand bookshop. He'd celebrated his new wealth with a spending spree of sorts, and the results were pleasing. Freshly shaved, with his unruly hair combed back ruthlessly and a few months of plentiful food and heavy lifting under his belt, he was in respectable shape, and his nearly-new jacket and well-polished shoes made him feel positively smart.

Not smart like the Smart Set, of course. He wasn't one of those, a fact that had been made abundantly clear to him, but still smart enough to take a fashion-conscious girl to a night-club. It would be nice to be the evening-dress type, rich and sophisticated, of course, just as it would be nice if he knew any girls who had ideas for the evening beyond dancing, but you couldn't have everything. He was solvent, healthy, and going out with his best friend as a thank-you for her unflagging support in some of the hardest times of his life, and all that made him a damned lucky man.

He took the omnibus to Maisie's lodgings. Her landlady, a woman artist who smelled of oil paint, let him in with an admiring look up and down and called out, "Your young man, Miss Jones!"

Maisie emerged into the hall. Will gaped.

Her frock was spectacular. It was silver with crimson fringes that shimmered over her at the tiniest movement, the colour contrast dramatic against her warm brown skin, and short enough to reveal most of a pair of plump and shapely calves. As if that wasn't enough flesh, it was also cut low at the front, and Maisie had a lot of front. Rather than a hat, she wore a wide silver headband with crimson silk rosebuds over her black marcelled waves; even her heeled shoes were silver. She was painted and lipsticked to the manner born, and looked like the brightest possible Young Person.

"You'll catch flies," Maisie told him with some satisfaction.

His mouth was indeed open. "Blimey." He struggled for words. "*Blimey*."

"You look all right yourself."

Will looked fine. Maisie *glowed*. He cleared his throat and said, "We'll get a taxi-cab."

"We can get the bus from here, can't we?"

"Not in that frock," he said firmly. "You deserve a taxi." Plus, if she showed that much leg on public transport, there might be a brawl. A riot, even.

He glanced at her as the taxi-cab took them through Piccadilly, bright and garish with the electric lights of advertisements blurred by the drizzle on the windows. "You really do look marvellous. I'm sorry I'm not smarter."

"Don't be silly, you look very nice. I thought I'd dress up a bit for this place, that's all. Are you sure it's all right, going here?"

"Of course it is. You deserve it."

Will was taking her to the High-Low Club. He'd never heard of it, but he wasn't a night-club sort of man; he'd simply asked her where she'd like to go for the evening out he owed her, and she'd named this on the grounds of having a voucher for free champagne. "Have you been before?"

She shook her head. "I've wanted to. Phoebe's been. Apparently the band is wonderful and it's awfully glamorous in a seedy way. There's all sorts of desperate characters as well as the Smart Set."

That didn't sound much of a recommendation to Will. "Do I count as a desperate character?"

"Only if I can be a gangster's moll."

The taxi stopped on Maddox Street. Will paid, and helped Maisie out. She really was showing a great deal of leg.

The High-Low Club didn't look like much from the outside: a tall, thin house that presented only a closed door to the world. This was opened by a large, suited doorman at Will's knock, and they descended a rather narrow and poorly lit flight of stairs down to the basement. If Will hadn't been able to hear the distant blare of the band, he'd have suspected they were about to be mugged.

The stairs led into a little cloakroom area, where they handed over their hats and coats and went through a set of double doors to the main room.

The music hit them with a blast as they entered. A band played at the far end, loud and frenetic, and the floor was filled with bright-coloured women and monochrome men, moving frantically to the rapid rhythms. It was an astonishingly tall space, the full height of the house, with two rows of gilt-railed balconies going round the walls. The lower balcony, at the level where a ceiling probably used to be, was supported by pillars all round the edges of the dance floor, and filled with people who talked, strolled, or leaned over the rails to watch the dancing. The top balcony, another normal room's height above, seemed to have mostly people sitting at tables. It was all cleverly lit with electric, giving just enough light to make the dance floor glitter.

"Oh, this is lovely," Maisie said. "What fun!"

A man approached. He wore a harlequin of a jacket of which some panels were white, and others a lurid striped green and pink material. If this was the new fashion, Will was leaving London and going back north right now. He heard Maisie inhale.

"Dancing, sir?"

"Sorry?"

The hideously-dressed man indicated the balcony. "Upstairs for conversation, down for dancing."

"Oh! Dancing, please."

The waiter conducted them to a table half way down the room, which made it just possible to speak over the music and the shouted conversations and raucous laughter from other tables. "And to drink, sir?"

"We've a voucher for a bottle of champagne," Maisie said, flourishing it. Will felt a bit of a skinflint, since he was taking her out and should be paying for everything, but Maisie was a frugal soul and, as she'd said, the voucher was no other use.

He glanced round while they waited for their drinks. There were a couple of well-dressed Indian men visible, plus the band, all of whom were black men, but the rest of the clientele was entirely white. He and Maisie had always gone dancing further east, where the dance-halls were a lot more mixed. He hoped she didn't feel looked at.

She seemed comfortable enough as she looked around with a calculating expression. Taking in the posh frocks, no doubt. Will assessed the room, trying to work out the point of the balconies. There seemed to be two spiral stairs from the floor to the top level, catercorner from one another. Both had a moderate flow of people going up and down. The lower of the two balconies was blocked midway on the back wall by a room with large glass windows overlooking the dance floor. Windows *inside* a house; what a thing. He supposed it would be the manager's office.

"What do you think?" he asked Maisie in the subdued shout required for conversation.

"Very grand," she said. "Except the waiters' uniforms, goodness me. How are you getting on, Will? I haven't seen you properly in ages."

"I've been pretty busy. Lots to do. I cleared myself a room to sleep in."

"How'd you manage that? Throw away all the books?"

"A fair few of them. I sold a pile as job lots to get them out of the shop, did some shifting of the rest—found a few good things in there—and now I have a proper bedroom above the shop. I even bought furniture."

"Look at you, Mr. Fancy."

"The best part is having a proper bed that doesn't fold up and drop you on the floor. I'd forgotten what it was like not to wake up with backache."

"And are books selling well, to pay for all this extravagance?"

"Some. More as I get the hang of it. How are hats doing? I like your thing." He indicated her headband. "Very smart."

Maisie, a milliner, took that as her due. "Thanks. I'm pleased with it. Phoebe loves it."

"Seen much of her?"

She beamed, a look of far more happiness than the casual enquiry merited. "We had lunch just yesterday, actually but I'll tell you about it when we've our drinks. She was asking me if you'd seen anything of Kim. Lord Arthur, I mean," she added conscientiously.

"Kim," Will said, because the title grated on his nerves. "Why doesn't she ask him?"

"*I* don't know," Maisie said. "She said he's been awfully funny, and not around much, and I said was there anything up, because the last time he disappeared off for days, well…"

She let that trail invitingly. Last time Kim had disappeared off for days, he'd been attempting to rescue Will, who had been kidnapped and held prisoner. Maisie adored the pulp serials, and remained bitterly envious that her involvement had been only tangential.

"Don't look at me," Will said. "I've no idea what he's up to. I haven't heard from him since I don't know when."

He knew exactly when: the second of January. It was currently the twenty-second of February. That was a sore point he had no desire at all to discuss, so he added, "I'm not sure if he ever uses the title. It's not compulsory, is it, if it's one of those whatsits?"

"Courtesy titles."

"I don't follow how those work."

"*Well*," Maisie said, taking the bait. "If you're a duke or a marquess, your oldest son borrows one of your titles, like Kim's brother is Viscount Chingford. Then your other children are called Lord or Lady with their Christian name, Lord Arthur and Lady Jane. The younger ones don't get any extra names, it's just a politeness to show who their father is."

"So if my old man was the Duke of Northants, I'd be Lord William Darling?"

"No, because you're an only child, aren't you? So you'd use a spare title he had lying around. Where is it you're from again?"

"Bugbrooke."

"You'd be Viscount Bugbrooke, imagine. I *wish* you were a lord." She switched to a terrifyingly upper-class accent. "'Oh, how mahvellous, Bugbrooke, old chap!' Except you'd probably say it Booray or some such if you were posh. Do you know how Phoebe's father's house is spelled and pronounced? You wouldn't guess it in a million years."

"You're Welsh," Will pointed out. "You've got no room to talk about spelling."

"Nothing wrong with Welsh spelling, thank you," Maisie said, with an edge on her accent.

"Come off it. You put two 'l's in everything and don't say any of them."

She stuck out her tongue. "You'll be sorry when my da is Marquess of Cardiff. Pronounced Caff."

"What would that make you? Lady Jones?"

"Lady Maisie Jones, but you can call me Lady Maisie." She sighed wistfully. "If only he'd gone into aristocracy instead of down the docks."

They laughed over that as the champagne arrived. The waiter made a production of opening it and pouring Maisie a foaming glassful, and by then her original question was entirely forgotten, which was a relief. Maisie was his best friend, but she was still a nice girl from Cardiff and there were some things Will couldn't talk to her about, no matter how much he'd have liked to.

He would have liked to very much. He wanted to tell her the truth, to have someone who'd give him good, sensible, measured advice, while also being entirely on his side. He couldn't risk it. That had felt increasingly like lying for a while now, but he simply didn't know how she'd react if she knew he was—well, not queer exactly, since he liked women very well. Open-minded? Whatever you called it, it wasn't a topic he could throw into the conversation and expect things to end well.

Anyway, they scarcely needed to discuss it since he hadn't so much as seen Kim in close on two months, so it hardly bloody mattered.

He forced that train of thought to a jarring halt. He was a blasted lucky man, and out with a girl who deserved a good time. That was a lot more important than an unreliable aristocrat who'd dropped him like a hot potato when he was no longer entertaining.

The waiter finished faffing about with the champagne. Will raised his glass and clinked it to Maisie's. "Here's to you. Best dressed woman in the room."

She gave a little shimmy that made the dress move intriguingly. "Do you really like it?"

Will began to give an 'of course' sort of reply, but managed to stop. Maisie knew he was an ignoramus when it came to clothes, so she didn't want a meaningless endorsement; she wanted moral support. "Can I have another look?"

Maisie checked she wouldn't bump into anyone, then stood and stepped back from the table. Will took her in, impressed. The frock was so stylish that he'd have thought she'd borrowed it from Phoebe, except Phoebe was the sort of tall, slim build that modern times were made for. She was very fine indeed, and he noticed a couple of admiring glances from their fellow customers, which might be for the dress, the curves it flattered, or the leg it revealed.

Any man would like it, he thought, or at least any man who liked ample bosoms. The fashion demanded women should be shaped like boys, skinny ones at that, and dresses went straight up and down accordingly, which didn't usually do much for curvier bodies. Maisie wasn't straight up and down from any angle, and her dress emphasised that in a way he could only appreciate.

"It's marvellous," he said. "You look top notch. Divine, darling." He imitated Phoebe, which made Maisie giggle. "What I like is, it's not exactly the usual sort of"—he mimed a tube—"but it still looks right for the fashion, only it's right for you. Does that make sense?"

"*Thank* you," Maisie said. "That was what I meant to do. It's ridiculous to squeeze women my shape into styles that don't suit, and I shan't follow some absurd grapes-and-water diet to whittle myself down to a stick. You need to dress for your own body, not pretend you've someone else's, don't you think?"

"Quite right. I wouldn't be seen dead in a flapper dress."

Maisie cackled. "I should hope not, with your shoulders. Well, I ask you: Phoebe said the other day that frocks now would suit Kim better than me, and what does *that* say?"

Will had a sudden picture of Kim in a flapper dress. He'd probably wear something shimmery in purple, and it probably *would* look good on his tall, slender frame, for a value of 'good' that Will didn't want to consider too closely. Phoebe would doubtless dress him up if he wanted, and Will felt a ridiculous pang of envy at that, because Kim and Phoebe loved each other so much that it hurt to be on the outside of it, looking in.

"It does seem a bit silly," he said. "After all, most women have, you know." He started to mime again and thought better of it. "Chests."

"Exactly, so someone ought to be making dresses that don't pretend we're a completely different shape that doesn't *work*. Sorry, I'm going on. I know you don't care about this."

"You listen to me talk about football."

"Which isn't easy, I can tell you."

"And that's not even my job, unlike you. Well, hats are your job—" Something clicked into place. "Wait a minute. Maisie, did you make that dress yourself?"

Maisie flushed. "It's my own design."

"That is cracking. Absolutely first rate. Have you shown Phoebe?"

Her cheeks darkened even more. "This is what I wanted to tell you about. I've been waiting to say in case it didn't come off, but I've been working on ideas for a while now, and I showed her them back in December, and Will, she loved them. She gave me some notes and we've come up with some more designs together, and she's going to take them to people. *We're* going to. You know she was a mannequin for Worth once, and she's friends with Lanvin—Jeanne Lanvin!—and Edward Molyneux?" She wriggled. "It's too exciting. And she's got marvellous ideas and knows such a lot and has such a good eye and she really thinks people would want my designs. That I could do it, that we might be able to do something together. And she asked her father, and he's going to lend her, lend *us* money to start up a venture!"

"Maisie Jones!"

"I know! And of course I'm not setting my heart on it working, but—well, it's worth a try, isn't it?"

"Of course it is," Will said. "Look at you, the newest Bright Young Person. This is wonderful."

"Touch wood." Maisie rapped the table. "We'll see, but I'm so excited. And look at you, with your own business and a house and everything. We're doing all right, aren't we?"

"Not bad for a couple of bumpkins up from the country." Will raised his glass again, and Maisie met it with hers. "Cheers."

They talked her plans through as they finished their glasses and had another, then Will led her onto the dance floor. The band was as good as he'd ever heard, and they danced for a solid half hour. Will loved dancing. He found it easy to lose himself in action, focusing on nothing but the movements of his own body and that of his partner, fitting together without the need for words.

Finally, too soon, the music came to a stop and they halted in a swirl of silver and crimson. Maisie beamed up at him.

"Excuse me." It was a woman standing next to her. "May I ask, *where* did you get that divine frock?"

"Maison Zie," Maisie said immediately. "This is an early model." She spoke in cut-glass English, disturbingly like Phoebe's accent, with no hint of her usual Welsh lilt. Will clamped his expression into the poker face he'd learned in the army.

"*Really*. And where—" The other woman leaned in to ask more, her attention clearly snagged, and a couple of other ladies gathered round. Will glanced over to see the musicians taking a well-earned breather. He caught Maisie's eye, jerked his head to indicate he was going off to find the lavatories, and received a tiny nod.

He wasn't sure where the facilities were, so he headed towards the back of the building. It was crowded, and very noisy. He weaved his way through the crowd, glanced around involuntarily as someone shrieked in his ear, and almost walked into one of the horribly-jacketed waiters. The man uttered a muffled curse and staggered back, grabbing at his salver to prevent the bottles on it from going flying.

"Sorry!" Will said. "I'm awfully sorry, that was my— *Sir?*"

The waiter's eyes snapped to his. They stared at one another with horrified recognition.

"Good God," the waiter said. "Darling? I mean, I beg your pardon, sir."

"Don't." Will had no idea what else to say, because the man in front of him, weary-eyed in his garish coat, was Lieutenant Michael Beaumont, who he had served with in Flanders.

He'd been a friendly young soul when he arrived in the trenches in '16, as naive as any other boy fresh from public school, but not too proud to learn from hardened men like Will, who was older by two years on paper and, by then, about two decades in experience. Beaumont had made a reasonable fist of things, and been a good fellow as brass went. But he was still an officer, a giver of orders, of a different class to the enlisted men. And here he was now, working as a waiter while Will drank champagne.

He wanted to say *What happened?*, but he could doubtless guess. Times were hard, jobs were scarce, land taxes and death duties had hit the upper classes to shattering effect. You heard stories of men getting into taxis driven by their old commanding officers, or going to a West End theatre for a night out and seeing them dancing on the stage. This was the first such encounter for Will, and he felt embarrassed on Beaumont's behalf and his own.

Beaumont gave him a brief, awkward smile. "You look well."

"Thanks. Yes. I, uh, I have my own business now."

"Congratulations."

Will scrabbled for something polite to say in return. "Have you been working here long?"

"A year or so. Needs must."

"It's rotten finding anything these days. I had a devil of a time before I got my shop."

"You look prosperous enough." Beaumont winced, as if he'd realised that sounded ungracious. "Which is jolly good. Look, I must dash, old chap—sir. The customers want their fizz."

"Wait. Can you stop for a drink?"

"More than my job's worth, I'm afraid. I can't just stand around and chat."

"How about lunch?"

Beaumont blinked. Will would have blinked in his position. He hadn't been a *how about lunch?* sort of man back in the trenches; he'd have suggested a pint, if anything, but probably he wouldn't even have thought of asking because Beaumont had been his superior. This was what mixing with the upper classes did to you.

"Well," Beaumont said. "Yes, why not?"

They quickly fixed up a time, choosing dinner rather than lunch because of Beaumont's peculiar schedule, and he went off with his silver salver laden with bottles. All champagne, Will noted, and the club charged thirty shillings for a bottle of the sweet, tinny stuff that couldn't have cost them ten. Nice work if you could get it.

He made his way to the gentlemen's facilities. The band had struck up again when he returned, and Maisie was dancing with a very youthful-looking man. Will didn't feel quite like finding another girl; he felt uncomfortable and self-conscious knowing his old officer was heaving trays around, pouring champagne for other people. He filled his glass and watched for a while, then decided to head up the stairs for a nosey around the balconies.

He went up at a leisurely sort of pace. The lower balcony was busy with chattering groups, except for a clear space between the staircase and the door of the office room. The tables up here were swanky marble-topped ones, heavier than the flimsy things downstairs, presumably in order that people didn't move them around. Will carried on up to the higher balcony.

This was a lot less crowded, and a lot of the conversations up here seemed to happen with heads together. It looked to be where Maisie's desperate characters gathered: there were some obvious tough customers, including a group in flash check suits talking louder than they needed to, much as if inviting other people to be annoyed by them.

Will took an empty table and sat down with his champagne to watch. The flash lot laughed raucously. A smarmy-looking bloke at the far end of the balcony was visited by three separate Bright Young People in ten minutes, each of them looking as though they wanted something rather urgently. It was fascinating people-watching, and he was startled when a voice by his elbow said, "Good evening, sir. May I join you?"

Will turned to see a tall, broad, powerfully built man of about forty, with a raddled look that spoke of late nights in smoky rooms, and the sort of very even, very white teeth that came out of a cardboard box. Will gestured to a free chair without enthusiasm, wondering if he was about to be touched for a drink.

"Thank you. My name's Fuller, Desmond Fuller."

"Evening," Will said, not troubling to sound welcoming. He'd taken against the teeth.

Fuller pulled out the chair and sat, apparently unsnubbed. "This is your first visit, I think?"

That suggested either Fuller was a habitué of the High-Low, or he worked here. "That's right. I heard good things of the band. All true."

"Mrs. Skyrme prides herself on quality in all she does. No

expense spared. She looks after her customers, and I look after her."

That sounded slightly like a threat, somehow. Will gave him a neutral sort of nod. "Is that the proprietor?"

"That's right. She takes a close personal interest in every part of the club." Fuller smiled, revealing his white teeth again. "I'm sure you'll meet her later. It's a busy night."

"I'd be glad to make her acquaintance. Are you management?"

"The floor manager. Second in command, though not a close second." Fuller gave a practised chuckle at what was clearly a standard line.

"Floor and balconies, I suppose," Will said, since they were doing weak jokes. "Interesting layout this place has. Did Mrs. Skyrme have it done?"

"The building was being gutted anyway. She's a remarkable thinker. A born night-club proprietor, nothing but the best. And you, sir. Are you here for the dancing?" Will nodded. "With the young lady in the remarkable dress." Fuller glanced down at the floor, where Maisie was happily shimmying with a different young man. "Is she a regular partner of yours?"

Will prickled instantly. It was something in the man's tone, the hint of quotation marks around 'partner'. "What's it to you?"

Fuller gave him a men-of-the-world smile. "We like to get to know our guests. It helps us provide what you want."

That sounded like an offer. Of girls, or perhaps dope: Will wouldn't put much past this chap, based on very little more than the instant personal dislike. "All I want is a place to take my girl dancing and have a drink without watching the clock."

Fuller's smile suggested complicity. "We remain hospitable at all times."

"How do you manage that? Because I've no desire to find myself in the dock in the morning."

"We take great care to keep on the right side of the law. No need to worry, Mr...?" He paused invitingly.

"Darling. Will Darling."

Fuller's eyes snapped to his. "Mr. Darling. I *see*. How good to meet you, Mr. Darling. And are you here on business?"

Will looked around. It was still a night-club. "I'm here for an evening out. Is that a problem?"

"We encourage a little separation between the levels. Private conversations on this balcony. So if you're just here for the dancing, you can rejoin your young lady now."

Well, that was him told. Will had absolutely no desire to move now he'd been ordered to, but he could see Maisie heading back to their table down below, so he made himself nod and stand.

Fuller gave him a toothy smile, and followed him back down to the ground floor where Maisie waited. He greeted her with ostentatious politeness. "Good evening, miss, and may I say how delightful it is to have such a fashionable young lady here. I hope you're enjoying the High-Low."

"It's lovely, thank you. I'm having the most delightful time."

Fuller stayed for a few moments more, larding her with fulsome compliments interspersed with enquiries about what clubs she usually frequented. At last he left, shaking Will's hand and bowing to Maisie.

She scootched her chair closer so she could speak in Will's ear. "Who was that ghastly man?"

"The manager."

"What was he up to?"

"Not a clue. He chucked me off the upper balcony. Well, not off. Out of."

"You wouldn't want off," Maisie agreed, glancing up. "Why?"

"That's where the trouble is. There's a dope dealer at work, plain as day, and a set of racecourse terrorists if I'm any judge."

"No!"

"And the manager fellow knows all about it. He came to snout out what I was doing up there and gave me my marching orders when I said I wasn't on business. This place is a pit."

"How shocking! Goodness me."

She looked thrilled, which was fair enough. Half the fun of this sort of place was seeing people behaving badly, at either end of the social scale. "Apart from that, how's your evening?"

"Wonderful. I've had five compliments on my dress, three requests for the name of the designer, and two indecent proposals."

"What?"

"Don't get on your high horse. Except if a fish-faced twerp in a blue blazer comes over here, you can get on your high horse with him any time. How about you?"

"I served with one of the waiters. He was an officer of my battalion."

"Goodness! Really?"

"Lieutenant. I used to call him sir, and now he's serving the champagne and I'm drinking it. It's pretty odd. I've arranged to have dinner with him. He couldn't stop and talk."

"Well, no, not while he's working," Maisie said. "We don't all have customers who like us to be rude. Shall we have another dance?"

They had several. Will was thirsty when they returned to their table at last, and tired of the cloying champagne. He ordered a beer, and a gin and tonic for Maisie. These arrived shortly, and so did a woman—middle aged, with brass-blonde hair, many strings of clashing beads, elbow-length satin gloves, and a frock made of layers of satin and net. She sat down uninvited, announcing, "Hello, I'm Theresa Skyrme," and smiled, red-lipped, at Maisie.

"Mrs. Skyrme?" Will said. "The owner here, yes?"

"That's right. So nice to meet you, Mr. Darling. And this is Miss...?"

"Jones."

"Miss *Jones*," Mrs. Skyrme said, giving a strong impression of amusement at a lazily chosen alias. "I don't think we've seen you here before, Mr. Darling?"

"First time."

"How charming of you to honour us with your custom."

She was still smiling, but Will would have put money the words were sarcastic. He could see Maisie's brows drawing together. "You're welcome," he said, and wondered what the hell sort of place they were in.

"Mr. Fuller tells me you were on the upper balcony," the lady continued. "Some people prefer the view from up there. Was there anything you wanted to see?"

"I like watching people. You've got an interesting sort of clientele here."

Her lips curved, but her eyes sharpened. "Oh, we have some wonderful visitors from all walks of life. Were you hoping to meet Brilliant Chang? Wally Bunker, perhaps? You never know: you might even bump into Tommy Telford some time."

Will met Maisie's eyes. She gave a tiny, baffled shrug. "Sorry, I don't know any of those people."

"What is it you do, Mr. Darling?"

"I run a bookshop."

"A bookshop," she repeated. "How lovely. And you like watching people. Do you have the chance to do much of that in your bookshop?"

"You'd be surprised." She was giving him the same grating feeling he'd had from Fuller, a sensation of hostile cross-examination. Maybe they had to be careful about their clientele; he didn't care. "It was nice to meet you, Mrs. Skyrme, but we won't take up any more of your time. Goodbye."

Mrs. Skyrme took that heavy hint and left with more protestations of how delightful it was to meet them both, and a last pat on Will's arm, assuring him, "I hope you'll tell your friends *all* about us."

Maisie took a long swallow of her gin and tonic. "What a dreadful woman."

"Rotten," Will agreed. "I don't like this place, Maise. The band's good, but I don't care for the management one bit."

"Let's not come here again. Are you sorry I picked it?"

"Course not. As long as you've had a good time, that's what matters."

She smiled at him. "It's been marvellous."

TWO

W ill met Beaumont for dinner a few days later. He looked worse under the brighter lights of the Lyons Corner House: the youthful good looks Will remembered from Flanders had been defeated by time and the ravages of late nights and cigarette smoke. Still, he wore a genuine smile as he approached the table, and they shook hands like old friends.

The conversation started off in the usual manner: listing of the dead and the scattered living, with suitable noises of commiseration.

"Do you recall Bill Taylor, Captain Taylor?"

"Poor old chap. Didn't he go to some shell-shock recovery place?"

"It didn't do much good. His family got him a couple of posts when he was out of hospital but he couldn't hold anything down. Blew his brains out at the end of last year."

"God."

"Not the land of milk and honey we were promised, is it?" Beaumont made a face. "I'm glad to see you well. How did you come to have a bookshop? I didn't have you down as a reading man."

Will gave a brief account of the miseries of his long unemployment, and the stroke of luck that had been reconciling with his long-estranged uncle. "He was delighted to see me. He was old and ill by then, and he'd never married. He gave me work, and said he'd teach me the trade, but then he fell sick."

"That's a shame."

"It was. I wish I'd known him better. But I was there to look after him in his last days. And he left me everything."

"I say!"

"Not that it's untold riches," Will hastened to add. "But the shop's a going concern and he owned the building, so I've a secure roof over my head. I'm blasted lucky."

"All right for some. Remember Captain Yoxall? He's an earl now, lucky blighter. I wish *I* had a wealthy relative on his deathbed."

Will wasn't sure how to respond to that. Beaumont made a face. "Sorry, I'm sure you weren't glad your uncle popped off. All the same, though—"

"I know what you meant," Will assured him, rather than waiting for him to dig himself further into that hole. "What's it like at the club?"

"Oh, I make ends meet. Awful hours, and the pay's only adequate, but the tips are astonishing. Bring some American bootlegger or South African diamond nabob a bottle of sweet fizz, bow and scrape a bit, and he might leave a fiver on the table. Not what I thought I'd be doing after the war but needs must."

"It seemed a bit of an odd place," Will suggested.

"How'd you mean?"

"Well, I can't say I took to that chap Fuller."

"Oh, God, who would." Beaumont gave a short laugh.

"And I went up to the top level and there were some pretty unsavoury characters there."

"It's a sink. A classy sink, one of the classiest, but there's night-clubs and night-clubs, and the High-Low is definitely the latter, if you follow me. There's two dope dealers who work alternating nights so the Smart Set can get their pick-me-up, and there's always one East End gang or another sniffing around looking for trouble."

"I saw some of them. Isn't that a bit of a problem?"

Beaumont puffed out his cheeks. "Not so much now. Those chaps you saw are Wally Bunker's lot, Mrs. Skyrme's pet gangsters. She has them around because of last year. We had a pack of thugs descend on us, smashed up the place one Saturday, and swaggered in the next to demand drinks on the house all night if we didn't want them to do it again. It's a hazard of the business, but they didn't reckon with Fuller. He had a set of his own thugs waiting for them and there was the devil of a scrap. He was wielding an iron bar, for God's sake. Caught one chap and broke his arm in three places."

"Are you serious?"

"Damned right. We didn't have any more trouble out of them, and Mrs. Skyrme brought in Bunker and his pals as regulars so it didn't happen again. Even she thought Fuller had gone overboard."

"Sounds nasty."

"He plays the smarmy floor manager well enough but he's a mad dog when she lets him off the leash. I recall when he found out some scrap of a barman was pocketing change—a matter of shillings, but it took two of us to pull him off the poor little sod. Flanders was a rest cure by comparison. I must say, I envy your bookshop. It would be nice to have a bit of peace and quiet."

Will agreed to this, rather than listing the multiple acts of violence that had taken place in or around his bookshop last year. Beaumont prodded unenthusiastically at his food. "So, that girl you were with, in the dress. Is that a serious sort of thing?"

"She's not my girl. We're just friends."

"Oh. Why's that?"

In part it was because Will had been down to his last shillings at the time things could have gone down that path, and by the time he was solvent enough to ask her out without losing his self-respect, their relationship had grown into a quite different shape. He didn't feel like explaining that. "She's the modern sort. Not interested in settling down. She's starting her own business."

"Good Lord. Do you ever have the feeling the whole world changed while we were away and nobody bothered to mention it to us?"

"All the time."

"And it changed us," Beaumont pressed on, staring at his plate. "One forgets how much. Do you know what I mean? I've gone about my business as best I can, day by day, and then I see someone from the old days and I suddenly think, what would I, the man I was back then, have made of me now? If you'd told me at demob *this* was where I'd be in five years—"

"It's not that bad," Will said, hoping to cut him off. "At least you're working. I'd have carried bricks or dustbins if anyone had let me, so champagne seems pretty good." That got a weak sort of smile. "We're doing the best we can. That's something to be proud of, isn't it?"

"Is it? How old are you, Darling?"

"Twenty-seven."

"And not married? Is there anyone special, if it isn't the armful in the dress?"

That was another question Will had absolutely no desire to answer. He took a mouthful of steak and kidney pie to give himself time.

Kim Secretan had unquestionably been special. They'd met back in November, in the course of dramatic events that had involved Will antagonising a criminal gang and upsetting the War Office, and they'd fit together. They didn't belong together—Will was a plain man with a knack for violence, while Kim was a twisty upper-class bundle of nerves—but they'd *fit*.

Will had walked out with a few girls, and had a few encounters with men during the war, but the intense crackle of attraction with Kim had been something altogether new to him: an overwhelming physical pull combined with a deep, instinctive liking. It had been an intoxicating combination of meeting minds and bodies and desires almost overwhelming in its power, right up until he'd discovered just how much Kim was lying to him.

And afterwards, if he was honest. Kim had lied and lied and lied again, and Will had fucked him in the full knowledge that he was a lying bastard. You might even have called it making love during one long, strange night for the pleasure they'd taken in pleasing one another, right before Kim had saved his neck and betrayed him all over again.

They'd fought, with each other and with their joint enemies; they'd fucked; they'd killed. When it was all over they'd gone to the pub once or twice, had another night together. It had felt like something that might go somewhere. Like a beginning.

Will hadn't thought twice when Kim had said he was leaving London to stay with Phoebe's family for a week around Christmas: that was what posh people did. And he'd returned promptly enough, dropping into the bookshop on the second of January, supposedly to offer belated compliments of the season though within about four sentences he was on his knees, pleasuring Will in the back room. It had been spectacular stuff, raw desire played out in desperate, panting silence, leaving Will with a dozen finger-mark bruises on his hips and a glowing warmth that was to do with more than just an excellent Frenching.

And then Kim had said, as he was leaving, "I expect to be rather busy in the near future," and that was it.

Will hadn't seen him since. Kim hadn't answered his telephone when Will had called to say he'd had his own 'phone installed, and he hadn't replied to either of the messages Will had left with his manservant. The only reason Will knew the bastard wasn't dead was that Phoebe would probably have mentioned it, since she was engaged to marry him in summer. He'd vanished like a ghost, leaving Will to realise how little there was between them: a lot of lies, a few fucks, a thread of intimacy and liking far too fragile to weave into anything that might cover the gaps.

He hated that this was still such a sore point. Kim had ended things, by deed if not word, close to two months ago. He ought to be no more than a pleasant memory by now, or an unpleasant one, depending on which part of their acquaintance Will was thinking about. He bitterly resented his continual awareness of Kim's absence, that he still thought about their three nights together when he was taking matters into his own hands, that he wanted to know why he'd been treated with such indifference.

That last was particularly stupid. Of course Kim had buggered off as unpredictably as he'd appeared, because he was an untrustworthy shit and a lord. There had never been any other possible outcome. Only, while he was around, he'd given Will a taste for starlight.

He'd finished his mouthful some time ago, and Beaumont was looking at him with a raised eyebrow. Will made himself smile. "Sorry. There was someone a bit ago. Didn't work out."

"That's a shame. Wrong girl, or right girl, wrong time?"

"Oh, everything wrong. Absolutely everything, right from the start. I should have known."

"No, you shouldn't," Beaumont said with startling vehemence. "We don't think about what's wrong when we meet someone special, do we? When you find someone who's absolutely, utterly right except for that thing that makes it wrong, you'd have to be some sort of plaster saint to resist, and why the devil should we? We've only the one life and we damn near lost that in Flanders, you and I. Why shouldn't we live now?"

Will gaped at him for a second, bewildered at what he could

possibly know, before he realised. "You mean you've met the wrong girl? Or is it the right one?"

"The utterly right girl, at the worst possible time. Oh Lord. What am I going to do?"

Will gave a small internal sigh, but there was only one thing he could say. "Do you want to talk about it?"

He walked home to stretch his legs. It was cold and wet in the drizzly way of London Februaries, but the exercise was a relief.

He hadn't spent time with an old comrade in while, and he rather thought he might not seek that out again. Beaumont was a reasonable sort of chap, if a bit inclined to moan, but they had nothing in common except their service and they'd both known it. He'd taken the opportunity to pour out his heart precisely because he expected not to see Will again, much as a man might confess all to a stranger on a train.

Will could see the appeal of that. He'd have loved to have someone nod along to his own complaints and agree that Kim was a disgraceful unreliable swine who was entirely at fault for the whole thing. He couldn't do that, so he'd played the sympathetic ear for Beaumont and got the expected story: an affair with a married woman who couldn't divorce her husband for reasons Will hadn't listened to. His mind had been elsewhere. It was both enraging and predictable where his mind had been.

Kim had disappeared from his life by choice. He'd decided Will was no longer interesting or useful or whatever it was, and he'd gone without troubling to say farewell. And if Will had been able to spill that out to Beaumont, he'd doubtless have sounded every bit as pathetic as his old lieutenant, whining about what might feel like a grand passion to the participants, but looked to anyone else just like every other sordid affair. It was a good thing for his self-respect that caution and the law had kept his mouth shut.

He was nearly home, and he didn't feel like going home. He surely deserved some sort of redress for what had been a rather disheartening evening, so he nipped into the Black Horse on the corner of May's Buildings. A pint, a game of darts, and a chat about the football scores would be just what the doctor ordered.

It did indeed make him feel better, so much that he stayed for another pint and didn't head down May's Buildings till past ten. The alley where his bookshop lurked was an obscure little passage off St. Martin's Lane, still not blessed by street lighting. Will let himself in the front door by feel and didn't put on the electric, not being made of money. He made his way through the maze of shelves and books to the back room, let himself into the yard to use the outhouse, locked the door again behind him, and headed up the stairs.

And stopped on the first turn, because there was a light on in his bedroom.

Zodiac, was his first and instant thought. He retreated three silent steps backwards, giving that urgent consideration.

Zodiac was behind the trouble he'd had in November, an organised criminal gang operating at a disturbingly high level. He'd killed one of their members and been instrumental in putting a stop to a very nasty scheme. They hadn't sought vengeance yet, but the thought they might was never far below the surface of his mind.

There was no reason they'd come for him now. It might just as well be burglars, except that his front and back doors had both been locked. Most likely he'd simply left the light on.

All the same, he backtracked soundlessly to his desk and picked up the Messer, his old trench knife, which he'd taken from a German sentry once he'd ensured the man would have no further use for it. Like him, it was a practical relic of the war: it had an eight-inch blade that took a razor edge, and if he'd been the sort who notched the handle for every kill, it would have looked like fretwork.

Knife in hand, he slid back up the stairs, avoiding the points that creaked, with a flutter of the old excitement in his gut. He paused outside the bedroom door and listened.

Not a sound. He was probably making a fool of himself over a forgotten light, though at least there would be nobody here to see him do it. Still, no point taking a risk. He adjusted his grip on the Messer, narrowed his eyes against the light, and slammed the door wide open.

It bounced off the wall, rather than hitting anyone on its way there. Will took two quick steps forward, keeping his back to the wall and the knife out, and scanned the room.

There was a man sitting in his armchair, reading one of his books. As Will stared he looked up, gave a quick flick of a smile, and unhurriedly marked his place with the dustjacket flap.

"What the bloody hell," said Will.

"Good evening," said Kim.

THREE

Will gaped at him, lost for words. Kim raised a brow. "Do you always enter bedrooms so dramatically?"

"I thought you were Zodiac. What's wrong with the front door?"

"I didn't want to announce my presence to anyone else."

"Why not? What are you doing here? And come to that, how did you get in?"

"Your back window."

"Again? For crying out loud. I only took the nails out last week!"

"For which I'm glad," Kim said. "It would have been unsubtle to smash it, and defeated my purpose."

Will glowered at him. "Which was what?"

"Getting in here without anyone noticing me."

"It's a shop. You can walk in without anyone paying attention all the time. *I* wouldn't pay attention if you walked in."

"You're a born bookseller," Kim agreed. "Sadly, I need to be a bit more careful than that."

That wasn't greatly surprising. As Will understood it, and subject to the very real possibility that Kim had misled him, he solved problems in secretive ways for British Intelligence in one form or another. "Who is it now? Zodiac? Did you annoy the Reds? Or is the War Office fed up of you? I wouldn't blame them."

"None of the above," Kim said. "I'm being blackmailed."

Will considered that statement, then put the Messer on his mantelpiece and sat down, on his bed since there was only the one chair and Kim was in it. "By whom?"

"That's the question, but let's not plunge straight in when I haven't even asked how you are. How *are* you?"

Will glowered at him. "We both know you're here for something. You might as well tell me what."

"We can still observe the niceties. And I am aware you might not care to hear my woes, in which case you should have a chance to say so, thus saving us both a tedious recitation."

"Is that your idea of an apology? It is, isn't it? You behave as though I never existed for months, turn up when you want something, and that's the best you can do?"

Kim gave a tiny shrug. "Do you want an apology?"

Will bit back a fervent 'yes'. He was deeply pissed off, but Kim didn't owe him anything and never had. It didn't work that way. Will wasn't a country girl, courted and cast aside by a London seducer, and it would not do to give the impression that he felt jilted. Kim's demeanour gave no indication of regret, still less a desire to resume relations, and Will was damned if he'd embarrass himself by behaving differently.

"What I want is a drink if I'm going to have to listen to whatever damn fool thing this is," he said. "I suppose you want me to hit somebody for you."

"I was hoping to approach the subject with a *little* more finesse."

"Wrong shop. Whisky?"

Kim was an amateur mixologist with a well-stocked cocktail cabinet in his mansion flat. Will kept a bottle of cheap Scotch on the mantelpiece. He sloshed it out and handed Kim a tumbler.

Kim sipped the neat spirit with a wince as Will kicked off his shoes and stretched out his legs on the bed. "Thank you. So how have you been?"

"Much as I was since you last popped in. Get on with it."

"No finesse at all," Kim said plaintively. "Very well, if you insist. I made what one might consider a small error of judgement last week. A young man got talking to me in the street and I invited him back to my flat. I'm sure I needn't go into details."

"Not really," Will said, as drily as he could. *Fucking hell, Kim. If you wanted to suck someone off, you could have come round here.*

"He stayed for two hours. I know the time exactly because that was what he said while informing me that he had someone outside who'd testify how long he'd been in my flat, while he would swear to the number and variety of acts committed."

"For God's sake." This stung like hell, no matter how he told himself it shouldn't. Kim could pick up trade in the street if he wanted; it was none of Will's business. "Still, it's your word against his and we both know you're a good liar. I hope you told him to clear off."

"I did not."

"You paid up? You bloody fool. How much did he tap you for?"

"I told him only had ten quid in the house, and he settled for that without much argument."

"It's not bad for two hours' work," Will said. "Especially since I expect you did most of the work anyway."

He regretted it as soon as he'd said it. He was entitled to be rude about this, extremely so, but Kim liked to oblige in bed and had taken abuse for his tastes in the past. For all he deserved, he didn't deserve that.

Kim's brow was arched, with a little sardonic smile on his lips, the sort of expression that said, *You can't hurt me.* Will clenched a fist, annoyed at himself. "Sorry. That was a shitty thing to say."

"You needn't worry about my feelings."

"I don't. I just didn't mean to hurt them that particular way."

Kim's brows twitched. "No offence taken."

"Yes, well, take this: you're an idiot for paying him a penny, because that's an admission. Now I'll have to beat the daylights out of him when he comes back."

A sideways sort of smile slithered its way onto Kim's face. "Is that an offer?"

Will sighed. "Just call me when he turns up."

"That is remarkably kind of you, Will." Kim sounded entirely sincere. "I really do appreciate it. But it's not necessary."

"It will be. You're a rich man, and he'll know that if he's been in your flat. I doubt he'll settle for less than a hundred."

"In his place I'd have demanded two hundred up front, no dancing around," Kim agreed. "The fact that he didn't suggests he cared far less about cash up front than about proving I'm vulnerable to blackmail."

Will sat up. "And why would he want that?"

"Because I've been nosing around some things people would prefer me not to."

"Of course you have. For the War Office?"

"I told you, I don't work for the War Office."

"You've told me lots of things, and at least two-thirds were barefaced lies," Will pointed out. "And I think you've just told me another, come to that."

"Me?" Kim said innocently.

"You're doing hush-hush work, someone tries an obvious bit of entrapment, and you expect me to believe you didn't realise what was going on, and paid up in a flap?" Will saw the twitch at the corner of Kim's mouth, which emboldened him to say, with certainty, "You prick. What are you lying about now?"

Kim's expression broke into the wolfish grin that brought up the hairs on Will's arms. "I do enjoy you, even if you ruin my fun. It is possible that I saw him coming a mile off, yes."

"So why would you fuck him? No, wait." Will took a quick mental skim back over the conversation. "You didn't say you did. So what happened, he just hung around chatting and making passes, and then said he'd accuse you anyway?"

"It's an incredibly common tactic," Kim said. "A youth wangles his way into a bachelor's flat and threatens to make claims on how the time was spent. The bachelors frequently pay up if they don't have a witness to the contrary, or at least that's their story and they're sticking to it. I expect a fair few of them are actually paying for services rendered, but who am I to criticise?"

"You're right there. And who was the witness to the contrary that five quid says you had lurking?"

"My man, of course. Peacock. You haven't met him, I think? Very discreet. He, ah, lurked in the kitchen and, may I say, finished my Times crossword while he waited, piling humiliation on top of embarrassment."

"Good," Will said. "I hope you never get a seven across again. Arsehole."

Kim grinned at him. He looked entirely as if they were playing a game and he was enjoying it, and the damn fool thing was that Will felt that way too. Of course Kim would turn up after two months with some bizarre story; of course he wouldn't tell it like a normal person. He was up to something, and he'd come round here to be up to it. A prickle of interesting possibilities ran up Will's spine.

He pulled himself together. "So you paid this toe rag because...?"

"I wanted to find out what would happen next. It seemed to me that my little blackmailer might provide a useful lead, so I gave him a tenner and had Peacock follow him when he left."

"And? Where did he go?"

"The High-Low Club on Maddox Street."

"You're joking. I was just there the...other..." Will sat up straight, his absurd enjoyment evaporating like spit on a stove. "Did you know that? You knew that, didn't you? Is that why you're here?"

"You were indeed there, with Maisie," Kim said calmly. "And then today you met one of the waiters for dinner. I wondered why."

Will didn't realise he'd propelled himself off the bed until his stockinged feet hit the floor. "What the fuck does that mean? Are you accusing me of something? What the *hell*?" He was staggeringly hurt, he realised, somewhere under the anger, horrified and appalled that Kim might be regarding him as the enemy.

Kim wasn't, though. Rather, he was rolling his eyes as though Will was the unreasonable one. "I'm not accusing you of anything, you idiot. The very opposite. Apart from anything else, if you wanted to hurt me, I have absolute faith you'd do it yourself and in person."

That was a very Kim sort of compliment, but it did smooth Will's ruffled feathers a little. "I *do* want to hurt you. Frequently. Damned if I know why I haven't."

"Your restraint is astonishing. Sit down, for heaven's sake. I have not been spying on you, but I *have* been keeping an eye on the High-Low for my own reasons. Imagine my delight when you turned up."

He said that with his usual light irony. Will had no idea how to take it. He glowered, as an all-purpose response. "What reasons?"

"What did you think of the High-Low?"

"Good band. Overpriced drinks. The manager and her second in command are a right nasty pair, they have gangs in, and there's a regular dope dealer on the top balcony."

"An excellent summary," Kim said. "It's a very dubious proposition indeed and I need to find a trustworthy inside man, which brings me here. How do you know the waiter? Or are you getting to know him?" He raised a suggestive brow.

Will returned a deeply unfriendly look. "I served with him, since you ask. Lieutenant Beaumont. I met him the other night when I took Maisie there, and we had dinner tonight to catch up."

"I see. How was it?"

Will shrugged. "Awkward. You know." Of course Kim didn't know; he hadn't served. "He's changed a lot since Flanders, but haven't we all."

Kim nodded. "What are his circumstances? I assume he isn't well off, if he's waiting on tables. Is he in need of money?"

"I am not putting you in touch with Beaumont so you can bribe him," Will said flatly. "We might not be bosom friends but he doesn't deserve that."

"Throw a dog a bone. I've got to get into this blasted place."

"Why? What is it exactly that you're after? What's this job you have on?"

Kim contemplated him for a long moment, as if weighing something up. At last he said, "How did you come to visit the High-Low? Were you invited? An advertisement, a recommendation?"

"Maisie picked it."

"And you didn't know this waiter chap worked there?"

"Of course not. I haven't thought of him since 1918."

"Was he surprised to see you?"

"Almost dropped his tray. Mind you, that was because I'd bumped into him. Are you trying to get at something? I went to this place because I'd promised to take Maisie dancing and she named it. Do I need more reason than that?"

Kim sighed. "Fate, then. *Our wills and fates do so contrary run,* and you are the most contrary of Wills."

"What?"

"The High-Low," Kim said, dropping the airiness. "It's linked to Zodiac."

They looked at each other. Will could feel his muscles tensing, readying for action. "Zodiac," he repeated. "What would they want with a night-club?"

"Consider the convenience of a night-club for a criminal enterprise. Vast sums in cash wash in and out regularly, making it impossible to trace the path of money. The most ill-assorted people can meet in a highly casual fashion. It's a notorious trade, and the High-Low attracted the attention of a colleague of mine, one Leinster, who specialised in following financial trails. He identified some profitable and highly illegal sidelines operating out of the High-Low and suspected it was being used by Zodiac to accumulate working capital. He had more suspicion than evidence, but he was a genius in his way. If he thought the High-Low smelled, I believe something there is off."

"You're talking in the past tense," Will said.

"Yes. Leinster is dead. He fell under a train on a miserable night in January. The platform was icy; he could very well have slipped."

Will's hairs prickled on his skin, not pleasantly this time. "But you don't think he did."

"No, I don't. He was working on linking the High-Low and Zodiac, and he fell under a train, and when I started attempting to retrace his steps, I contracted a nasty dose of blackmail. I'm not chalking both of those up to chance."

"No. Damn."

"Problem?"

Will made a face. "This might be just imagination, or an inflated idea of my own importance, but..." He told Kim briefly about his visit to the higher balcony, and the odd conversations with Fuller and Mrs. Skyrme. "I felt as if they were getting at something, trying to find out what I was up to—which was nothing. Maisie thought the same. And now you're saying they might be Zodiac, and they might be after you—"

"And you wonder if, knowing Kim Secretan was in the picture, they recognised the name Will Darling. As you say, damn."

"I was hoping you'd say 'nonsense'."

"Sadly, no. You made your presence felt to Zodiac last year. If someone in the High-Low is sufficiently high up, they will know your name, and they might very well have wondered what you were doing there."

"Mrs. Skyrme was wearing long gloves." Will didn't need to fill that in. Zodiac's inner circle sported little wrist tattoos, a brand of loyalty.

"She usually does. I don't suppose you saw Fuller's wrists?"

"Didn't look. I thought I was having a night out, not sticking my head into the lion's mouth. Hell's teeth, Kim. You said Zodiac would leave me alone if I left them alone, and now I've turned up at their place and they clearly thought I was asking questions. Mrs. Skyrme even said something about me telling my friends about the place. That meant you, didn't it?"

"Probably. You said she was trying to find out what you were up to. Any specifics?"

"She gave me a list of names, people I might know. I think she was watching for a reaction. I hadn't heard of any of them."

Kim frowned. "Can you remember the names?"

"Tommy someone. Teller? Brilliant Chang, I remember that, and Wally Bunker, who Beaumont said was a racecourse terrorist."

"He's behind any amount of illegal gambling, and wears a check coat that should be on the statute books as a serious offence."

"He was on the top balcony. Nasty-looking piece of work."

"Brilliant Chang is a dope merchant," Kim went on. "A very pleasant and cultivated one, at least if you meet him socially, and does not operate from the High-Low, which suggests she didn't want to name her own people. Might the third have been Tommy Telford?"

"Rings a bell."

"Ask not for whom the bell rings," Kim said. "Damn, and also blast."

"Who is he?"

"A professional purveyor of violence and intimidation. If you'd recognised his name, you'd have understood you were being threatened. Your visit was clearly seen as an act of aggression. I'm extremely sorry, Will."

"It's hardly your fault."

"The link between your name and mine is what puts you at risk. That looks like my fault from here."

"Oi," Will said. "I made Zodiac dislike me all by myself, thanks. So should I expect blackmailers?"

"It probably depends what you've been up to."

"Is that up to with you, or up to in the two months since you buggered off without a word?"

Kim's eyes snapped wide. Will felt fairly startled himself: he hadn't meant to say that. "Never mind," he muttered.

"Not at all, it's a valid question." Kim sounded smooth and urbane, as if he was discussing something that didn't matter at all. On the other hand, he was a liar. "I don't know what Zodiac know about your personal life but any association with me tends to stain reputations. What you've done in the last two months is your own business, but I hope it was discreet."

"Jesus Christ." Will found himself briefly speechless. "You come round here, suck me off, disappear for months, and now you're telling me how *I* should have been behaving?"

"Purely as a practical matter."

"Practical matter!"

"You'd prefer a moral judgement?"

"I'd *prefer* you not to be an arsehole, but apparently—"

"I don't claim any say over what you do," Kim said over him. "I apologise if I gave you that impression."

"That isn't an apology, and it's not what you should be apologising for!" Will caught himself there before he said something really stupid, like, *What happened? What went wrong? What did I do?*

He hadn't done anything. Kim was a rich man with a fashionable fiancée and a background of eye-watering privilege, and five names plus the title, and beautiful manners when he chose to use them, and elegant hands unmarred by calluses and scars. Of course Will had no place in that glittering world. Their lives had intersected because of Zodiac; there had been nothing to keep them in the same orbit without that threat. Kim was back here now because of Zodiac.

And that was his right, and Will had no more say over what Kim chose to do than vice versa. Not to mention he'd already refused the offer of an apology, so he oughtn't bang on about it. Kim might be an arsehole but that didn't mean Will should become one in his company.

He put a hand up. "Forget I said that. I'm pissed off but this High-Low business isn't your fault. No, I have not done anything indiscreet, as if it's any of your business, but I don't suppose that'll stop Zodiac if they want to get at me."

"Indeed not. You might want to watch your back."

"So should you."

"The best defence is a good offence," Kim said. "And I am nothing if not offensive. I'm going to have a look at what Mrs. Skyrme is up to, and if I find links to Zodiac, things will become interesting. Leinster always said we'd get them by following the money."

"Was he a friend?"

"I worked with him several times. He didn't give a damn for my past as long as I did my job. He was a good man, and I owe Zodiac something on his behalf."

"I owe them a kicking on my own," Will said. "Do you want your back watched?"

He realised too late that he really could have phrased that better. He'd had a bloody good look at Kim's back that long night locked together in his bed, and he was pretty sure Kim had the same memory now from the way his eyes widened.

Or not, because when Kim spoke he sounded as smooth as ever. "I thought your score with Zodiac was settled."

"You keep your scores, I'll keep mine."

"Fair. Are you sure you want to be involved, though? You might do better to continue living the life of an innocent book-seller and hoping they conclude you're harmless."

"Did you just call me harmless?"

"If it's convenient for them to think so—"

"No," Will said flatly. "I am not going to roll over and play dead, or sit around and wait to see what they're going to do to me. I had enough of that last time."

"You're simply forced to take pre-emptive action. I quite understand."

Kim's voice rippled with amusement. That was probably fair because Will wasn't fooling anyone, including himself.

The fact was, he was bored. He bought and sold books, sometimes read them; he shifted stock around, did repairs, went to the pub or the football or the cinema. He had no projects, no horizons, no plans, just a comfortable life doing the same sort of thing every day. It would have sounded like paradise back in the trenches, but he had a knife slowly losing its edge and a worrying sense he was doing the same, and the placidity was starting to scrape his nerves.

He *liked* action, that was the problem. He'd spent his formative years at war, and he'd got used to it as a man got used to cigarettes. You could stop, for years even, and then you remembered how it felt and you found yourself reaching for it all over again.

"I'm not going to sit and wait," he said. "So if you think you can strike a blow at the bastards via the High-Low, I'm in if you want me. By the way, the floor manager is a vicious piece of work." He repeated what Beaumont had told him. "If you're planning to get in there, you'll need backup. Me, the War Office, whoever."

"I'm not working for the War Office and there is nobody I'd rather have with me than you," Kim said. "I would very much like you at my back, please. And by back I probably mean front."

Will blinked. Kim tipped his head. "You needn't look so startled. You can look out for yourself, you're quick on the uptake, and I trust you. I hope I haven't made you think otherwise."

"I'm not even going to answer that," Will said with feeling.

Kim gave a quick smile, there and gone. "Fair warning: I will tell you now that this won't be clean. I'm going to be very unpleasant to people who deserve it, and probably to a few who don't."

"What about Beaumont?"

Kim shrugged. "I'd be most grateful if we could use him to get into the High-Low."

"What would you need from him?"

"Any information he has on the people who run the place. A layout, weak points—it's not obvious how one would break in, and I don't want to show my face there while casing the joint, as the Americans say. Assistance, if he feels so inclined. If we can't use him I'll find another way, but since you have the connection—"

"I'll see if he wants to talk to you. No more than that."

"That would be marvellous. Don't tell him I'm official, will you? Tell him you've a pal in a spot of bother and ask if he can help, perhaps."

"Do you think it's safe?" Will asked. "Him being seen with me, I mean. I wouldn't want to get him in trouble."

Kim considered. "Did you have any sense he was pumping you for information when you met?"

"No. He mostly talked about himself."

"And I take it you don't feel you've been followed or watched? Nothing suspicious since you met him?"

"Well, there's this dodgy bastard who broke into my shop..."

Kim grinned at that. "Then it doesn't sound as though there's a problem. You might tell him to be discreet, but better he meets you here than at my flat."

"Fair enough."

Kim rose. "Let me know when to pitch up. I like the room, by the way."

It was an improvement on the crowded back-room of the shop where he'd lived for months but that was about all you could say for it. Kim had stained-glass lamps and original Pre-Raphaelites. Will had whitewashed walls and second-hand furniture. "It's not much."

"It's bare and efficient. Just how I think of you," Kim said, and slipped off down the stairs without a farewell before Will could think of anything to say in reply.

FOUR

W ill had an arrangement to meet Phoebe for lunch the next day. He hadn't mentioned that to Kim. Some might think it was a bit much to be lunching with a man's fiancée without telling him; Will was of the opinion that Kim could go whistle.

The Honourable Phoebe Stephens-Prince was a strikingly lovely blonde, tall and slender and wildly out of Will's class. She dressed in the most dashingly modern fashions, smoked cigarettes in an ebony holder, painted her face, called everyone 'darling', and seemed to be exactly the sort of empty-headed Bright Young Person who got in the newspapers unless you listened to her.

They met at their usual place, a small French restaurant on the Charing Cross Road. She had arrived before him, and Will was unsurprised to see her deep in conversation with the proprietor. All the staff were hopelessly in love with her, and looked at him with a mixture of envy and bewilderment that he fully understood. He found it hard to believe he got to lunch with Phoebe too.

"How absolutely lovely to see you," Phoebe said, once they'd ordered. "You must tell me everything about how you've been and what you've done. How did you like the High-Low?"

"We had a good time, but it's a funny sort of place."

"Isn't it? And the proprietress, too dreadful."

"When did you go?"

Phoebe raised a brow. "Oh, goodness, months ago. I was there with—now, who was I there with? Binkie Huckaback and Gloria Glade, so it was summer, of course. A little party for Binkie's birthday, which to be honest isn't entirely something one would expect him to celebrate, being a juvenile."

"He's too young to drink?"

Phoebe gurgled. "No, darling, a *juvenile*. An actor who plays delightful young men, so his feet are very firmly planted on this side of twenty-five. Johnnie Cheveley was awfully cross about it, but he would be."

Will was well used to the flood of names that meant nothing to him. It became oddly soothing after a while, like the Shipping Forecast on the radio. "Who's Johnnie Cheveley, and why was he cross?"

"Oh, well, darling, *that's* a long story. Who he is, I mean, not why he was cross. That's a very short story: he didn't want to go. *He* said the High-Low was a rotten place and *Gloria* said he'd enjoyed it well enough before, and there was very nearly a fight when Binkie and Gloria went off to meet a friend of theirs. I say friend; Gloria looked awfully refreshed afterwards, if you take my meaning."

"Would the friend have been on the upper balcony, at all?"

"I think he might have been, because Johnnie was very unkind about her breaking her neck coming back down the stairs. Not that she did of course. Well, you know she didn't."

"I do?"

"Darling, you know her!"

"No, I don't."

"Yes you do, she's in the pictures. She was in that thing with

Louise Brooks last month as the girl who wouldn't, *and* the one with the man with the hair."

Incredibly, this brought a face to Will's mind. "Oh, *her*. Right. Yes, I've seen her a few times."

"I hope not in the High-Low," Phoebe said. "She really ought to be more discreet. But it still isn't Johnnie's business."

The waiter arrived with their first courses. Will waited for him to stop making puppy eyes at Phoebe and clear off before asking, "So why's this Cheveley fellow on your mind?"

"You *are* clever, darling." Phoebe took a sip of her soup. "He wants me to marry him."

"You're engaged. To Kim, I grant you, but still engaged."

"Darling, I know! It's too absurd. The thing is—can I bore you with the story? You see, his family and ours are connected, and I was desperately in love with him when I was quite little. He was in Signals in the war and I embarrassed us both writing him heartfelt letters. And by the time he came back his father and oldest brother had died, in that order so the death duties were iniquitous, and everything that's left went to the second brother to keep the house up. Johnnie was the third son, so he doesn't have anything at all and he has to work. He was furiously angry about that, but Daddy offered him a post as his secretary, with a generous salary and plenty of free time so he could live as he used to. I met him a great deal, and he was always terribly offhanded with me, which I very stupidly took as a challenge. I was rather wild then, and a dreadful fool in a lot of ways. We all were, I suppose. You know what it's been like since the war, with parties and everything changing."

Will's post-war experience had not included parties, but you couldn't miss the rules being rewritten all over. "Mmm."

"Anyway, eventually—well, I was very silly and careless and got badly in trouble, and Daddy made Johnnie a generous offer if he'd marry me. But what with one thing and another he refused, which was quite his right, of course, but he wasn't kind about it.

Not kind at all." She was looking over Will's shoulder then, not meeting his eyes. "And Kim *was*. He was the only person who didn't tell me how dreadful I'd been. Of course he was in disgrace himself, so he knew how it felt. He offered me his hand and I said yes and told my parents, but then the—well, the pressing need to get married didn't come about, you know. But after all that, I rather felt like *staying* engaged for a while, and of course it's useful for Kim. So we were privately engaged for a few months, and we got on so marvellously that I thought, why not stick to it and get married?"

"I can think of a couple of reasons," Will said, with some understatement.

"Perhaps, darling, but you aren't in my position. So we announced it last summer and planned to marry this summer. And then, quite unexpectedly, Johnnie proposed to me at Christmas, and he hasn't stopped since."

Will blinked. Phoebe made a comical face, but her eyes weren't laughing. "He's proposed *five times*. In two months! He keeps saying he made a terrible mistake and not to let it ruin our lives, and so on and so forth. He even asked Daddy for his blessing."

"When you're engaged to someone else?"

"Johnnie knows my parents don't think much of Kim. But Daddy told him it was up to me, which put Mother in an awful bind, since she naturally wants to support whichever man Daddy likes least."

Will stared. Phoebe gave him a little joyless smile. "My parents don't get on. I have thought of becoming one of those women who goes to Africa to shoot buffalo in trousers—me in the trousers, obviously—but I'm their only child since my brother died, so..."

"I didn't know. I'm sorry. War?"

"Goodness, no, darling, he was only seven. Diphtheria, the poor heart. It was a dreadful blow to my parents but by then they weren't speaking at all so there was no prospect of a replacement. Anyway, here we are. Daddy won't make me decide between my suitors but he won't call Johnnie off. Mother loathes them both. And Johnnie won't stop proposing."

"What does Kim say?"

"He's always said, if I want to end the engagement and marry someone else I should do precisely as I please." Phoebe turned her wineglass in her slim fingers. "But he doesn't like Johnnie."

"I know you've thought about this," Will said. "But there are men in the world who aren't queer *or* arseholes. Have you considered marrying one of them instead?"

There was a strangled noise from behind him, and he realised a waiter had come to top up their wine glasses. He said, "Uh." Phoebe clamped her lips together, shoulders shaking, and let out a splutter of laughter once the scandalised man had retreated. "Will, darling, really! Shocking the staff."

"Sorry. Point stands, though."

"Johnnie isn't that bad."

"He sounds awful," Will said, not mincing words.

"He was very…oh, war-weary for a long time. And I didn't behave well, and mostly, he was entitled not to be in love with me. Loving someone doesn't oblige them in the slightest. It's not like 'good morning', when you have to say it back."

Will couldn't imagine not loving Phoebe, but she had a point. "Er, are you still—"

"Oh, not in the slightest, darling. Not at all. I know so many people who are in love with people who treat them appallingly, and I used to think that was such a glamorous way to go on. And then Johnnie was truly unkind to me and whatever I felt for him positively *evaporated*. Like salt on a slug, withering it up."

"Kim can be pretty unkind."

"Not to me," Phoebe said, with breathtaking simplicity. "And I love him but I'm not *in* love with him, and maybe that makes a difference."

Their main courses arrived. Will waited impatiently for the waiter to go; Phoebe, as ever, gave the man a charming smile. She picked up her knife and fork. Will ignored his. "So this chap's changed his mind. You don't have to listen to him, though, do you?"

"Well, this is the problem. I suppose Maisie told you about our plans? She's been dying to. She is so extraordinarily talented, and I know the people she needs to know, and she has a vision, and I really think I can help her make it happen. It's desperately exciting. I'm going to introduce her to everyone. I want us to go to Paris, for her to work with people—I want Teddy Molyneux more than anything—and to be *someone*. She's far too talented to waste her time in that dreary unimaginative hat shop which is a positive what-do-you-call-it for someone of her potential. You know. Awfully depressing place. In Gloucestershire?"

"You don't mean the Slough of Despond?"

"I should take you everywhere," Phoebe said. "Of course it's a risk for her, but I truly believe she can do it if she just had the chance, and I know how to get her the chance, so we really only need the money to start, and Daddy has that. So I asked him to lend me what I needed for us to go, and Maisie to have her start, and if it works, for us to set up in business. We could do it. *She* could do it. She's so good, Will."

Phoebe's blue-grey eyes were alight, her face transformed. Will found a rather hard sensation in his chest when he breathed in. "And he'll lend you the money?"

"Darling, he said he'd give it to us! He told me yesterday. He wants to meet Maisie, which is quite reasonable, but he's very happy to fund me. Mother doesn't want me to go into commerce, of course, which is probably his reason, but I can't help that. So it's all wonderful except that he said that he wants Johnnie to, what's the word, to handle the accounts."

"Are there strings attached?"

She made a face. "Not as such. Nothing spelled out. But I'll have to apply to Johnnie for funds and send him accounts for approval, which I think *he* thinks means he can tell us what to do."

"Why's your father doing this?"

"Matchmaking, I expect," Phoebe said wearily. "Because I wanted Johnnie before and he said no, and now I could have him *I'm* saying no. He thinks if Johnnie and I spend time together I'll learn to forget my pride and accept his guiding hand or some such."

"Does that work outside novels?"

"I shouldn't think so. I'm desperately annoyed with Johnnie."

Of course Cheveley was exploiting such an unfair scheme. That seemed bloody typical of this man Will hadn't heard of an hour ago and thoroughly disliked. "Can't Kim lend you the money instead?"

"It's an awful lot. And there's reasons it wouldn't be right. Or at least… Well, take my word, it might make things dreadfully awkward."

"It sounds pretty awkward this way. I suppose you really do need the money?"

Phoebe's jaw firmed. "I promised Maisie. I already told her Daddy had agreed, before he came back with this. I shan't let her down." She looked quite fierce for a moment before her usual sunny smile returned. "And it needn't be awkward if Johnnie is reasonable about it. Only, is there a way to persuade a man to stop proposing?"

"A half-decent one would stop as soon as you told him to."

"Darling, how optimistic of you. Or perhaps I don't know enough half-decent men."

"Then tell Kim to have a word with this fellow. He's your fiancé. If this chap won't listen to you, he'll probably listen to him."

"You would think so, except Johnnie dislikes Kim so very much. I'm sure that's part of it, you know, wanting to get one over on him. Ugh. Oh, well, I'm probably making a mountain out of a molehill, and if he misbehaves awfully I shall appeal to Daddy. I'm sorry to bore on about this."

"You haven't at all. I'm sorry I can't help."

"But you've listened beautifully, darling, and been on my side, which is all I wanted. It's just that I usually bore on at Kim, and I have no idea what he's up to these days. I've barely seen him in weeks. I don't suppose—"

"Actually, I saw him last night," Will said, and could have kicked himself as her eyes rounded. "Not socially. He turned up. Work."

"He's up to something, isn't he? You needn't answer if it's one of his secrets, but you're up to something, with him? That *is* exciting. I shall forgive him for not answering his telephone."

"Even better, tell him to answer it."

"Oh, I *know*. What's the point in having a receiver if you aren't going to receive? I'm glad though, Will. He's been very Kimmish for a while now, but I think he's missed you."

That seemed implausible. "I've seen him twice this year, by his choice. And I can't say the most recent meeting improved matters much."

"Oh. Would it make a difference to know that he asks about you?"

"It would make a difference if he talked to me," Will said. "And since he doesn't—"

"But he doesn't talk to me either, not properly. I understand him by looking at the holes in what he says, and you've been nothing but holes since New Year."

"That's about how I feel," Will said, surprising himself. It was horribly easy to talk to Phoebe. She chattered about whatever was on her mind, so you did too, and before you knew it things that should have stayed as unexamined thoughts were out there in front of you, impossible to ignore.

"Oh, darling, I'm sorry. I wish—"

He didn't want to hear what she wished; it might hit too close to home. "Save your wishes for you and Maisie to become the newest Paris fashion house. That's what I want."

Phoebe blushed, a charming rosy shade. "Really?"

"Of course really. And don't let any men get in the way."

Phoebe lifted her glass in a toast. "No, darling," she murmured. "I shan't."

FIVE

Beaumont returned Will's phone call that afternoon, sounding exhausted and a little wary. He probably hadn't expected to hear from him again. Will didn't even try to explain, simply telling him there was a fellow he ought to meet. Kim could make up his own lies.

Beaumont made negative noises. "I've no money to invest in any get-rich-quick schemes."

"It's nothing like that. Or racing tips, or anything else of the sort. It may be you and this chap can help each other out."

"What do you mean?"

"He can explain better than I can. He's in a spot of bother, and you might be able to do each other a good turn."

"I don't see how, and I'm not promising anything," Beaumont said grudgingly, but he agreed to come round at five. Will gave him the address, and immediately phoned Kim, who actually answered for once, with an aggressive rap of "Secretan."

"It's Will."

"Oh, hello," Kim said, audibly adjusting his voice to warmth.

"I've got that meeting with Beaumont for you. Today at five, my place."

"Thank you. What did you tell him?"

"Nothing. I didn't know what lie you had in mind."

"You could tell him I need his professional advice, and bask in a warm glow of honesty."

"You tell him, so I can watch you choke on your own tongue as you attempt to spit out something like truth."

Kim laughed, a warm, infectious sound despite the crackly line. "Harsh, Will, harsh. I'll be with you, shall we say half an hour before? Call me if he arrives before then, and unlock the back door if you would."

"You don't ask much," Will muttered. "And I never—" He stopped. Kim had already hung up.

The afternoon dragged, as would any period sandwiched between time with Phoebe and Kim. He sold a few books, wrote a few letters, dealt with a few orders to go by post, and otherwise occupied himself until he heard faint sounds from the back room at around half past four. Will ignored them until he'd got rid of his sole customer, then strolled through to find his erratic sort-of partner lounging on the camp bed with a book.

"You're here, are you?" he said in lieu of greeting.

Kim gave him an up and down look. He seemed a bit worn in daylight, Will thought, with a touch of tension around his eyes and mouth. "Good afternoon to you too. Any chance of a cup of tea?"

Will tugged his forelock. "At once, m'lord."

"Oh, shut up."

"Tired?"

"A bit." Kim gave a sudden yawn. "I was prowling the streets around the High-Low in the small hours, keeping an eye out for opportunities, which were not vouchsafed to me. The place is surprisingly secure for a quite ordinary night-club, especially one with such a cavalier attitude to the licensing laws. One usually expects an easy and discreet route out, and the High-Low has both a back door into the yard area behind, and a fire escape coming down from what I assume is Skyrme's office, yet both seem very firmly locked even when it's open."

"You sound like an expert. Been in many night-club raids?"

"Three," Kim said resignedly. "All Phoebe's fault. She used to make me take her to the most appalling places; I got quite used to ending up in the cells for the night and the dock in the morning, getting the fish-eye from a magistrate. But all of them were fly-by-night operations, while the High-Low is on a different scale. It's worth noting that Mrs. Skyrme has plenty of experience of raids. She's run three night-clubs, as well as a couple of bridge-clubs with high stakes. The first two night-clubs were closed down by the police within months. The High-Low, by contrast, has been open for three years, and is succeeding triumphantly. It has never been raided, and judging by the lack of easy back ways out, it doesn't look like they expect to be."

"I wonder what she did differently this time."

"Took better advice on which policemen to pay off, I expect. Is that the door?"

"It might be Beaumont. I'll tell him you're here."

Kim nodded. Will went back into the main room, and saw his old lieutenant looking around.

"Hello, there," Will said. "Thanks for coming."

Beaumont gave him a perfunctory smile. "Look here, I'm not awfully sure what it is you want."

"Best if my pal explains. I asked him to come here." Will went to lock the door and put up the Closed sign.

Beaumont looked uneasily around. "I don't think..."

"He's got a problem that's linked to the High-Low. I'm wondering if there's anything you can tell us that will help us deal with it."

"Deal how?" Beaumont demanded. "What are you up to?"

"That very much depends what you can tell us." That was Kim's voice. Beaumont jumped a foot. Will looked round to see him leaning against a bookcase. "Beaumont, yes?" He swung forward, holding out a hand. "Arthur Brabazon, good to meet you. It's my opinion there is something very wrong at the High-Low. Would you disagree?"

Beaumont looked a little startled by that abrupt opening. "It's a night-club. What would you expect?"

"I'm talking about more than that. I think you know what I mean."

Beaumont's eyes widened. Kim went on, "Of course you can say, *Not my business*, or *More than my job's worth*, and perhaps that's true. But Darling has told me enough about you that I believe that you'll do the right thing, if you'll just hear me out."

His voice was steady, serious, so intensely sincere that Will almost forgot he hadn't told Kim anything of the sort. Beaumont's eyes flicked between them, uncertain, and Will suddenly remembered the boy from 1916 trying to hide his fear behind his lieutenant's uniform.

"The kettle's boiling," he said. "How about a brew-up while we talk about it?"

Beaumont straightened his back. "All right."

In the back room, Will put the tea on while Kim unfolded the old camp bed to serve as a divan since there was only one chair. They'd fucked on that their first night together, a fact Will put firmly to one side. Kim perched on it while Beaumont took the chair.

"Brabazon, was it?" Beaumont asked. "Darling said you wanted me to help you out. I'm not sure what you think I can do."

"I'd better give you the story. The fact is, I'm being black-mailed," Kim said, with charming ruefulness.

Beaumont's jaw dropped, as well it might. Kim shrugged. "I did a damn fool thing and I'm not greatly proud of myself, but I don't think I deserve to be bled white by some grasping swine."

"No. Er. I'm sorry to hear it. You can't go to the police?"

"Not easily. It would cause a great deal of difficulty and

painful embarrassment, which I might deserve, but others don't. I'm damned if I'm going to pay up, though, and I see no reason to be civilised about this. I'd rather take the fight to the blighters."

"And face the consequences?" Beaumont said, a little sceptically.

"Let's say, spread the consequences around. My intention is that the blackmailers will regret this a great deal more than I will."

"He's not joking," Will said. "They picked the wrong target. Sugar?"

"No. Thanks." Beaumont took the mug. "You're planning to go off the rails? Are you in this, Darling?"

"I didn't get mentioned in Dispatches for sitting on my hands."

"No. No, you were one of the hard nuts, weren't you?"

"This is of course between us," Kim added. "I'll happily swear you were never part of this conversation if need be. But I felt you should know where we stand."

"Why? Why are you telling me this?" Beaumont demanded.

"Because the blackmail is coming from the High-Low Club," Kim said. "And I don't think you're surprised to hear that, are you?"

Beaumont's lips parted. "What—how—" He darted a look at Will. "What did you tell him?"

Will hadn't told him anything, which raised all sorts of questions. Kim came in smoothly. "Merely that you were in a sticky situation, which makes two of us. And the High-Low Club is in the middle of the web. Am I wrong?"

Beaumont passed a hand over his face. "Let me think a moment."

Will sat on the bed with his tea. He didn't look at Kim, though he was very aware of him there, a foot away, in his element.

"Look," Beaumont said at last. "I do know something. But if I tell you and you act on it, it might come back on—well, me, but on someone else too."

"That's the risk," Kim said. "I give you my word as a gentleman that if you help us we'll help you. We'll do our best to deal with your problem, and the police won't be involved if I have anything to say to it. I operate better under cover of darkness."

Beaumont's eyes widened. "But this is someone else's secret. I can't just go around telling people willy-nilly."

"But you need to tell someone," Kim said. "You need help. If you could deal with this alone, you would have done so already. You need allies. We're here."

Beaumont looked from one to the other again, then his eyes narrowed. "I know what Darling did in the war. What did you do?"

Kim grinned. It was a wicked, conspiratorial grin that bore no resemblance to any real expression Will had seen him wear while discussing his past. "An excellent question, to which I can give no answer. If you're asking, do I know what I'm doing and do I know the right people to get away with it—yes, to both."

"You're one of the hush-hush people, aren't you?"

"Certainly not. I'm a gentleman of leisure these days, nothing more."

Will could almost see Beaumont's mind working. He knew Will was a dab hand with a blade, Kim was clearly some sort of dark-arts merchant, but he was being blackmailed so this couldn't be official…

It was fascinating to have a clear view of Kim manipulating someone else: the half-truths, the implications left trailing to be picked up. He was somehow managing to lie his arse off without technically telling a falsehood. Will was reluctantly impressed, and not at all surprised when Beaumont gave a decisive nod and took a fortifying swig of tea.

"All right," he said. "But I want—the other person—to be free and clear of this. No police. It can't come out, any of it. I need you to promise me that."

"Absolutely," Will said, before Kim could speak. "You've my word on it."

Beaumont's face relaxed, which was nice because Kim's had tightened a fraction. "Thanks, Darling. Christ, I hope this is a good idea. Well. The thing is, there's a lady." He went through the story again for Kim's benefit, and this time Will listened.

Her name was Flora Appleby, and her husband, Peter Appleby, was a Foreign Office functionary. He'd first been unfaithful less than three months after the wedding, and their marriage had long outlasted any affection. He had his career to think of, and their relationship was distant rather than hostile, so Mrs. Appleby had continued to accompany him on various diplomatic trips for the look of the thing. And then she met Mr. Michael Beaumont.

"We met in the park." He had gone rather red and wasn't making eye contact. "We started speaking casually, but soon—I make no excuses, of course, but she is the most wonderful woman, and that swine Appleby—"

"No need to explain yourself," Kim said. "The heart has its reasons which reason knows nothing of."

"He doesn't deserve to kiss the ground she walks on," Beaumont said hotly. "We saw each other as often as we could. I've never felt this way. I'd do anything for her. And then that blessed Act passed in summer, and we had our chance."

"What Act?" Will asked.

"Matrimonial Causes, I assume," Kim said. "Permitting women to seek divorce on the grounds of adultery alone, without the additional requirement to prove cruelty, sodomy, or incest."

"Exactly," Beaumont said. "She had no way of doing it before, and he didn't want a scandal because of his precious career. But now she can seek a divorce herself: goodness knows she has plenty of evidence. I told her I'd marry her like a shot, of course."

Kim frowned. "Forgive my question, but is there not a possible obstacle here, if the lady has been indiscreet?"

"What happens then?" Will asked. He wasn't up on divorce law.

"The law holds that if one party is unfaithful, the marriage may be considered broken. But if *both* parties have strayed, a divorce cannot be granted and they must stay yoked together forever."

"How does that make sense?"

"The point isn't consistency, it's punishment. Respect the holy and sacred institution of matrimony, or have it enforced as an instrument of torture."

"It's farcical," Beaumont muttered. "Cruel. But we didn't think it would arise. Appleby wants to avoid scandal, and it will be far less noteworthy if he accepts the divorce than if he contests it."

"Oh, everyone's divorcing these days," Kim assured him. "It's positively fashionable. The papers scarcely have room for all the announcements."

"He was resigned to the idea. She was speaking to a lawyer. And then—"

He seemed to stick there. Kim said, "I will help you if you give me the information I need. And I will do my best to protect Mrs. Appleby against consequences. I know what it's like to be in a hole. You can't get out alone."

Beaumont looked at Will, silently pleading. Will wanted to say something reassuring, and found that *You can trust him* stuck in his throat. "He knows what he's about," he said instead. "And you've got my word we'll do our best for you. What happened?"

Beaumont took a deep breath. "Mrs. Skyrme. She threatened to tell the court about us, to ruin Flora's chance of getting a divorce. She's holding our future over our heads."

"How distressing. Why?"

"She wants to force Flora into doing something for her."

"Really?" Kim said. "What would that be?"

"Does it matter?"

"It matters to Mrs. Skyrme, clearly."

Beaumont nodded. "I suppose so. Well—"

Flora Appleby had first met Mrs. Skyrme a few years ago, at her bridge club. The play was high and she ran up debts she couldn't pay. Appleby was to be sent off on a trip to Hungary, his wife with him, and she found herself pressed to settle up before she went.

"Flora didn't have the money, so Mrs. Skyrme made her an offer," Beaumont said. "She was to bring some furs back from Hungary—very valuable ones, matching cream mink, but she'd be given papers that certified them as cheap rabbit. All she had to do was add the chest to their luggage. She didn't realise she was doing anything wrong."

"By smuggling?" Will said involuntarily.

"Evading import duty," Beaumont said. "And yes, but women never understand this sort of thing, do they?"

Kim met Will's eyes briefly. "Regardless of what she understood, this was doubtless a welcome way out of her predicament. Go on."

Flora Appleby brought back the chest of furs. She was given to understand that she would be required to carry out this favour on future trips as well, and duly did so, making two trips in 1922, two more the following year.

"Then this January Appleby had another trip to Hungary booked. With the divorce coming up, Flora didn't want to go. She went to see Mrs. Skyrme and told her she wouldn't be doing any more trips. Mrs. Skyrme asked her to go one last time, said it was all arranged. Flora refused, Mrs. Skyrme said she still owed her money, and they had an awful row. And finally Mrs. Skyrme told her that if she didn't do it, she would lay a complaint, letting the divorce court know that there was fault on both sides. Flora and Appleby would be stuck for life."

Will whistled. "Nasty."

"Flora couldn't believe it. She thought Mrs. Skyrme had spoken in anger, but she went back the next day, when tempers had cooled, and apparently she was quite serious. Flora said it was like speaking to a different woman. She felt afraid of her. So if you want to know who at the High-Low is capable of blackmail, there you are."

"How did she know about the affair?" Kim asked.

"Flora told her," Beaumont said wearily. "That's how I got this job in the first place. She asked Mrs. Skyrme if she had anything going for me—we weren't awfully discreet before the Act passed; there didn't seem any point. And if you're wondering why I haven't told the woman what to do with her damned job, it's because I don't dare. I hadn't had work in over a year before this. I suppose that's contemptible. I can feel her looking at me as I go about the place, with a saccharin smile and a sneer in her eyes."

"It's not contemptible," Will said. "Starving wouldn't help."

"The truth is, I don't know if I'd have the guts to confront her anyway," Beaumont blurted. "She's a snake, and Fuller is a brute, and he does as she tells him. While she holds this information over our heads, we're stuck. And it's got even worse."

"How?"

"There was some man sniffing around Flora last month. He asked her some damned impertinent questions about her trips and her friendship with Mrs. Skyrme and the things she brought back. She thought he might have been police or Customs or some such."

"Was there really?" Kim said. "What did she do?"

"Sent him off with a flea in his ear, the dirty little snoop. But she told Mrs. Skyrme she thought she was being investigated, begged her again not to make her take the trip, and the damned cat of a woman wouldn't listen. She took the fellow's card and told Flora she'd deal with it, and I dare say she did—everyone knows she pays the Old Bill to turn a blind eye to the after-hours drinking—but the fact is, she wouldn't care if Flora got into trouble with the law. She doesn't give a damn for anything but her blasted furs. But what if he comes back? What are we to do?"

"Let Uncle Arthur sort it out," Kim said, with reassuring firmness. "Has the fellow returned?"

"Not to my knowledge, but of course Flora's been away."

"Of course. Tell me more about the smuggling."

"What do you want to know? Flora goes with Appleby. A man delivers the chest of furs along with a bill of sale pricing them cheap and showing all the expected duty has been paid at that end. She adds it to her luggage and brings it back."

"Has she ever checked what's inside the chest?"

"Of course. She isn't a fool," Beaumont said indignantly. "It's just the furs, and Mrs. Skyrme's treats."

"What treats are these?"

"A carton of Hungarian gaspers and two boxes of chocolates. She has Flora bring them to her as a present when she returns, and that's when she arranges for the furs to be collected."

"I see. Does she share her little treats with Mrs. Appleby?"

"What does that matter?"

Kim shrugged. "It gives me a picture of the woman. If someone smuggled a chest of furs across Europe for me, I'd offer them a chocolate, or a cigarette."

"You'd think so, wouldn't you? As it happens, she doesn't. Flora was quite offended by that. She said Mrs. Skyrme has never so much as opened the boxes in front of her. Typical of her. I dare say she's stuffing her face with violet creams while we're all sweating away downstairs."

"I dare say," Kim said sympathetically. "So Mrs. Appleby is abroad now. When does she return?"

"They're expected back on Sunday week. Why do you care about a bit of playing the fool with import duty? You said this was about blackmail."

"It is," Kim said. "And isn't it interesting that Mrs. Skyrme chose Mrs. Appleby's personal indiscretion to blackmail her with, rather than this serious legal offence?"

"Oh. You mean..." He frowned. "No, I don't know what you mean."

"Don't worry about it. Thank you for trusting us with this, Beaumont. You won't regret it. I will give you my card. Call one of us if there are any developments at all, and don't confront Skyrme or otherwise act without our instructions. Got it?"

"Yes, but what are you going to do?" Beaumont demanded.

"From what you've said, it seems clear your problem and mine are linked, so Darling and I are going to stick in a crowbar, lever the top off this thing, and drag Mrs. Skyrme out kicking and screaming. When I've finished with her, she'll have other things to think about than your lady's marital affairs. Take my word for it."

"Gosh. But what about Fuller? He's dangerous."

"That's what Darling's for," Kim said. "Can we count on you?"

"Well... Oh, curse it. Yes, I suppose so."

"Glad to hear it." Kim grinned at him. "So tell us. What's my best way to get into the High-Low Club and raid her office?"

They spent a good twenty minutes with Beaumont detailing the security arrangements of the High-Low through night and day. It sounded more like a fortress than a night-club to Will. He added his own observations, helped Beaumont sketch a plan of the interior, and seethed inwardly with the questions he had a pressing urge to ask Kim.

He had to escort Beaumont to the front door to let him out and lock up behind him. That involved a few words of reassurance and a farewell, and when he walked into the back room with hard conversation on his mind, Kim had gone.

SIX

Two days later, Will sauntered round to the tradesman's entrance of Gerrard Mansions in Holborn, where Kim lived. He had on a flat cap and his oldest coat, carried a brown paper parcel, and felt ridiculous.

Kim had sent a brief note instructing him to stay away till then, not 'phone, and take these precautions when coming round. Will didn't know if that was fear of Zodiac or just dodging questions. Probably both, and he intended to have serious words about the latter, but he turned up as per orders all the same, and was admitted at the mews door by an inexpressive bald man in a severe black coat.

"Mr. Peacock?"

"Mr. Darling." Peacock the manservant let him in. "I shall take you up the back stairs and advise Lord Arthur of your arrival."

He led the way up a set of plain stairs that brought them into Kim's little kitchen. Will had breakfasted here, once, after they'd spent the second of their two nights together. He wondered if Peacock had cooked their food then.

"Excuse me, sir." Peacock inclined his head, rapped on the kitchen door, and opened it, proceeding into the lounge in a stately manner. "Lord Arthur, the delivery you mentioned has arrived."

"Will?" Kim called. "Come through."

Will did, passing Peacock, who gave him a very correct bow on his way out. Will glanced after him.

"Don't mind him," Kim said. "He loves the cloak and dagger stuff, it's why he tolerates me."

"But at least he *does* tolerate you," Phoebe said from the sofa. "He regards me as an incapable one step from Colney Hatch, and doesn't he let me know it. Hello, darling."

Will bit back *What the blazes are you doing here?* "Hello Phoebe. I wasn't expecting you."

"Do you have the jacket?" Kim asked. Will tossed him the parcel. Kim unfastened the string, and produced a white jacket panelled with green and pink stripes: the livery of the High-Low Club. Beaumont had brought it to the shop early this morning in a very furtive manner before sloping off home to bed.

"Oh dear," Phoebe said. "I'd forgotten quite how bad it was. Goodness, Kim, must you?"

"I regret I have but one hideous garment to wear for my country." Kim stripped off his own coat and slipped it on. "A bit large, but better that than tight. Peacock should be able to adjust it. Right, shall we get on? As per Beaumont, the High-Low Club remains open until the small hours on an entirely irregular schedule. Fuller, the floor manager, lives above the shop, as it were, in a room at the front of the building on what remains of the top floor, and closes the place up exceedingly securely, with bolts, locks, and metal shutters. Mrs. Skyrme lets herself in at any point between eleven and two; the cleaners come at three. All together that makes for an extremely unpromising target; I imagine that's no accident. So—"

"Hold on, hold on," Will said. All their collaboration in shady activities so far had taken place in private. Speaking in front of

Phoebe felt exceedingly exposed. "Are we going through the plan now?"

"Of course we are," Kim said. "As I was saying, the High-Low is well protected against burglary, so I don't want to burgle it."

Phoebe pouted. "Oh, darling, what? You *promised*."

"I'm not going to burgle it because I'm going in through an open door," Kim said patiently. "The aim, ideally, is to get in and out unobserved."

"Pretending to be a waiter. Why not a guest?" Phoebe asked.

"Because Skyrme and Fuller observe their guests. A uniform is a good way not to have one's face looked at."

"Except by other men in the same uniform," Will pointed out.

"A risk, I grant you, but I'm hoping you and Phoebe will mitigate it for me."

"Oh, am I still doing it?" Phoebe perked up. "Marvellous. I have such a good plan."

"For what?" Will asked with foreboding.

"My grand entrance, darling. I shall come in like what's-his-name, that delightful shiny person, though probably not in purple *or* gold. Purple is Kim's colour and I really think that in gold, with my hair, I'd look like a candlestick, don't you?"

"The Assyrian," Kim murmured.

"What's that?"

"The Assyrian. Came down like the wolf on the fold. It was his cohorts who were gleaming in purple and gold, though."

"I dare say you're right," Phoebe told him with motherly patience. "The *point* is that I shall make the most enormous spectacle of myself and attract everyone's attention from you, which I consider a good deed. You look like a hurdy-gurdy man."

"You wound me," Kim said. "Then while all eyes, particularly those of Fuller and Skyrme, are drawn her way, I shall sidle upstairs unnoticed and, I trust, let myself into the office."

"What if it's locked?" Will asked.

"I hope that shouldn't be an obstacle. I've been taking lessons, since I realised last year it was a skill I needed to master." Kim's eyes flicked to Will's, just for a fraction of a second but it was enough. Will knew he was thinking of the endless minutes when he'd been chained up in a Zodiac hideaway, and Kim had probed the lock of the manacle with a wire in an effort to free him. He hadn't believed it would work; he'd almost wept when the lock clicked.

Kim had come to get him when he'd thought he was a goner. He'd cared, and the memory was a punch to Will's chest.

"So you'll let yourself in while Skyrme is busy downstairs," he said, trying to keep his voice businesslike. "Sounds a bit tight. And how do you get out?"

"Carefully," Kim said. "That's where you may or may not come in. I don't know how long I'll need, or what the situation will be on the floor, so I will require a look-out to intervene if another distraction is required. If it isn't you can simply have an enjoyable evening's dancing."

"What sort of intervention?"

"Whatever seems appropriate. Use your ingenuity."

"Right. Phoebe, are you sure about getting involved in this?"

"Well, of course, darling, why not?"

"Because it's not safe," Will said with all the patience of which he was possessed. "Skyrme is mixed up in very bad business, she knows Kim, and you're his fiancée. I don't think you should bring yourself to her attention."

Phoebe's eyelids drooped. "How Victorian of you. I don't intend to sit at home doing needlework, darling. It is 1924, after all."

"*Kim*," Will appealed.

"Phoebe will be quite safe," Kim said, with extraordinary certainty. "It is hardly out of the ordinary for her to attend a night-club. You're more likely to attract adverse attention than she is. You needn't come if you feel it's a risk."

That was gratuitously provocative. "I said I'd back you up," Will said. "I don't see you need to put Phoebe in danger."

"*He* isn't, darling. *I* am."

"You don't know what you're getting into. I don't like it."

"Then don't," Phoebe said, and her cut-glass voice was sharp enough to hurt. "Because it is neither your business nor your right to tell me what to do. Is it?"

Will felt himself redden. Kim cut in while he failed to find a response. "If all goes well, Skyrme won't even know I've been there. If it doesn't, Phoebe won't be the one in trouble."

"There's no need to fuss," Phoebe added, sounding more like herself, less like the upper-class alien who'd just put him in his place. "I've got out of any amount of night-club raids, you know."

"And been arrested three times," Kim pointed out.

She widened her eyes at him. "But only three, darling, and I've been in positively *dozens* of raids."

"That would put anyone's mind at rest. With a bit of luck I'll be in and out unnoticed while you dance; with slightly less luck, Will might end up having to buttonhole Fuller with a complaint about overcharging for the champagne. It really ought to be an entirely uneventful evening."

"No trouble at all," Phoebe agreed. "Talking of trouble, dearest, have you booked that table? I thought the Criterion but I'll leave it to you of course. Saturday at the High-Low, then. Quarter past ten, you said? Goodbye, darlings."

Kim went to escort her out, and they exchanged murmured words, leaving Will standing in the sitting room alone and wretched. He would have rather liked to disappear down the back stairs the way Kim did. Running away from problems was a lot easier than facing up to them.

Kim shut the front door, and returned alone. "May I say something?"

"I don't know if anything's ever stopped you." Will knew it

was ungracious and didn't care. He felt stupid, and snubbed, and very obviously not part of Kim and Phoebe's rarefied circle.

Kim ignored that. "Phoebe wasn't really talking to you then. She's in a rather unpleasant situation thanks to her father, and it's wearing on her nerves."

"This Johnnie Cheveley character?"

"Oh, she told you? Yes. He thinks she'll come to heel if he tugs at the leash hard enough, and her father has handed him the power to do it. She isn't happy."

"So do something about him."

"She doesn't want me to." Kim gave a mirthless smile. "The sooner she goes to Paris the better. She's fizzing with enthusiasm about Maisie's talent, and the prospect of this joint venture. I haven't seen her this excited in a long time."

"Then why let this arsehole spoil it?"

Kim shrugged. "So far, he's just a nuisance. If he's fool enough to apply too much pressure, he can take the consequences. Do you know about this dinner? I am to host a group of the extremely fashionable Saturday week, all for Maisie to meet. Couturiers, designers, professional clothes-wearers, and so on: Phoebe knows everybody. You're welcome to join us—the Criterion does a very decent table—though I will quite understand if you'd rather find something rusty with which to poke yourself in the eye."

Will had no intention of being lured away from the topic at hand by this very clear bait. "Have fun. Let's talk about you sending your fiancée into Zodiac territory."

"Believe me, she'll be fine."

"How can you say that?"

"For God's sake. This is Phoebe, do you think I don't care about her?"

"How the hell should I know what you care about?"

Kim's nostrils flared. He started to reply, and stopped himself. "I suppose you have good reason to say so."

Will opened his hands in lieu of response. Kim winced. "No, wait. You've found yourself in the middle of a mess again, and I'm sorry. I really do understand your concerns about Phoebe, but you must appreciate her situation. She's had a bellyful of people telling her not to do things because they're stupid or risky, and some of those people were right, which is unforgivable. Her parents treat her as a child to be rebuked or indulged. I don't do that."

"Yes, but—"

"I'd say *trust me*, but you'd make a rude remark. Trust Phoebe, because she has a genius for people. And, to be honest, my options are limited. We're on a tight deadline here, with Mrs. Appleby due to return from her travels on Sunday week. I need to know what's going on before she's back in the country."

That was what he was here for, Will reminded himself. "Is there anything going on beyond a bit of customs evasion?"

"That remains to be seen. But she's a Foreign Office wife: she should know a great deal better than to play the fool like this. You probably shouldn't have promised Beaumont we'd get her off scot free."

"That was his condition for talking. I wasn't going to watch you leave him twisting in the wind. And that reminds me. How did you know he was being blackmailed?"

"I didn't."

"You bloody did. You knew there was something up: you all but told him you knew what was going on. How?"

"More fool him for believing a stranger's meaningful statements," Kim said. "It's a well-known technique: tell someone you know what they did and watch the blush of their guilty conscience. You know that old story? Someone sends a telegram as a prank to White's with no name, saying *Fly, all is discovered*, and six of the members leave the country?"

"So if I say to you that I know you're lying to me right now, you'll admit it?" Will countered.

"Sadly, one must have a conscience at all in order to have a guilty one. Which I suppose is a point in Beaumont's favour."

"You didn't like him. You didn't like him from the moment he walked in. Why not?"

"Good God, you're like a dog with a bone," Kim said. "All right. I didn't know what was up with Beaumont, but I knew there was something because when my colleague Leinster fell under that train, he had a High-Low matchbook in his pocket. And across the matchbook he had written Beaumont's name."

"*What?* Why the blazes didn't you say so before?"

"Because when I went to look into the man, I discovered you dining with him. And once you told me your connection to him, I wanted you to continue approaching him as a friend."

"Which I did! I persuaded him to trust you; I gave him my word. Jesus, Kim! What the bloody hell are you playing at?"

"Let me spell something out," Kim said. "Leinster had Beaumont's name. He asked questions of Beaumont's mistress. She took his card to Mrs. Skyrme and said, *This man is investigating our smuggling,* and Mrs. Skyrme said she would look after it. And now Leinster is dead."

That stopped Will's building anger in its tracks. "Oh," he said. "Oh, shit."

"Quite."

"It's not just customs evasion, then."

"No. I have some idea what it might be, but it's only an idea thus far. I'm sorry I didn't tell you before, but subterfuge isn't your strong suit. Could you have lied to his face, knowing this? Or even looked him in the eye as you did before?"

That was a fair point as far as it went. He wasn't much of a liar, and people rarely had trouble telling when he disliked them. He wouldn't have spoken to Beaumont the same way. "No. And I see why you wanted to reel him in. But I still don't like being used."

"I know," Kim said.

That was all. He didn't apologise, because they both knew there wasn't much value to an apology for a thing you'd done entirely on purpose.

"I don't like it," Will said again. "You can trust me, or you can leave me out of it, but don't use me again, Kim. I'm not your tool."

"No." Was that shame on Kim's face? Hard to say; it wasn't an expression Will had seen often. "You aren't. I do know that."

"Try to keep it in mind," Will recommended. "But, look, Beaumont can't be involved, surely? He told you all that stuff easily enough."

"Agreed; it does seem unlikely. Leinster was something of a misogynist and it's quite possible he assumed Mrs. Appleby's lover must be directing her actions. I'll try to find out. But Will, promise or not, if Mrs. Appleby knew what she was doing when she handed Leinster over to Skyrme, I will see her hang."

He sounded like he meant it, and Will couldn't blame him. "*If* she knew," was the best he could say. "Damnation. I'm sorry."

"What on earth for?"

"Well, you. This looks like a rotten job."

Kim's face twisted, a sudden, shockingly open movement that made him look dreadfully like a child. It lasted a fraction of a second before his face smoothed over, but Will could see the tension in his jaw and neck still. "Kim?"

"You startled me with sympathy. Ah, Christ, Will."

"What?"

Kim hesitated. "Only that I'm grateful to have you with me thus far. And." He exhaled. "And I don't flatter myself that you'll care, but I ought to say that I disappeared on you in January for purely professional reasons. You deserve to know that."

"What reasons?"

"I had—call it omens of trouble with Zodiac at the end of last year. I thought I would do well to keep my distance rather than draw attention to you, and subsequent events proved me right. I'm rather afraid things are coming to a head."

"And you didn't think to tell me?"

"What, and expect you to sit tamely at home, keeping out of danger, because I said so? You aren't famous for your obliging nature."

That phrase struck at Will's gut. Kim had used it about himself, here in this flat. He had an exceedingly obliging nature, at least in some areas. And Kim had noticed that resonance too, because his eyes were on Will's deep and dark.

"I'll decide what to do for myself," he said, hearing roughness in his voice. "Stop playing silly buggers."

"Silly buggers is what I do. There's no point waiting for me to do otherwise. There's no point waiting for me at all."

"I haven't been *waiting* for you," Will said indignantly. "I haven't happened to meet anyone else I wanted to fuck, but that's not the same thing."

"No. Nor have I, since you. I wish you would. I wish you'd meet a nice girl and settle down and grow roses around the door. A decent, respectable life. Why don't you go and get that instead of being here?" There was a strained note to Kim's voice. "Why aren't you doing that now?"

Will opened his mouth, and realised he had no answer.

He *did* want to live decently, in theory. He had always expected a respectable life with the trappings of church, children, brass doorstep, vegetable plot, just as his mother had dreamed of for him. Those were things any man, or most, would want to have.

The blood-red uncivilised streak of his nature that had blossomed in the war didn't want them. That streak wanted someone who would ask him to infiltrate night-clubs and kick people's heads in. That streak wanted Kim, who offered none of the things that appealed to Will's respectable ambitions and everything that fed the wolf.

Infinitely unreliable, oddly vulnerable, painfully desirable Kim, who he could neither understand nor forget. His abrupt disappearance had been a constant, daily prickle of disappointment and hurt that Will hadn't wanted to address because it was easier to bundle those thoughts up and shove them into the back cupboard of his mind, even if they kept spilling out again, even if they got still more tangled that way.

It was absurd that the pulsebeat of desire was as strong as ever. It was absurd that Kim was looking at him now with something raw and painful in his eyes after buggering off for two bloody months. It was absurd that Will couldn't look away.

"Will?" Kim said softly.

"I used to have an idea what I wanted," he said. "If you'd asked me ten years ago, I'd have said I'd be a joiner by now—I was apprenticed to the local man—and married to Mary Alice Goodman. Instead I've got a bookshop, and I've killed eighteen men."

"Eighteen," Kim repeated.

"Confirmed. It's not that I'm keeping score," Will felt compelled to add. "That would be—"

"Worrying?"

"I had the choice between remembering how many or forgetting. I didn't feel right forgetting."

"No," Kim said, the flicker of humour gone. "No, I see you wouldn't. Sorry."

"It doesn't keep me awake at night. I had a job and I did it. But it changed me, I know it did. I'm not the man I might have been, not any more. That's all." It had been on his mind since meeting Beaumont. Speaking the words aloud felt like a confession.

"I'm sure you're right about that," Kim said. "But I really can't bring myself to regret the man you might have been, given the one you are."

The breath caught in Will's throat. He was sure Kim heard it.

"You could have the respectable life," Kim said again. "You truly could, Will, if you wanted. Sell the bookshop, throw away the knife. Go home. Marry Mary Alice."

"She's already married."

"Use your ingenuity. Go and find the life you were supposed to have."

"What if I don't want it any more?" Will asked. "What if there's something else I want instead?"

"Is there?"

Their eyes were locked. The silence rang like crystal.

Oh, what the hell. "You sodding know there is."

Kim's throat moved in a swallow. He had a fine-boned throat with a hollow at the base; he'd groaned, before, when Will had licked it. He didn't say anything for a long second, in which Will wanted to move and didn't quite dare, and when he did, his eyes flicked away from Will's face. "I stayed away."

"I noticed."

"You deserve more than I have to offer."

"I know."

"God's sake, Will. Haven't you learned your lesson yet?"

He hadn't. He was beginning to wonder if he ever would. But he knew how to make everything feel simple and obvious again, if only temporarily, so he said, "The door's locked."

It was what they'd said before, to mark out a space for themselves in the maelstrom of last November. No guilt, no thought of anyone else, no obligation, just a little place in time.

The look on Kim's face showed he remembered. "Damn you."

"Same to you."

He wasn't sure who moved first. It didn't matter. They rose and came together in silence, kissing with an intensity that pulled the marrow from Will's bones. Kim was kissing him hard, his long fingers in Will's hair, Will's hand round his lean arse. His mouth was hot and hungry, and Will kissed him ferociously in return, almost angrily, with a knot of need and frustration and fearful desire roiling in his gut.

After a few frantic moments, Will pulled away. They'd crashed down on the sofa at some point, Kim underneath, Will over him with one leg on the floor for balance.

"What do you want?"

"You," Kim said. "In my mouth, if we're doing this. I have thought about you fucking my mouth on a near-nightly basis since November."

"Same." Will started undoing his buttons, watching Kim watch him. "I keep thinking about the way you look when you suck me. The way you sound."

"How do I sound?"

"Desperate."

"That's about right," Kim said, as Will knelt over him.

Kim's lips came round his stand. Will rocked forwards, hearing Kim's little strangled grunt, felt his prick rub against lips and tongue. He groaned. Kim moaned agreement.

"Christ, I love this," Will rasped. Kim's arms were above his head. Will trapped the slender wrists, watching his own tanned hands with their calluses and scars and fight-thickened knuckles, rough and ugly against Kim's smooth skin. Kim arched under him and Will thrust a little harder into his mouth, and again, finding a slow rhythm that set Kim rocking under him. He'd be stiff as a post, Will knew.

"I love watching you do this," he whispered. "Knowing you love it. Knowing it's making you hard."

Kim made an urgent noise. Will leaned in, just a little harder, prick rubbing deliciously against the roof of Kim's mouth. He was on the back foot with Kim most of the time, what with his wealth and class and brains and limitless capacity to lie, but in these moments when he was bare and raw, exposing the desires Will knew shamed him for all the bravado, the balance tipped.

It flooded Will with an urgent, absurd tenderness. He pulled back, dragging his prick from Kim's receptive mouth, holding his hands down still.

Kim moved underneath him, a slow undulation of the hips. He was still entirely dressed. Will let go with one hand and shifted back, unfastening Kim's trousers and freeing his erection, stiff and leaking. It was slimmer than Will's own, not intimidating in size, hot to his touch as he wrapped his fingers round it. He stared down.

"Will?"

"Can I—" He didn't know how to voice this, which was ridiculous, because he had no trouble with the words when Kim was doing it. "Do you like being sucked off?"

"Don't be kind to me, Will."

"I'm not. I want to make you beg."

"Oh. Well, then."

That sounded like a yes. Will leaned down and tentatively put his mouth on the prick he held.

He hadn't done this in a long while but it was like riding a bicycle: you were unlikely to forget. He explored a little with his tongue, feeling the smoothness of the head and the ridged shaft. Kim inhaled sharply, but stayed quiet, for once. Will licked around it, put his mouth over it, claiming the end, and Kim's hips jerked.

"Mph?"

"Don't mind me," Kim said, rather breathily. "Carry on. Oh God. You could use your hand if you wanted."

Will slid his hand up and down, finding a rhythm. There was a musky, organic taste in his mouth, from the viscous stuff that came before you spent, but other than that it was easy enough. He wouldn't say he found it particularly arousing as an act, not in the way Kim did, but his own cock was hanging heavy as he moved, and Kim's moans were enough to keep any man going. "God. So good. Christ, you can do what you want with me. Christ Jesus, Will."

Will's toes were curling. He tried sucking, rather than just moving his mouth up and down, and Kim convulsed against the sofa. "God, yes. Please. No, stop, I'm going to come."

Will moved his head away, enjoying the anguished and frankly dramatic noise Kim made. He crawled up to kiss him again, tasting both Kim and himself from Kim's mouth, letting his hips rest over Kim's. Their lengths rubbed together. Kim mewled in his mouth like a baby.

"God. That."

Will moved his hand down and met Kim's. Their fingers interlocked around both cocks, breathing hard, moving not quite in synchronisation but very nearly. The feeling of Kim, hot and hard and smooth, the shift of skin and flesh, the sound of his breath.

Kim shifted his head and his lips closed on Will's ear, sending a shuddering wave through his nerves. He gasped aloud. Kim dragged his teeth over the lobe, traced his tongue around the folds of flesh, sucking and licking until Will was squirming with the absurd pleasure of it, rubbing up against the body under him. "Jesus. Kim."

"You are beautiful," Kim rasped. "So beautiful. My God."

"Come with me," Will whispered. "Oh God, I can't—"

He bucked, unable to hold back, his spend hitting hand and belly. Kim groaned in Will's ear, bit the lobe again, and buried his face in the crook of Will's neck, gasping as he came.

After that, there was a very long silence.

Will didn't want to move. Their hands were still locked over both pricks, free arms around each other's necks, Kim's hair in his face. It wasn't exactly comfortable but it was comfort, of a sort Will hadn't realised he needed.

At last Kim let out a long, warm breath against Will's skin. "Well, that confirms that."

"What?"

"My inability to see you without something like this happening."

"You didn't want this?"

"Of course I did. Painfully. I hoped that you wouldn't."

Will blinked. "Uh...why?"

"For all the reasons that come swarming when the door is unlocked, of course. I did hope I'd make an effort not to cause you harm, but apparently I'm not capable of that."

"This wasn't harm."

"You say that now."

Will considered that. "If there's a nasty surprise waiting around the corner, you might warn a chap."

"When isn't there? Ugh. Will you promise me something?"

"What?"

"Promise first."

"Like hell. I'm not buying a pig in a poke from you."

Kim gave a huff of amusement. "Fine. Promise me, if you decide this was a mistake, if Mary-Alice gets in touch to say she's divorced or you've just had enough—promise me you'll say so there and then?"

"Excuse me? Seeing that you didn't even bother to tell me this was over—"

"It wasn't over." Kim stated the words like an axiom. "Not for me. I'd have left it alone if you had the common sense to move on. Or if I had a scrap of decency, of course."

Will twisted round. "What? Why would you say that?"

"Because I know myself. It's more than you do."

Will couldn't really argue. He'd had a bare-bones account of Kim's wartime shame that had led to the death of his younger brother. He knew from experience the shitty things Kim was capable of, and he was aware they sprang from a streak of warped, quixotic honour that was probably more destructive, certainly self-destructive, than simple amorality could ever be.

He was also spending his life in an effort at atonement, and when Will had been kidnapped, Kim had scoured the country for six days to find him, saved his life, and made sure his kidnapper came to a protracted and unpleasant end.

"Rubbish," he said. "Firstly, stop talking as if you did anything but what I wanted. Secondly—well, you're a slippery bastard, granted. You've made plenty of mistakes and done a lot of bad things and told an incredible number of lies. You're an utter shit. Sorry, what was I saying? I got carried away."

Kim choked. Will leaned in and kissed him, putting a gentle hand to his face. "Look, this part is all right, isn't it? You and me, here, door locked—that works, even if it's a mess outside, right?"

"I don't want to bring the mess in," Kim said, a little stifled.

"Then don't." Will shifted so they lay together, squashed on the sofa, his arm tight round the slim shoulders. Kim leaned into him, hiding his face, and Will stroked his fine hair with the quiet compulsion he'd feel for a cat on his lap. His heart was painfully tender in his breast.

All his tangles were tugging tighter, and he couldn't blame anyone but himself.

SEVEN

W ill arrived at the High-Low Club around half past nine on Saturday. The band was in full swing. A waiter escorted him to a side table and brought him a pint of beer with the resigned expression of one who didn't expect much of a tip, and Will sipped it as he looked casually around. Mrs. Skyrme's office was lit. As he watched, someone moved between a lamp and the blind, casting a momentary shadow on the slats.

It only took a few moments for one of the club's hostesses to say hello, an over-painted young woman with weary eyes. She introduced herself as Cynthia, paid him a couple of insincere compliments, took him for a dance, and then plunged into the subject that was really on her mind: where his lady friend from last time got that beautiful dress. Will dredged up everything he could remember about the subject of fashion, ordered a bottle of champagne with an internal wince at the cost, assured Cynthia it was fine for her friend Doris to join them, and managed to play his part in an animated conversation, interspersed with more dances.

He was pretty sure this was how men were meant to behave in night-clubs: flirting with women who were being paid to do it, splashing his cash. He felt like a bloody idiot, but at least he had something to think about that wasn't Kim.

He danced, drank champagne, and chatted to the girls. There was no sign of Mrs. Skyrme or Fuller. Beaumont was moving around a set of tables on the other side of the dance floor; Will tried not to look at him. He just kept a smile on his face and let the clock tick.

He and Doris returned to the table together after an energetic foxtrot. They sat, and Will poured out the last of the bottle.

"Shall I order more?" Doris said, unsurprisingly. Doubtless she got a cut; quite possibly her job depended on sales. Mrs. Skyrme would make a lot of her legitimate profits this way.

Will made a unilateral decision that Kim would be paying him back for this one. "Go on, then."

She gave him a wide professional smile. "You're a gent. Here, Bob!"

Will handed over the notes without obvious wincing, and glanced at his watch. It was five past ten; he had ten minutes before Phoebe's arrival.

"Tell me about yourself," he suggested to Doris.

"What, me? Nothing to tell."

"How'd you get into this line of work?"

Doris bridled. "I don't know what you mean."

"Look, I don't mind," Will said. "You're great girls and I'm having a good time with you. I wanted a drink and a dance with someone pretty and I've got double what I bargained for." Cynthia giggled, but Doris's eyes were wary. Will added, "Just dancing, no funny business, you needn't think that. I'm from the Midlands and it's a bit lonely in London, that's all."

"You poor lamb," Cynthia said, going motherly.

"It *is* lonely," Doris said. "I'm from Selly Oak myself."

Will hadn't needed telling that, from her vowels, but he expressed gratification at meeting a countrywoman anyway. "So what's it like to work here?" he asked. "Bit more fun than a shop floor, or are you always wearing out your shoes?"

"Shoes!" Doris said with feeling. "Bane of my life, they are. It's—well, it's not so bad." Her eyes flicked to the side as she said that. "You don't half go home tired sometimes, but the pay's good. The Mrs. is—"

"Fair," Cynthia said over her, quickly. "Never takes the tips and lets us mind our own business as long as the customers are happy. There's a lot to be grateful for, Dorrie, and worse places to work."

"I expect so," Will said. "What about that fellow Fuller? Can't say I took to him."

If he'd never met Fuller, he'd have learned all he needed from the girls' reaction. They both stiffened, faces flattening into neutral, the responses of people who expected to have their answers used against them.

"The Mrs. relies on him ever so," Doris said. "Oooh, here's the champagne. You pour. Talking of shoes, Cynnie—"

That was the subject very firmly changed. Will accepted another unwanted glass of fizzy muck and sat back, rather than press them for answers they didn't feel safe to give.

It was near quarter past now, Kim was due to arrive at the back door any moment, where Beaumont would let him in, and there was still no sign of Phoebe. She was often late, but surely she wouldn't let them down tonight? Ought Will cause some sort of ruckus and draw all eyes his way if her promised diversion didn't materialise? And how the devil would he do that?

"I might just visit the gents," he said, rising, and at that moment realised he needn't have worried. Phoebe's arrival was impossible to miss.

The party crashed in like a wave, making enough noise to be

heard over the band, especially since one of them appeared to have a hunting horn. It was a gaggle of young people about thirty strong, dressed with a startling combination of Bohemianism, extravagance, and grime. The men were mostly in tailcoats, some in lounge suits or exaggerated Oxford bags. Most of the women's hemlines barely skimmed their knees; all of their dresses dipped extremely low at the front, or even lower at the back. It was a radiant mass of bare flesh, sequins, fringes, bright colours, shining fabrics, painted faces, except that some of them looked as though they'd been rolling in the gutter, with streaks of dirt up bare arms, on white shirt fronts and waistcoats, across cheeks and costly fabric. A few had ripped hems, or bedraggled trouser legs.

Next to him Cynthia sucked in a long breath. "*Those* won't be worn twice."

Doris nodded agreement without looking round. They both watched the newcomers with appalled envy, lost in the spectacle of so much glory thrown so casually away.

The Bright Young People gathered in the middle of the dance floor, tightened up into a group, then darted away in all directions like starlings scattering, leaving only Phoebe standing, tall and slender in a shimmering blue dress, face lit with glee.

"God," Will said involuntarily.

The newcomers were everywhere, chattering and shouting, accosting people with what seemed to be demands. Some of them were diving under tables, others shouting at the band. One of them attempted to wrest away the clarinet-player's clarinet. Several waiters were remonstrating with them. Mrs. Skyrme emerged from the office and hurried down the stairs as Fuller started to sprint down from the top balcony.

Will tore his eyes from the spectacle, looked the other way as casually as possible and saw a waiter—or, rather, a man in a waiter's jacket, slim and dark-haired—emerge from the depths of the room behind Mrs. Skyrme, and set off up the stairs with a tray. Unmistakable to Will, unobtrusive to, he hoped, anyone else. Kim looked quite as though he was meant to be there, as long as the people who hired the staff didn't see his face.

Will forced his attention back to the dance floor in case anyone followed his gaze. He would much rather have watched Kim's progress along the balcony, watched him sidle up to the office and try the door. Had Mrs. Skyrme locked it? If she had, would Kim be able to deal with it?

He'd find out, damn it. Will forced himself to concentrate, and saw Phoebe was talking to Mrs. Skyrme, hands fluttering. He could almost hear the word 'darling'. A man in Oxford bags had climbed on a table despite the mass of material flapping round his legs, and seemed to be examining one of the columns holding up the balcony. The people sitting at the table seemed to accept this with remarkable equilibrium. The same sort of thing was going on across the entire dance floor, while some of the new revellers charged up the stairs.

"What the blazes are they doing?" he asked aloud.

"Treasure hunt, I bet," Doris said. "It's the newest craze. They look for a clue, then when they find it, they go to the next location. They go on all night. Don't use language like that."

"I didn't say anything."

"I could see you thinking," she told him, and her painted face cracked into an entirely real smile.

On the dance floor, Fuller's mouth was clamped into a far less convincing expression of goodwill, while the set of his shoulders suggested he wanted to start throwing people out by main force. He gestured at the band-leader, who made a few gestures of his own and changed the tempo of the music to something more sedate. That would doubtless calm the new arrivals down a bit. Admirable management, but not in Will's interests.

He glanced up to the balcony again. There was no sign of Kim in his waiter's garb, so presumably he'd got into the office by whatever means. The trick now was to ensure Mrs. Skyrme and Fuller stayed out of it for long enough that he could do whatever needed doing.

Phoebe's Bright Young People seemed to be achieving that in their insatiable demand for attention. Waiters darted round the dancefloor like sheepdogs, urging those of the party they could corral to a hastily assembled set of tables. Beaumont was one of them, bearing two trays of champagne and glasses. Phoebe hooked her arm through Mrs. Skyrme's and drew her to the tables, talking unstoppably. The High-Low's manager wore the slightly bewildered look of anyone blown away by Phoebe's breezy conversation. She wasn't likely to get out of there any time soon.

That left Fuller. Will gave it some thought, then leaned over to murmur his excuses to the girls. He left them at the table, and strolled over to the set of spiral stairs nearer to Mrs. Skyrme's office. Fuller was still busy with the revellers so Will went up the stairs, feeling appallingly visible, and leaned on the balcony rail, a man with nothing better to do than watch the world go by.

He was at the corner of the room, overlooking the dance floor, the tables along the long side of the balcony to his right, and the office to his left. From here he could see the smoked glass window of the office door, and make out a shape moving within. The glass obscured most detail, but the pale blur of the jacket was all too visible.

So his job was to prevent anyone, but especially Fuller, heading for the office, in case they saw Kim. And he'd definitely need to cause a distraction when Kim emerged—God, he was taking his time—because he'd be entirely visible to half the room on this side when he did.

The band started playing dance tunes again. Desmond Fuller was still below. Mrs. Skyrme laughed at something a man in a filthy striped blazer had said. On the down side, Phoebe's battalion of young idiots seemed to have stopped their game in order to drink champagne. They were still making an incredible amount of noise, but they'd lost their fellow customers' attention. That was the trouble with these night-club people, Will decided, they were jaded. Still, nobody was coming up to the office. A bit longer and they might get away with this.

Will watched and waited. It was smoky up here, irritating his lungs. The band played on. A waiter cleared his throat, and Will turned with a pulse of hope, but it wasn't Kim or even Beaumont, just a stranger in a garish jacket.

"Would you care for a drink, sir?"

"I'm all right for now."

"Perhaps I can take you to a table?"

"I've been sitting all day. I'm fine here."

"If you're sure, sir."

Downstairs, Mrs. Skyrme was disengaging herself from the Bright Young People. Will watched her for a few seconds, made sure that she was off on her rounds of the floor, chatting to customers, then cast about for Fuller.

He couldn't see him.

Will scanned the floor frantically, looking for one sleek head among dozens. He couldn't find the bastard, but Phoebe was standing by the far edge of the dance-floor, chatting to a man in a blazer. She looked up, caught Will's eye, and moved her hand in a casual gesture, pointing.

Will tracked along the room, and found him. Fuller was on the spiral stair, heading up. Will crossed his fingers the man was on his way to the upper balcony, but he didn't keep climbing the stair. He headed off towards the office door, and Will.

The band blared below. Will flexed his fingers.

Kim was still in the office, and if he came out now, Fuller would see him. Will stepped in front of him as he approached. "I say. Just the chap."

"Ah, Mr. Darling. It's good to see you back. I hope you're having a good evening? Excuse me."

He swung nimbly around Will. Will sidestepped to get back in his way. "Very decent, thanks. Can you get me a brandy?"

Fuller raised his hand, making a wiggling gesture with his fingers. "Someone will be along in a moment. Excuse me."

"No, not in a moment." Will let the bonhomie drop out of his voice as he raised the volume. He'd seen plenty of belligerent drunks in his time, and how their moods turned on a sixpence. "I said I wanted a bloody brandy. D'you work here or not?"

"There's a waiter just coming," Fuller said, with a practised stretch of the lips. "A brandy here, right away, on the house. I'm sorry for the delay."

That was beyond reasonable, and Will wasn't in the habit of picking fights without provocation. He simply couldn't think of anything to take further offence at, and in that second Fuller slipped by him, moving towards the office, with Kim still in it.

Will shot a frantic look down at the dance floor, and saw Cynthia edging towards the group of Bright Young Things. A woman looked her up and down, expression mocking, while a tall man in evening dress with grime over his shirt-front made no effort to hide the fact that he was ogling her cleavage.

"Get your hands off her, you dirty bastard!" Will bellowed, loud enough to make people jump two tables away. To make his point, he snatched a wine bottle from a passing waiter's tray, turned, and flung it towards the office. It sailed over Fuller's head and exploded in a shower of shards against the wall, causing quite a lot of screams.

"Hoi!" Fuller shouted. "What the—"

That should do it. Will charged down the stairs, roaring threats and curses and shoving people out of the way. Speed was of the essence: he needed to draw Fuller down, so he barrelled ruthlessly into the crowd on the dancefloor. Someone behind him grabbed at his arm, digging fingers in. Will swung round, dislodging his grip, and Fuller's fist just brushed his jaw as he turned.

Dirty bastard, hitting from behind. Will feinted, and hit him with a straight right, feeling Fuller's nose crunch in a satisfactory manner. The man staggered back, and, since he liked Doris and Cynthia, Will landed a second punch in those offensive teeth. There was an audible crack and a sproing of wire as the dentures broke. Fuller gave a yell of pain and clutched his mouth.

Will swung back to the gaping Bright Young Things. "I'll bloody kill you, you filthy swine!" he shouted at random. A chinless young man grasped his shoulder with a reproving bleat. Will jabbed at his face, making no great effort to pull the blow —*someone* should punch them—and slammed his other elbow sideways, landing it in a soft gut. At that point someone collided with him from behind, and that was when things got hairy.

He was frogmarched out, Fuller on one side, his mouth concave from the broken dentures and bleeding heavily from the nose, and a burly doorman on the other. A waiter hurried after with his coat and hat. They shoved him sprawling onto the wet pavement with what Will felt was unnecessary force.

"Don't come back," Fuller told him thickly, and spat on the pavement.

Will heaved himself to his knees, then his feet, once they'd gone inside. It was drizzling, the cold wet air a relief after the heat of the club and the fight. If Kim hadn't been able to get out without that distraction, he deserved to get caught.

He'd taken a fair few punches, including a glancing one that landed just over his eye, and Fuller had added some vicious kicks when he'd gone down. It was a damn good thing he'd been pulled off by watchers, because Will's ribs hurt. He stretched the pain out for a moment, waiting to see if Phoebe would emerge, but the door remained firmly shut. He hoped that meant she was all right but he lingered on the other side of the road a little longer anyway, keeping a weather eye out for policemen.

Nothing happened. He shrugged on his coat, muddy where it had been thrown in a puddle, slapped on his equally battered hat, and set off down the street.

There was a figure waiting under the lamppost at the end. Kim had on a large topcoat and an opera hat; Will supposed it must be the folding kind. He looked self-possessed and well put together. The bugger.

"Ouch," he said as Will came under the lamplight. "That looks painful."

"You should see the other fellow. Got out all right?"

"Entirely unnoticed, while you were drawing all eyes your way. Thank you, Will. That was spectacular."

"Did you see what happened to Phoebe?"

"Safely surrounded by idiots."

"I whacked a couple of them."

"Good," Kim said wholeheartedly. "You probably need witch hazel on that cut."

"Am I cut?"

Kim indicated his own eyebrow. Will wiped his brow with the back of his hand, and saw the wet skin smeared with blood. "Blast."

"Here." Kim stepped in front of him, bringing them both to a stop on the dark street, and turned to face him. He drew out a handkerchief, glimmering pale in the gloom, and reached out to dab gently at his eyebrow.

"You'll ruin your handkerchief."

"That's all right." Kim pressed the handkerchief to Will's face with light touches, eyes intent. He was a fraction taller, nothing worth noticing, but you couldn't help seeing it up close like this. Will's breath was coming a bit short.

"Nasty cut," Kim said, voice barely more than a whisper. "Perhaps you should come back to my place. Let me clean it up."

"All right."

They walked in near silence. Will didn't want to talk about what was going on, what Kim had found, or been looking for. He wanted them behind a locked door. Everything else could wait.

Kim led the way round to the mews behind his mansion flats without discussing it. He had keys to the back door. They went up the stairs, and Kim let them into the kitchen, relocked the door, and put on the light.

"Sit down. Let me deal with that cut."

"Sod the cut."

Kim touched a finger to his lips. "Sit."

Will sat. In truth his brow was throbbing quite painfully now they were out of the rain.

Kim stripped off his topcoat, and the ugly waiter's jacket. He fetched cotton wool and a bottle of witch hazel, rolled up his sleeves, and carefully cleaned the cut above Will's eye. The witch hazel stank, and it stung.

"Ouch. *Ow*."

"I know you've had worse. I've seen the scars."

"I complained about those too," Will pointed out.

He had no real reason to complain. Kim's hands on Will's face and shoulders were very gentle, and did not feel like a nurse's impersonal touch at all. They both smelled of cigarette smoke and damp cloth, not to mention the witch hazel, but Kim's subtle cologne threaded its way through everything.

"Are you done?"

"Your hand." Kim took Will's right hand, running a thumb over the grazed knuckles almost too lightly to feel. "Let me just—"

"My hand will be fine. I've got better things to do with it."

Will stood. Since Kim didn't move away, that put them face to face and body to body. Will ran his hands down Kim's arms, feeling the muscle under his touch, closing his fingers round the slim forearms with their faded white lines of healed cuts.

The drink and the backwash of fighting had fuzzed his head, and he didn't know what to say. *I want. I need.* His mouth tasted of blood and witch hazel and bad champagne. He wanted it to taste of Kim.

"Will," Kim said on a breath. "There's something I should tell you."

"Is it going to piss me off?"

"You certainly won't be happy."

Will shut his eyes and rested his forehead against Kim's. "So we wouldn't want to fuck afterwards?"

"Well, *you* might not."

Their faces were so close, Will could feel his own warm breath rebound against his skin. "Can it wait till tomorrow?"

"As long as you don't say I didn't warn you."

"Let's go to bed."

He'd only been in Kim's bedroom a few times. It felt more familiar than it should. Kim switched on some of his many lamps as Will struggled out of his coat, then walked over and pulled him into a kiss without a word. His mouth was hard and demanding. Will got a hand on his taut arse, then the other. Kim snarled against his lips, and moved his head to bite gently at Will's earlobes, clutching his shoulders.

"God. Kim. Can I—"

"Yes," Kim said into his skin. "Please do."

They both stripped quickly. Will wasn't sure where the urgency was coming from. Maybe they were trying to outrun whatever trouble followed; he didn't care. He kicked away his trousers and stepped out of his drawers.

Kim sucked in a breath, almost a hiss. "Every time I see you naked…"

"What?" Will was in reasonable shape—he did a lot of manual

work, and he'd filled out in the last few months—but he was solid, not graceful, and he had some ugly scars.

Kim tipped his head. "Many things. Every time I see you naked, I marvel at the gift. I discover a structural weakness in my knees that makes them want to bend. I consider and reject joining a gymnasium." He stroked a very light finger over the ridged line on Will's belly. "I wonder how close you came to not being here."

"That wasn't the bad one."

"Which was?"

"My leg. If it hadn't been for the bravest stretcher-bearer in Flanders, I'd have died out there. A month in hospital."

Kim's fingers trailed down over his hip, to the gnarled skin on his thigh. "This?"

"Mmm."

"Does it hurt?"

"Not any more."

Kim's fingertips were skimming the rough surface of the scar, round and over. "Beautiful."

"The scar?"

"Yes."

"You're bloody odd."

"Scars are always beautiful," Kim said. "They're proof we lived." He ran his fingers back up to Will's stomach, skirting his groin in a way that made Will very aware of it. "What was this one?"

"I walked into a bayonet. What are the ones on your arms?"

"I walked into a razor."

Will looked at the thin white lines. "A razor?"

"I used to cut myself," Kim said, quite calmly. "When I was fourteen, fifteen. It…how can I put this? It let certain feelings out that would have been worse if they stayed in."

Will had no idea how to respond to that. He'd known a fellow in the trenches who'd taken to pinching himself viciously, so his wrists were a constant mess of half-moon nail marks. He didn't want to think of a young Kim hurting his body to escape his mind, or of these scars as proof he had lived through whatever it was. The idea gave him a vast, aching sorrow too big for him to contain.

"I thought you got them when you learned knife fighting," he said, inadequately.

"Don't be absurd. I used wrist protectors."

Will opened his mouth, looked at the thin, faint scars again, and said "But—"

Kim gave a sudden choke of laughter. Will caught his eye and spluttered, and then they were both laughing, stupidly because it wasn't funny, and gloriously because it was.

"A foolish consistency is the hobgoblin of little minds," Kim said. "Shut up."

Will wanted to hold him, to wrap his arms around him and find out what was wrong and make it right. That wasn't in his power and Kim probably wouldn't have welcomed it anyway. He said, instead, "Come to bed," because he didn't know how to say anything else, and took Kim's hand.

There was no hurry. That was important, somehow. He took his time, kissing and touching, and Kim did the same. Hands over each other, using touch because words were large and frightening things. Forgetting about scars, for now.

After a while Kim sat up on Will's spread thighs, took his left hand, and very slowly took a finger in his mouth. Will sucked in a breath. Kim drew the ring of his lips steadily up and down, with obvious symbolic effect but also providing a world of sensation in itself. Will had no idea his battered hands had so much feeling left in them; his prick jerked painfully. Kim seemed in no hurry, taking each toughened finger in turn, running tongue and teeth over the knotty joints and hardened skin, drawing his manicured nails across Will's palm, slow and lingering and making his toes curl.

"You have beautiful hands," he murmured. "I'm sure I mentioned this."

"You did. You're wrong, but you did."

"I'm not wrong." Kim kissed the inside of Will's wrist. "I'm never wrong."

Will managed a snort that turned into a yelp when Kim leaned forward and captured a nipple with his mouth. "God!"

"You're remarkably sensitive tonight," Kim purred. His teeth rasped over the nub, hardening it. Will squirmed under him, the more when Kim's hand slid down his side, over his hip, between his legs. Kim's mouth and hand moved together, sending pleasure spiking up and down, his cock rubbing hot and hard against Will's leg in time with the movements.

Will moaned. Kim lifted his head away. "Can I suck you off?"

"No. Don't." He didn't want Kim kneeling between his legs, face hidden, feelings unreadable. He reached for the dark head. "Stay up here with me."

Kim's lips parted a little. Will pulled him up and wriggled down to kiss him, cupping the back of his skull to keep him there, thighs and hips and pricks bumping beautifully together. Thank God for being the same height. He clamped his other hand on Kim's smooth arse, feeling the muscle work, the vibration of his groan. Kim shifted over him, clamping Will's cock between his legs, his own rubbing between their stomachs, and they rocked and kissed, kissed and rocked, fingers gripping and tongues duelling, until first one then the other groaned and jerked and came.

They lay together, a tangle of arms and legs, body heat and wet spunk. Kim let his head drop to the crook of Will's neck, leaving him with a faceful of fine hair.

"Not sophisticated," he said at last, muffled. "But good."

"Did you want sophisticated?" Will asked, with a stab of self-consciousness.

"Not tonight. I think I wanted honesty. Thank you."

Will dropped an arm over his shoulder. They lay together in silence for a moment until Kim shifted, which made it apparent that the sticky mess on Will's belly had started gluing them together. "Ugh. This must be what they call a mess of frottage."

"Jesus *Christ*. Had you been planning that long?"

Kim grinned and rolled off. "I'll get a cloth."

EIGHT

Sleeping with Kim was always good. Waking with him had, to date, been a more mixed experience.

On this occasion he was still in bed when Will woke with a mild headache, a sense he hadn't had enough sleep, and a tight patch on the hairs of his stomach where he'd missed a bit of spunk. He dropped an arm over his eyes. Kim said, "Hello."

"Morning."

"Sleep well?"

"Not bad. Is your chap likely to wander in with a cup of tea for sir?"

"That's 'my lord' to you, and no. Peacock does clothes, cooking, and occasional espionage. I make tea myself."

"Is that an offer?"

"I walked into that," Kim said with mild disgust, and rolled out of bed. Will took the opportunity to admire his back view until he covered it with his purple gown and went in the direction of the kettle, and then took himself off to the bathroom to borrow Kim's toothbrush and make himself rather more presentable.

By the time Kim returned with a tray, Will was sitting up in bed flicking through a book and feeling civilised.

"Tea," Kim said, handing him a cup. Will took a sip. It was horrifyingly weak. "Are you reading *The Waste Land*?"

"No, you are." It had been the only thing on Kim's bedside table. Will didn't consider Modernist poetry much of a bedtime story. "I've read it already. I had a copy in the shop a couple of months ago."

"Thoughts?"

"It doesn't rhyme."

He closed the slim volume and put it on the table as Kim got into bed, a feat he managed without spilling his tea, and sat with his knees up, so their shoulders didn't quite touch.

"Are we talking now?" Will asked. "Or is the door still locked?"

"It is locked, but—as you wish."

"Tea first." The tea was undrinkable, but he didn't really want to know what Kim had been hiding about the job either. It would doubtless be infuriating, but he was less concerned by that than by whatever pain had driven a boy, a privileged marquess's son at that, to let it out with a blade. Kim had no fresh scars, nothing within the last decade or more. Will had a crawling sort of worry that was because he'd found less visible ways to hurt himself.

There were a lot of things he wanted to know, and he wasn't sure he could ask most of them. They were private, secret things, and physical intimacy didn't automatically open the door for those. You could ask a lover for them, but he couldn't call Kim his lover in any conventional sense. Or even a conventionally unconventional one.

"I don't know what the rules are," he said aloud.

"Sorry?"

"The rules for us. What we are, what we're doing. I don't know how we're expected to behave in this situation."

"We're expected not to do it at all," Kim said. "That being the case, behave as you like."

"Rubbish. There's still rights and wrongs and expectations. Things you ought to do, lines not to cross. The things you won't change, the things I won't put up with, the things we both want. I'd like to know where I stand."

"Wouldn't we all. I'm not sure where I stand either, Will. I had an equilibrium before you turned up."

"I didn't turn up. *You* turned up. You hired a thug to wreck my shop."

"Moan, moan, moan. He didn't break anything expensive."

Will made an offensive gesture. Kim gave him a rueful half-smile. "How do we set rules for the game when neither of us is sure what we're playing at? You have no idea what you want, and I don't know how I'd give it to you."

"Start with this: I want to know what you do."

"You already know that."

"No, I don't. You were a Bolshevik once, unless you weren't, and now you work for the War Office, or maybe you're a free-lance spy. What are you, exactly? What does it mean for you? If I'm helping you, who else am I helping?"

"Is that the most important thing to you?"

Far from it, but it was a truth he thought he could get, which would be a start. "You keep lying to me about it, so it probably matters. I want you to trust me with this."

"I do trust you."

"You've a funny way of showing it."

"Too true." Kim turned the cup in his hands, round and back. "Ugh. In confidence, Will. Not to insult you, but it has to be said."

"Understood."

"All right, then. You may know that there's a patchwork of what are flatteringly called intelligence agencies—Special Branch, SIS, the Private Bureau, and so on—which were set up by various people before the war on a more or less amateurish basis. Most of them are now being swallowed up into either Military Intelligence or the police force; some remain as independent operators of sorts. I work for the Private Bureau, which as the name suggests is very much a relic of the Edwardian era, and which has carved out a very specific niche dealing with problems that need brushing under the carpet. If the powers that be want a problem solved without such tiresome trivia as written records or court cases, if they don't want official fingerprints on the scene of the crime or it's important that a minister should be able to swear he never gave any such order, they come to the Private Bureau. Whereupon someone like me will slither around doing things that couldn't possibly be countenanced by those paid to uphold the law—entrapping innocent bookshop owners, and so on. Making sure things don't come to light."

"Cover-ups?"

Kim shrugged. "The well-connected are protected, that goes without saying, but there are other issues. We deal with a fair few cases of extortion." He waved a hand, indicating the bed they shared. "One might be disinclined to report a blackmailer to the police for fear of consequences, whereas the Private Bureau has no compulsion to punish the victims."

"What about the perpetrators?"

"Consequences happen," Kim said. "Sometimes officially, sometimes not. Jobs are lost. Bank accounts are emptied. Words are dropped in ears, and decisions are made to leave the country and start a new life in South America. The passive voice does a lot of work in my line."

Will frowned. "It sounds a bit dodgy."

"It is; that's the point. The Bureau offers a certain amount of leeway. I don't know if it's a good or useful thing for society in general, but it's certainly handy if—for example—one has made a miserable hash of one's life. And if you don't mind owing the chief a favour, up to and including your soul."

Will examined his face, the little lines at the corner of his eyes. "That seems a bit of a leap from being a paid-up Bolshevik."

Kim didn't reply for so long that Will began to think he wouldn't. At last he said, "I really did believe in it, you know."

"You don't seem the fanatic sort."

"Fanatic, idealist." Kim waved a hand. "I thought there was a better way for everyone. I believed—still do—that the war was nothing but empires squabbling for resources, with the blood of millions used to keep the engine running. I refused to be involved in mass murder, and tried my hardest to be gaoled as a conscientious objector, though my father put paid to that. I sincerely cheered the Revolution in 1917 and looked forward to the British equivalent. And then reports started coming in of the bloodbath."

"You thought it would be a bloodless revolution? Because you don't get many of them."

"I know. But the fact of children lined up and shot—I told myself the aristocracy had brought it on themselves, that they had sowed the wind and were reaping the whirlwind, but by 1919 and the atrocities of the civil war, I couldn't hide behind that any more. I couldn't persuade myself mass slaughter was the beginning of a fairer society; I could only think of how the French had guillotined their king and created a vacancy for an emperor."

Well, yes, Will thought. Obviously whoever came out on top of any society would be a power-hungry arsehole: that was how the world worked. "You really were an idealist," he said aloud.

"Is that so surprising?"

It was, considering his grimy goings-on these days. Or maybe it wasn't; maybe spoiled innocence tarnished faster than healthy cynicism. The thought gave Will the same uncomfortable feeling as Kim's scars.

"I was sickened," Kim went on. "Whereas my comrades, the ones with whom I'd planned a British revolution, were positively thrilled. They talked with enthusiasm about setting up a British Cheka. They *wanted* a secret police and summary killing of class traitors. Most of them were Oxford and Cambridge men of birth, I should observe."

"Of course they were."

"They revelled in the idea of mass execution, bodies in the streets. I can't convey what it was like to watch civilised people go through the intellectual gymnastics necessary to persuade themselves that state murder was first a regrettable necessity, and then a high treat."

"I suppose you'd need to," Will said. "If what you believe in goes wrong, either you let go the belief, or you believe even harder."

"And it hurts to let go. God, it hurts. My ideals were a bad joke. My family had disowned me over them. My brother, my little brother had called me a coward and gone to war in my place, and he was dead. If I'd gone he'd be alive now, but he was dead because of what I chose, and every piece of news from Russia made it clearer that I'd chosen poorly. My idols were false, and for all my principles, the only person I had saved by not going to war was myself. Everyone who despised me for it had been right." He breathed out hard. "And it all rather came crashing down."

Will put both empty cups on the bedside table and reached for Kim's hand, squeezing his fingers. They felt cold. "Kim—"

"Don't insult me with comfort. If I'd enlisted, Henry would be alive now, but since I refused, he's dead. It's as simple as that."

"No, it isn't. You might as well say *If Henry had stood a foot to the left, he'd be alive,* and blame him for being in the wrong place. I was there, Kim. I knew a chap who tripped over a rock and his pal behind him took the bullet that went over his head. He never got over it to my knowledge. Was it his fault?"

"He didn't duck it deliberately. I did."

"And your brother signed up deliberately. He was a grown man who chose to march into a meat-grinder that had already chewed up millions of us. It *was* mass murder; maybe if more people had stood against it, fewer would have died. I know why he went to war, I signed up too, but that doesn't make either of us clever."

"Nobody ever claimed Henry was clever," Kim said. "But he had to go because I did not. It really is that simple."

"It bloody isn't. I'm trying to tell you. You can't just say *if this then that*, and decide what would have happened when the whole thing was a sodding lucky dip. What if he'd gone anyway and you'd both got killed? What if he'd stayed home and died of the 'flu? What if there's some German lad right now discovering a cure for the common cold because you weren't there to put a knife in his ribs? What if one of the men I killed was going to be a great leader, but he met me in a trench? If you want to start on *They'd be alive if only I hadn't*, we'll be here all day."

"Yes, but—"

"Not 'but'. You're talking as if you had some sort of control, like if you'd behaved differently, the whole world would have been different. Don't flatter yourself."

Kim gave a short laugh. "I had no idea that was what I was doing. You cannot talk this away, Will. I did harm. Henry went to France as a direct consequence of my refusal to enlist, and he died there. I lived, he died, and it was all for nothing. I'm not asking for absolution: I took the wrong path, and there's no comfort in pretending I didn't. Christ, I made a hash of things."

That part was inarguable. "So you joined this Private Bureau to make them right?"

"I can't even claim that. I couldn't see any way ahead. But I'd met a fellow socially who, little did I know, was the Bureau chief. He paid me a visit, and said he had a use for me. I told him it was more than I did, that I didn't care if I lived or died, and he said excellent, that was exactly what he wanted."

"Charming."

"He saved my life. For his own purposes, of course, but he never claimed otherwise. He set me to join an actively dangerous

Bolshevist group—as it turned out, one run by Zodiac—and I turned out to have a knack for the game. Between that and Phoebe, who needed a keeper, I managed to believe I was doing something useful while I put myself back together. So there you are."

Will nodded slowly. He'd asked the question, but the last thing he'd expected was a comprehensive answer, still less one that felt so rawly honest. He felt like he'd stepped into an unseen pit.

They sat for a few minutes in silence. Will had no idea what was happening in Kim's head, but he'd spent plenty of time with men whose wounds weren't on the outside, so he waited. Sometimes that was the only thing you could do.

At last Kim shifted. "Sorry. I don't talk about this very well. I hear what you said to me, and I appreciate it."

"I don't mean to tell you how you ought to feel about your brother. Only that, if you go around counting up the cost of lives from what we all did and didn't do, the numbers aren't going to be pretty for anyone."

"Perhaps that's a reason to count them."

"True. But then, if your lads had come through, if the Bolsheviks had brought in what they promised and made things better for everyone, wouldn't it have been worth the cost?"

"Also true."

Will sighed. "Fucking war." He looked round at Kim's huff of laughter. "Well, that's what it comes down to, isn't it? So when you said you worked for the War Office before..."

"It was true as far as it went. I was on loan. DS—that's my chief, intelligence men have a fashion of going by initials—sits like a spider at the centre of a web of obligations, occasionally pulling threads. I am a resource to be used, just like everyone else."

"So if I help you, I'm working for the government, but not getting paid?"

"The Private Bureau very definitely isn't the government. I doubt most of the Cabinet know it exists: they don't have to. It ticks quietly away in a corner of Whitehall without anyone paying attention. I've a long leash, and a free hand."

"And authority?"

"In what sense?"

"I just helped you commit a burglary—"

"Unlawful entry, at most."

"Still unlawful. Are you allowed to break the law? I stabbed a man on your behalf last time; I'd like to know."

"Murder is not encouraged, and best avoided," Kim said. "I am absolutely not empowered to break the laws of the land, so I try not to get caught at it. But when push comes to shove, DS protects his own, is owed a great many favours, and knows where the bodies are buried."

Will contemplated his profile. Kim had been looking ahead throughout the conversation, not once making eye contact. "Do you feel right about what you do?"

"I've done things that needed doing. That's a significant improvement."

"All right. I see. Thanks for talking to me."

"I wish you wouldn't put it like that," Kim said. "It rather emphasises how bloody awful I am at this. I'm sorry, Will. You deserve better."

"I deserve you not to lie to me about what I'm doing. I'll work with you, but I want to know who I'm working for and against. And something else." Their hands were still touching, had been throughout all that. Will interlaced their fingers deliberately. "This is a rule for you: you don't use me to punish yourself. You don't decide not to talk to me for two months to keep me out of danger or because you're a terrible person who deserves to be alone, or any of that. I'll tell you what I deserve, and what I want to be involved in, and I'll let you know when I've done with you, same as you can me. Got that?"

Kim looked round at last. "What does that mean, 'when I've done with you'?"

"Like we said the other day. When I decide I don't want to keep on, I'll tell you so, and you can do the same. Only, actually tell me next time, all right?"

Kim gave a half smile. "When you don't want to keep on. When will that be?"

"How should I know? I don't know what I'm doing. Nothing's gone like I thought it would since 1914. And all I can think about is you."

Kim's mouth opened. He looked just a little desperate, and just a little hopeful, and then he reached for Will's head, leaned over, and kissed him hard.

Will grabbed his shoulder, feeling the tension, still holding his other hand. They kissed savagely, tongues tangling, need rising fast, and if this was a way for Kim not to talk about things any more, Will could live with that for now.

Kim threw a thigh over Will and pulled himself across so he was sitting over his lap, leaning forward to keep their mouths joined, hips and pricks rubbing together. Will freed his hand and grabbed Kim's dark head, the stupid beautiful lying hurting bastard that he was.

"Just..." He didn't know what to say. *Stay with me. Talk to me. Hide in me if you have to. Don't be alone.* "Jesus. Kim."

"I need you to fuck me," Kim said against his mouth. "Please."

"So do I."

Kim leaned over to get the Vaseline from his bedside drawer, clamping his thighs over Will's to keep his balance, with interesting effect. Will took the opportunity to run his hand over Kim's arse, buttocks tense with the movement. Kim purred, and Will hauled him up with one arm to keep him sprawled over his lap, stroking the bare flesh, feeling the prick hot and hard against his leg. He ran his fingers lightly over Kim's skin, down the cleft of his arse, between his legs. Kim spasmed under him.

"Tell me again," Will said, hoarsely. "Let me hear it."

"I want you to fuck me. I want you in me and all over me."

Will pressed up with his thigh. "You're hard for me. For this. You know how much that makes me want you?"

Kim whimpered. Good. Will wanted him mewling, and desperate, and not thinking about anything else. More, he wanted to take charge. Last time, which had been Will's second go at the act in his life, Kim had had to talk him through it. He planned to do better now.

He got his rough hand over the muscle and flesh of one arse cheek, squeezing it. "Christ, I want this. And I'm having it."

Kim widened his legs obligingly. Will let his fingers delve between, over the crinkled skin of his balls, up and down the divide of his arse, stroking and rubbing as Kim rocked on his lap. He took the Vaseline from the bed where Kim had put it and scooped out what seemed even to him an excessive amount, just in case. "Suppose I get a finger up you."

Kim made a needy noise. Will steeled himself—it was all very well talking like he knew what he was doing, but Kim had done this bit last time—found the opening, and gently eased a very slippery finger in.

It was tight, and hot. He slid the fingertip in and out, tiny motions, gaining confidence. Kim moaned.

"You want this," Will told him. He pushed a little further, feeling the muscle around the digit. "And I know how much you want it, and that is driving me out of my mind. Tell me again."

"I need it. I need you. I want you to fuck me till I forget my own name."

"What, all of it?"

"Take that as a hint."

Kim was squirming on Will's lap, rocking back and forth

against the exploring finger. Will pushed it in to the knuckle, brushing against a hard knot.

Kim made a high-pitched noise, muscles stiffening. Will rubbed the nub, watching him jerk. Kim had taught him about this last time, that men had something like a woman's clit up there, and that seemed about right given the reaction he was getting. He had a sudden urge to find out for himself, because Kim's fingers were clutching at nothing and his toes were curling. Maybe one day. Right now he had Kim Secretan writhing like a landed fish, and Will had never felt so powerful in his life.

"God, you love this. You should be ashamed of yourself, how much you love this."

"Oh, I am," Kim assured him breathlessly. "Utterly. Now embarrass me till I can't walk."

Will withdrew his hand and scooped up another glob of Vaseline. "Up."

Kim manoeuvred himself up one lanky limb at a time. It seemed to take some effort. He sat back on his heels, watching as Will smeared the petroleum jelly over his own cock, taking his time because of the expression in Kim's eyes at the display.

"Christ," Kim said. "Are you trying to kill me?"

"Might be."

"Carry on."

"Pleasure." Will knelt up. "What's the best position for me to ram it right through you?"

Possibly that was a bit much. Then again, Kim's eyes widened quite magnificently, so maybe not. He moved silently to hands and knees, and Will got behind him, steadying himself with a hand to the shoulder. He eased forward. "Tell me when?"

Kim breathed out. "Now."

Will pushed in, felt the ring of muscle give. Kim was tight around him, his back rigid under Will's hand. Will took it slowly, in part because he was wary about causing hurt, in part because his ribs hurt considerably from Fuller's kicks, and in part because he was about an inch from coming, which would be a poor show after all the big talk. He paused to give himself a minatory squeeze, and carried on, listening to Kim's harsh breaths, working his way deeper, in and out, until they were both ready. He got hold of Kim's hips. "All right?"

"More than."

"Still remember your name?"

"There's an Aloysius in there to forget. For Christ's sake—"

Will thrust in, pulling with his hands at the same time, slamming in almost harder than he'd meant. Kim cried out, a yell that rang off the walls, and snarled, "Again, you bastard," before Will could question him. So he did it again, finding a rhythm, Kim shouting with each thrust as if it hurt but shoving back hard against him for the next.

"Legs wider," Will rasped, shoving one thigh. "I want you—" He couldn't think of a word. "Spatchcocked."

Kim made a noise that could have been a laugh or a sob and obeyed, going down to his elbows for balance. Will leaned forward, making him take his weight, and wrapped an arm round his hip, under his belly, capturing his prick. He lost some of the leverage this way but gravity made up for it, and he fucked Kim frantically in a call-and-response of cries and thrusts until he heard the timbre of his lover's voice change in a way he recognised.

"Oh, there you go," he gasped. "What's your name?"

"Who fucking cares?"

"You love it. You're going to come with every inch of me in you and love it."

Kim's legs gave way and he fell forward onto the bed, trapping Will's arm under his belly. Will thrust hard—*I'll break the bed for you if that's what you want*—giving up on holding himself back as he heard Kim gasp and sob his pleasure, driving for his own climax, emptying his balls and his bone marrow and his heart into Kim.

He fell forward over the other's back, face in his neck, wondering vaguely if he'd had a stroke. There were multicoloured dots swimming in his vision.

"Good Lord," Kim said after a few moments. "You're a man of your word."

"Was that—"

"It was. It really was."

"Did I hurt you?"

"Not in any way I wouldn't pay good money for."

Will heaved himself up onto his elbows and eased out with a wince. "Bit of a mess."

"Don't worry about it."

His manservant must be extremely understanding. Will flopped onto his back. Kim rolled far enough onto his side to sling an arm over him.

He'd fallen asleep within seconds, the only other time they'd done this. Being awake made a fellow a bit self-conscious. He wanted to ask again if Kim had really liked it that way, but it seemed too close to fishing for compliments.

"Was that good for you?" Kim asked abruptly. "I know it's not your preference."

"Bloody good. It's strong meat, but God, Kim. The way you are." He put his hand up to meet the one draped over him. Kim's fingers laced into his so easily and naturally. "You make me feel like a prize bull."

"You have reason to," Kim assured him. "And on that note, I am going to claim the privilege of first wash." He pulled Will's hand over, kissed the knuckles, and swung himself out of bed, not without an intake of breath. Something probably stung.

Will lay back in a warm haze of sated desire. Like the sheets, it began to cool fairly quickly.

He wasn't fool enough to think that a good bout in bed solved anything, or that Kim's wounds were in his power to heal. He didn't delude himself that asking Kim to tell him the truth meant it would happen, either. They'd been honest with one another as far as it went, and that was something, maybe even a lot, but Will had a feeling all it had achieved was to dig their foxhole deeper.

Kim was taking up an alarming amount of space in his mind. If he was thinking this much about a woman, he'd have no trouble finding a name for it. He dropped an arm over his eyes and pushed the thought down with the rest of the more troubling Kim thoughts—how he kissed, how he smelled, how he cried out when he climaxed, how his mouth felt on Will's cock and his fingers on his skin, and how very much Will didn't want to know what he'd been lying about.

He needed to stop. This way madness lay, probably literally.

He sat up when he heard Kim emerging from the bathroom. He entered, hair wet and wearing nothing but a towel slung very low around his lean hips, which still bore faint red marks from Will's fingers. "Bathroom's free."

Will got up, naked and badly in need of a wash. As he passed, Kim caught his face with a damp hand and kissed him open-mouthed, and he fell into the pleasure of it all over again.

NINE

Kim had run him a bath. Will had a good scrub and emerged feeling a lot more decent. He borrowed Kim's spare gown, and poked his head into the kitchen, where he discovered his partner in crime frying sausages.

"Better?" Kim said. "Breakfast shortly, if you want to get dressed."

Will donned his rather mud-splattered trousers and once-white shirt, regrettably aware that he looked like a treasure-hunting Bright Young Person, only not so young or bright. Kim had put on the kettle again and they sat at the kitchen table eating sausage sandwiches.

Will broached the subject first. "So are you going to tell me whatever it was from last night?"

"There is a certain amount."

"I bet there is."

"First of which is that our exploits had only limited success. Skyrme has a large safe with an exceedingly modern combination lock, and she's disciplined about keeping anything of interest in there. Her desk and filing cabinet contained nothing useful. If there's anything juicy, it's in the safe. Which means we have to go back."

"Blast," Will said. "So if you don't have anything to tell me about that, what's going to piss me off?"

"An excellent question. What I *did* find was a small notebook she had left in her handbag, which I had a flick through but didn't take for fear of giving her warning. It contained names, initials, dates, sums of money. I looked for dates that seemed meaningful to me, including those Beaumont gave us for Mrs. Appleby's previous trips."

"And?"

"There were two entries with dates around the times of her return, the initials FA, and very large sums of money. About thirteen thousand pounds in total."

"Jesus," Will said. "For furs?"

"It was never furs. Mrs. Skyrme gave Appleby's boy friend a job to keep her sweet, then made her a lifelong enemy to force her to take this last trip. That's not about dodging import duty."

Will scrubbed a hand over his eyes. "Blast and damn. Dope?"

"We'll find out."

"A lot of money, anyway, and all of it going through Mrs. Skyrme's hands. Which were gloved again last night, by the way."

"I'm sure they were," Kim said. "I think she's Aquarius, the water-carrier. Zodiac's money-washerwoman."

"Jesus Christ. Let me think a moment."

Will had half a sandwich left. He finished it while turning matters over in his head.

It looked like Beaumont's lover was so far up a gum tree, she was liable to snap her neck on the way down. If Will was instrumental in her facing the consequences of her actions, he'd have served Beaumont a truly shitty turn.

"What about Mrs. Appleby?" he asked.

"What about her?"

"I promised Beaumont—"

"She killed Leinster," Kim said. "When she gave him up to Skyrme, she killed him as surely as if she shoved him under the train herself."

"She didn't know that would happen."

"What do you imagine she expected when she asked a black-mailing smuggler to deal with a threat for her?"

"I don't imagine she thought about it at all," Will said. "She thought she was paying off a bridge debt with a bit of under-the-table work."

"She's a grown woman. She knew she was committing an offence and abusing her husband's position, and she knew Skyrme was a ruthless bitch when she gave her Leinster's name. She might not have known exactly what would happen to him, but she wasn't expecting an invitation to afternoon tea."

"Maybe. All right, yes. But I still promised Beaumont."

"Which is why you should have let me make the promises," Kim snapped.

Will glared at him. "Don't make me a liar."

Their eyes locked, not in a good way. Kim's lips were pressed together.

He'd known the dead man. He'd probably imagined a hand in the small of his own back, a sharp push on a rainy night, the rush and clamour of an oncoming train. Will breathed out. "I'm not saying you shouldn't be angry. But make it with the people who did this, not the ones they lured in and twisted up in their nets. What happened to Leinster is down to Skyrme and Fuller, and the greedy bastards in Zodiac, and I'm ready to go after them. But give me this."

"Why?"

"Because you might have learned to betray people, but I don't want to."

Kim inhaled, a tiny sharp hiss. Will shrugged. "Sorry. I'll use a knife for you but I'm not putting it in a friend's back."

"How very moral." Kim's voice had a clipped, almost sneering edge. "Would you prefer her to suffer no consequences at all for the misery to which her smuggling has contributed, or shall we help her obtain her divorce as well? Flowers at the wedding, perhaps?"

"If you hadn't lied to me in the first place, we wouldn't be having this conversation," Will reminded him. "So don't push it."

They glared at each other a moment longer. Finally Kim rose, an irritated movement. "I can't let another shipment of whatever the hell it is fall into Zodiac hands."

"I'm not suggesting you do. And if Mrs. Appleby knew for a fact Leinster would come to harm, you can hang her out to dry with my goodwill. But I made a promise, and Beaumont wouldn't have talked without it."

Kim stalked to the kettle. "All right, all right. Let me think."

"While you're thinking, you can tell me what we do next," Will said. "Go after the safe?"

"Yes. I have to get at Skyrme's files. If she's the money woman, she must be inner circle. She's connected to Capricorn. She'll know who he is."

"Capricorn's the head, right?"

"And where there's a head, there can be a guillotine."

He knew that note in Kim's voice and it set the wolf in Will howling. "Let's do it. Can you open safes?"

"Of course not: that's rather the point of the things. It's a combination lock, and short of drilling, which takes hours, the only way to open it is to get the combination."

"Any ideas?"

"Well, since Mrs. Skyrme lacks the common decency to keep it written on a piece of paper in her drawer..." Kim grinned harshly. "We'll just have to ask her."

They met Beaumont a few days later. Will had arranged for him to come to the bookshop at five. Kim arrived via the back room a little before the appointed hour, Beaumont rather later, collar up and hat pulled well down. Will let him in, locked up, ushered him through to the back room, and leaned casually against the door to the shop.

Beaumont was looking decidedly twitchy. "What's going on?" he asked without preamble.

"We're looking into the High-Low still," Kim said. "And we need a little more help from you."

"You must be joking. All hell broke loose last time. Fuller interrogated the whole staff about Darling and whether any of us knew him."

"Did you tell him the truth?"

"Of course not. I need this job."

"You shouldn't count on it lasting much longer." Kim sounded as cool and collected as if he wasn't talking about a man's livelihood. "There is a great deal of funny business going on at the High-Low. Now would be a good time to start looking for new employment."

"Easy for you to say!"

"True," Kim agreed. "Nevertheless, I'm giving you the best advice I can, which is to get out before the people asking the questions are wearing uniforms."

"You didn't say this would happen!" Beaumont objected. "I said I'd help you with this blackmail business, not have my whole life upended."

"I'm sorry about that, but it turns out Mrs. Skyrme has her fingers in a number of pies." Kim's voice was urbane as ever, his eyes expressionless, and Will had the oddest sensation of hearing a violin string pulled too tight. "Consider yourself fortunate that I can attest to your cooperation. It will look a great deal better for you if things go bad."

"For me? What have *I* done?"

"You've looked the other way for a long time. Whether that's enough to support a charge of aiding and abetting, I don't know, but if I were you, I wouldn't wait to find out. It is, of course, your mistress who will face the full force of the law."

Beaumont sprang to his feet. "What? No! Absolutely not. You can't bring her into this."

"She is in it up to her neck," Kim said. "She has been abusing her husband's position in the Foreign Office to smuggle illegal goods."

"Import duty on a few furs—"

"It isn't furs." Kim's voice was cold and hard. "It's a great deal worse than furs, and you must have realised that."

Beaumont's expression made denial implausible. "You don't understand. She's innocent—trusting—"

"She's an active participant in a smuggling operation, and she has done a great deal of irreversible harm." He paused, holding Beaumont's gaze. "But she could help put some of it right. I need her to hand over those cigarettes and chocolates when she returns."

"Why?"

"Because that's what Mrs. Skyrme wants, and I can use them against her."

"No," Beaumont said. "No, no. If you do that, Mrs. Skyrme will know Flora gave them to you. All hell will break loose."

Kim laughed, a short and mirthless sound. "You think that can be avoided? If Mrs. Appleby hands over everything to me tomorrow, I will do my best to keep her name out of it; if the authorities get involved, I will ensure her cooperation is noted. That's the best I can do, but I will do it. *If* she hands them over."

"And if she doesn't?" Beaumont demanded, and squared his shoulders. He was Kim's height, a little broader. Will shifted slightly at the door, enough to make his presence felt, and Beaumont sent him a look of something like hatred.

"Then I do my worst rather than my best," Kim said. "I will

personally ensure that she faces the full legal consequences for everything in which she has been implicated, which extends far beyond mere duty fraud. She will be gaoled, she will be ruined, your affair will come out, and being trapped in her marriage will be the least of her problems. I'd take the first option if I were you."

"Or maybe we'll do what's best for us and you can go to hell. I'm not playing your damned game, and if you're being black-mailed you should think twice about forcing other people into things. Suppose I tell the authorities to take a close look at you, eh? What about that?"

"Be my guest," Kim said. "But if Mrs. Appleby does not oblige, she'll pay."

Beaumont was white-faced. "You shit." He swung around to Will. "Are you just going to stand there? This man is threatening me! You entrapped me!"

"Your decisions led you here," Kim said. "I suggest you take responsibility for them."

"I'll speak for myself," Will told him. "Beaumont, you don't know what your girl friend has been mixed up in. If I were you, I'd do what he's asking. I'm sorry, but that's how it is."

"Damned if I will. What the devil do you mean, what she's been mixed up in? All she did was bring in a few bits and pieces!"

"Quite," Kim said. "And when my colleague, a man called Leinster, came to ask questions, she told Mrs. Skyrme all about him, and now he—a British agent—is dead."

Beaumont's mouth opened soundlessly, fishlike. Kim's lip curled. "There is blood on your mistress's hands. If she wants to wash it off, she should help me now. If she doesn't, I'll make her pay in full for her part in Leinster's death. Let me know which you prefer."

Will had rather expected Kim to vanish again while he let Beaumont out of the shop, trying to ignore his look of open hatred. But he was still there, seated on the camp bed, back to the wall, waiting.

"Get what you want?"

"I think so. I'm sorry, Will. This is a dirty business."

"You warned me it would be." He hesitated. "Does it get easier?"

"Betrayal? Not much."

Will came and sat next to him, resting his shoulders against the chilly plaster, hearing the bed's familiar creak. There was very little he wanted to say, so he didn't, just listened to Kim breathe.

"My first time was in 1920," Kim said after a while. "Well, I say that: some people might place my first betrayal a great deal earlier. And I dare say I betrayed my family and my class very thoroughly when I changed my allegiances and refused to go to war. But the first time I set out to do it, quite deliberately to an individual..." He made a face.

"Was this the Bolshie lot, the one you mentioned?"

"Yes. Maclean, who you knew as Libra, had a little group with large ambitions. I, let us say, persuaded one of them to trust me, sufficiently that he introduced me as a new recruit, and with what I learned, DS and the Private Bureau turned them inside out. Maclean got away, but three of them received hefty prison sentences, and my—the man I'd entrapped hanged himself before trial."

"Jesus Christ."

"Quite."

Will wondered if he had the right to ask, and did it anyway. "How did you feel about that?"

"Not much worse than I did every other day. That was the great advantage of my situation for DS, you see: it hardly mattered what sort of job he gave me."

"I'd like a word with this fellow."

"Don't blame him," Kim said. "The group in question was planning a large-scale bombing campaign, my dear friend included, so finer feelings be damned. If I had to do it again, I would. Some things need doing."

"You still have to live with yourself afterwards."

"How many men did you stab in the dark?" Kim flashed. "Is the dark so much better than the back?"

"I've got to live with myself too. I'll take your word you did the right things, or at least did things for the right reasons."

Kim's shoulders dropped. "I wish you would, then perhaps you could persuade me of it. I'm truly sorry about Beaumont. He'll loathe you now, and I dare say you'll feel responsible if his girl friend pays the price. I should have found a way to get at him that didn't involve you."

"You should, yes. Though you didn't know what would come up."

"I knew it would be bad." He sighed. "I have a lowering feeling I was giving myself an excuse to see you again."

Will had to take that in for a second. "Were you?"

"Probably. Yes. Of course I was."

"That's…" Will didn't know what to say. "You couldn't have just answered the 'phone? Oh, hell, Kim. Sometimes you have to get the job done. I understand that. Some things don't happen in a gentlemanly way. You can't stay clean if you're knee deep in mud, and that's all there is to it."

"Some people would call that an argument not to get in the mud in the first place."

"Except the mud is where the work is," Will said. "Or the war. Clean hands were for people who didn't go."

"I didn't go, and look at my hands now."

Will took Kim's manicured fingers in his own toughened hand. "Yes, I know. Put a lot more work in and they might end up like mine. Do you know the thing about stabbing people in the back?"

"What?"

"They don't scream."

Kim twisted round to give him a look. Will said, "They just groan, can't help it. It's like the blow takes the breath out of them. So if you need someone to die quietly, that's what you do, and never mind being honourable about it."

"I'll...bear that in mind," Kim said, and they sat together in silence.

TEN

Mrs. Appleby didn't arrive in the country until Sunday and Kim had preparatory work to do. That left Will at a loose end for a bit, until he learned that he was non-negotiably invited to the couturiers' dinner at the Criterion on Saturday evening.

"But why on earth do you want me there?" he asked Maisie. "I'm no use to you. I don't know anything about fashion."

"I know, but..." Maisie gave him a frantic look. "Edward Molyneux and a lady who works directly for Jeanne Lanvin are coming, Will! And Adela Moran, who Coco Chanel sometimes uses, and Gloria Glade the film star, and Kim and Phoebe will be there being Lord Arthur Secretan and the Honourable Miss Stephens-Prince—all in the Criterion, for *me*, and I'm terrified. You won't be terrified. I need you there *not* being terrified, or I might be sick."

"You do want to do this fashion thing, right?"

She gave him a look. "Yes. It's what I've dreamed of for years, and now it's not just a dream but a thing that might happen. A real hope. Is there anything more terrifying than getting what you hope for?"

What Will might hope for wasn't even something he could think about properly. "Fair point."

"It will be all right once I've started. Phoebe's doing it for me, she'll make it work. But I desperately don't want to let her down, and it's the first time, and everyone else will be posh, and—I need someone like me there, on my side. Please?"

Oh God. But this was Maisie, so Will set his shoulders. "Any idea where I can get evening dress before Saturday?"

"Phoebe said she'll arrange it. Oh, thank you, Will, thank you. I know you won't enjoy it."

"I just hope you do."

"If it kills me." Maisie grinned wryly. "I do have to get used to mixing with these people and the sooner I do that, the better. And the sooner they get used to me, the sooner they'll look at my designs instead of my skin or my shape or my accent."

"Aren't you changing your accent? Only you were talking posh in the night-club."

"It's one less way to be different. I think I might have to. My da would hate that." She cocked her head at him. "You wouldn't change how you talk to make other people more comfortable, would you? Not at any price."

"Probably not," Will said. "We won't find out because I'm not a brilliant young person, so nobody cares. Anyway, how many times have you told me I'm too stubborn for my own good?"

"Almost every time you do anything."

"Exactly. Talk however you want."

Maisie screwed up her face. "Maybe when I have my own fashion house I'll switch back. Or just make Welsh fashionable." She adopted an accent so cut-glass you could shave with it. "'Oh, bore *da*, darling, do give me a cwtch, it's been positively *ages*.'"

"Please, no."

Will spent the next couple of days preparing, having borrowed some of Maisie's magazines to read up on fashion houses and designers in the vain hope that he wouldn't look completely ignorant. He ploughed through half a dozen copies each of *Smart Set*, *Vogue*, *Harper's Bazaar*, and *London Life*. Jean Patou and Coco Chanel jostled for page space with Lucile, Travis Banton, and a dozen more, amid reports of high life and film stars. The details slipped out of his brain as quickly as he read them, and he couldn't summon up any interest in the Louis vs Cuban heel debate no matter how hard he tried. He was, however, pleased to learn that hemlines would continue rising, presumably taking spirits with them.

He did stop dead at a piece on country houses.

Pictured: The Hon. Phoebe Stephens-Prince and fiancé Lord Arthur Secretan with friends at the Viscount Waring's graceful Hertfordshire home, Etchil.

There were a couple of photographs of the house—it looked old and grand—and of elegantly dressed people standing around in it. Phoebe was in one, holding the arm of a handsome older man who the caption identified as her father, the viscount. He could see the resemblance and it made him uncomfortable all over again.

He knew Kim and Phoebe were aristocracy. He thought he'd got used to it. But there was something about seeing them in print next to pictures of Noel Coward and Mary Pickford and Clara Bow that got right under his skin. He couldn't reconcile Lord Arthur Secretan smiling blandly out of the pages of *London Life* with Kim naked and gasping under him.

A suit arrived for him: evening dress, not new but nearly so, with shoes, tall shiny hat, and white gloves. It fit well enough, and made him feel like a circus chimpanzee, dressed in his betters' clothing. Will tried it on a couple of times to see if he could do the tie properly, and also get used to his appearance. The answer to both was no.

Overall, he was feeling decidedly apprehensive on Saturday morning, so he didn't want to consider how Maisie must feel. It was a welcome distraction to hear the two-note cry that resolved itself into "Knives to grind! ... Sharp'ning!"

He hailed the knife-grinder as he pushed his cart up the lane, and brought out the Messer. The wizened little man looked at it with a professional eye. "Looks like this saw some service, guv. German, ain't it?"

"Mine now."

"It'll do to cut your nails with, anyhow," the knife-grinder said, and went off into a wheezy laugh.

Will stood and watched as he worked the treadle that set the grindstone spinning. He'd always loved watching knife-grinders as a boy—the shrill noise, the sparks—and he wasn't particularly surprised when another man, strolling down May's Buildings, stopped too.

The knife-grinder withdrew the Messer and turned it assessingly as the grindstone slowed. "That'll cut anything needs cutting, I dessay. Thruppence, guv."

Will fished out the coin. The watching man said, "That's a proper blade."

"Yes."

"What's a bookseller do with a thing like that?"

"Picked it up in Flanders," Will said briefly.

"Get a lot of use out of it, do you?"

Will turned to look at him as the knife-grinder trundled on his way. "What was that, mate?"

"I said, you like using your knife. Right, Mr. Darling?"

The watcher was a man in unremarkable clothes, maybe in his forties, but could be ten years older or younger, with nothing to suggest an occupation. Bland was the only word for his featureless face, down to a pair of indeterminately coloured eyes that held no expression at all as they looked at Will. He might have been any of a million men in London, anonymous to all but their own loved ones, except the nape of Will's neck was prickling viciously, and he didn't think this fellow had loved ones, somehow. He settled the Messer into a comfortable, usable grip.

"You know my name," he said. "What's yours?"

"Telford. Tommy Telford."

"Is that right. I've heard of you."

"I've heard of you." Telford's hands were in his coat pockets, which were deep ones. Will glanced down in case he could spot the outline of a gun, and up again to see Telford's blank eyes on his face. "Worried?"

"Should I be?"

"You tell me, Mr. Darling. You're the one shoving your nose in where it's not wanted."

"How've I done that?"

"More to the point, why?"

They were the deadest eyes Will had ever seen, eyes that said *I don't care* without recklessness or dash or resignation, just a void where human feeling ought to be. Will had a sudden urge to stab the fucker now and get it over with.

"Why what?" he said. "Or, no, let's just stop asking each other questions and you tell me why you're here."

"It's a public street. A free country. Why shouldn't I be here?"

Will sighed heavily. "We both know you're here to threaten me, so crack on. I've work to do."

Apparently Telford didn't often get asked to hurry up with his menaces. He looked even blanker for a second, then narrowed his eyes. "You need to mind your own business, Mr. Darling. You've caused plenty of trouble. It's time to stop."

"Who says?"

"I do."

"I'll hear it from your boss, mate. The organ grinder, not his monkey."

The air between them was thick with aggression now. *Better not get hit in the face*, he thought. Maisie would not be pleased if he turned up to her posh dinner with a top hat and a shiner.

"You need to listen better," Telford said throatily. "And you and your posh friend need to watch yourselves, because you've had all the chances you're going to get. Stick your fingers into our business again, I'll cut 'em off."

"I'm the one with the knife," Will said softly.

Telford jabbed a hand forward without taking it out of his pocket, so that the cloth was visibly distorted. It looked like he had a gun in there, unless it was two fingers held together. Either way, Will tensed, swaying his weight to the balls of his feet, and nearly jumped out of his skin as Norris, the walking-stick seller next door, said, "Ah, Mr. Darling, there you are! Am I bothering you? Only it's about those stray cats—Oh!"

He had bustled up to them and was looking wide-eyed at the Messer. Will managed a laugh. "This? I just had it sharpened. My pal Tommy wanted a look. Didn't you, Tommy?"

"Lovely piece of kit," Telford said, the words right, but the tone so flat and dead that Norris recoiled. "I'll be off. Don't forget what I said, will you?"

He strolled away. Will nodded in his general direction, and turned to his neighbour with some relief. He couldn't solve the local cat problem either, but at least it wasn't life-threatening.

He could have done without this bloody dinner after that, especially since, walking into the Criterion, he felt only slightly less apprehensive than about some battles he'd been in. The restaurant was a grand place, artistic and Bohemian in an extremely expensive-looking way. Kim was there to greet him in the private room he'd booked, unbearably sleek in his perfectly fitted evening dress. He shook Will's hand, flicked a look over him, and said,

"Very nice. Very nice *indeed*," in a purr that tingled all the way to Will's toes.

"Pretty smart yourself," he managed.

"I try." Kim's eyes settled on his face, and his brows angled in a flicker of concern. "Is everything all right?"

"Tell you later."

By Kim's side, Phoebe wore a spectacular blue-grey dress that shifted and shimmered around her like mercury. She greeted Will with both hands and a kiss on the cheek, and breathed, "Sorry for snapping, darling," in his ear.

"Sorry for dictating," he said equally softly.

She squeezed his hands. "And thank you for coming. You're a poppet. Have you told Maisie she's beautiful yet? Go and do that."

Maisie wore a dramatic beige and gold creation. She was perfectly groomed and painted, and grey with nerves.

"You look absolutely wonderful," Will said, with entire truth. "You'll be the best-dressed woman in the room by miles."

"Watch it. I made Phoebe's dress too."

"Equal first, then. She's stunning."

"I know," Maisie said on a breath, then gave him a nudge. "Oh, and my name's Marguerite, all right? Marguerite Zie. We're calling me that, so don't forget, and don't laugh. Because 'Maisie Jones' doesn't sound like a couturier, and my name is Margaret, actually, so it's close, and everyone else uses professional names so it's not as if I'm turning my back on where I come from—"

"I don't know who you're arguing with, but it's not me," Will said. "It sounds fine. Good idea. Oh God, they're coming, chin up."

A gaggle of elegant people had arrived, young and rich and braying. Phoebe swooped around the room doing introductions. "Now, Adela, you know Marguerite already, don't you? But Will doesn't know anyone, so this is Will Darling, darlings, which terribly easy to remember, and Will, this is Binkie Huckaback and Gloria Glade, who you'll know from the pictures."

"Of course," Will said, identifying the brassy blonde. She was perhaps a bit less perfect in reality than on the silver screen, and the juvenile by her side was stretching the definition of that term, but they were both extremely good-looking and dramatically dressed. "I saw *Top Hat and Tails* just the other day. You were both marvellous."

"Very kind of you," Huckaback said with a manly sort of nod.

"And Adela Moran, and her fiancé Bubby Fanshawe, who it's quite delightful to see because I thought you weren't coming, Bubby."

Miss Moran had an aggressively shapeless bright yellow dress, the sort of shingled hair that came to sharp points round her face, and lips painted an arterial shade of red. She was probably the height of fashion, and the least of Will's worries, because Fanshawe was a chinless young man with a nasty black eye, and he was staring at Will.

"Decided to toddle along, what," Fanshawe said. "I say, we've met. This feller, I mean. He's the chap from the night-club. The one who popped me in the eye."

"He did *what*?" Maisie said.

"Uh—"

"Night-club, Will?" Kim asked, materialising at his side. "I didn't think you'd set foot in one of those in your life."

"No, Will isn't a night-clubber, are you, darling?" Phoebe said. "And this is Johnnie—"

"It is him," Fanshawe said obstinately. "I blasted well remember being popped in the eye by a feller for no reason!"

"I think I'd remember popping you in the eye," Will said, since he had no choice but to follow the lead he'd been given. "It's not my habit to assault strangers."

"Well, a chap who looked exactly like you dotted me one in the High-Low last week."

"Never heard of it," Will said, cursing everyone involved.

"Bubby, darling, he doesn't look anything like him," Phoebe said reproachfully. "Will, I mean, like that awful man who popped you in the eye. He was *dreadfully* common, and much taller."

"Also, Will is an antiquarian book dealer," Kim said. "I dare say he'd fight you to the death over an incunabulum, but the breed isn't known for night-club brawls. What were you doing to provoke assault, Bubby?"

"He didn't do anything," Miss Moran put in. "Some fellow went simply berserk in the High-Low for no reason at all, shouting and swearing. It was desperately fear-making. Bubby tried to stop him and got a thump in the face for his pains."

"Serves you right," Kim said. "You shouldn't interfere in other people's business."

"Serves me right?" Fanshawe repeated incredulously. "Listen here, Secretan—"

"He did look like you, though," Miss Moran remarked, as Fanshawe turned his full attention to Kim.

"I have one of those faces," Will said apologetically. "I constantly get strangers asking me where they know me from, or if we went to school together."

"You do, rather," Phoebe agreed. "Well, that explains it."

"And Bubby was hopelessly blotto that night," Miss Moran added, without criticism. "Which explains it even better. Imagine if it *was* you, though. Perfectly scream-making!"

"Too hilarious," Phoebe said. "And this is Johnnie Cheveley. Johnnie, Will Darling."

Cheveley was well built, good-looking, radiating the air of an English public schoolboy grown up into a cricket-playing gentleman. Will would have formed an instant dislike for him if he hadn't already had a head start. Cheveley gave Phoebe the sort of affectionate look that should be reserved for a fiancée of his own, and said, "Thank you, my love. Good to meet you, Darling. So you aren't a habitué of the High-Low, then?"

Will wasn't sure if he was being mocked, or if that was just his guilty conscience. Phoebe had said that Cheveley disliked the place, though, so he felt reasonably confident in saying, "Never been, I'm afraid."

"You haven't missed much," Cheveley assured him. "A rotten noisy Negro band, and a thoroughly vulgar woman in charge. Not worth anyone's time. What's an incubus, or whatever it was?"

Will launched into an explanation of incunabula, as if this was a conversation he wanted to be having or a man he wanted to be having it with, and kept half an eye on the room around him. Another group had arrived, this lot older, sharper and sleeker, and Phoebe had whisked Maisie off to join them. Those must be the fashion people, the makers rather than wearers of clothing; just as alien to Will as the Bright Young People but potentially less irritating.

Maisie stood out as the only one in the room who wasn't white, as well as by far the curviest. Will couldn't blame her for switching her accent. If he'd been able to do a posh voice that was remotely convincing, he might have tried it himself.

After a few moments of forced conversation with Cheveley, someone came and took him away, and Will had a moment to survey proceedings. Phoebe was in effortless control of the room, laughing and talking. She introduced Maisie as a brilliant young designer, with the proof being the frocks the two of them wore, and that seemed to work for their guests. Will didn't follow much of the conversation, but these were people at the top of their field: his input wasn't required. He smiled and shook hands and watched: Phoebe laughing and glittering; Maisie launching herself into this unknown, privileged world with an easy smile that covered her dogged determination to get it right; Kim being Lord Arthur. He'd never seen that before.

Not that Kim was being snobby. Everyone called him by name. But there was something different in his demeanour, an easy, charming social manner that indicated he was granting them all permission to behave as his equal. This was the wealthy son of a marquess, with his fiancée the daughter of a viscount, both of them scattering starlight everywhere. This was a man Will had no right to touch.

At dinner he found himself at the end of the table, opposite a strikingly handsome chap whose name he'd missed. He'd have been happy to concentrate on his food and let his neighbours carry on gossiping about people he'd never met or heard of, but after a few minutes, the man remarked, "Forgive me, but would I be right in saying this isn't entirely your sort of thing?"

Will wondered if he meant the Criterion restaurant, the world of fashion, or just upper-class socialising. "It's not," he admitted with the best smile he could manage. "I run a bookshop, I'm afraid."

"The printed word is nothing to apologise for. I used to illustrate for magazines."

"Oh, really? Which?"

"*Smart Set.*"

"I've read a few of those," Will said, feeling pleased with himself. "And now…?"

"I have a Paris salon," the man said kindly. "Edward Molyneux."

Will cringed. "Right, yes, sorry. You used to work with Lucile. Lady Duff-Gordon." That was an effort to show he'd done some homework, and a bloody stupid one because Molyneux already knew. *Shut up, Darling.*

"Yes, that's me. You read your bumf, poor chap," Molyneux said with a twinkle that only reached one eye.

Will noted that, recognised something in his tone along with the slang, and said, "Were you at the Front, at all?"

"Signals intelligence." He indicated the eye that didn't twinkle. "Got this, or rather lost it, at Arras. Where were you?"

Will hadn't expected war talk this evening. He slipped into the familiar world with guilty pleasure, established a few names they had in common, and exchanged stories. Molyneux proved to be a sharply intelligent man with a wicked sense of humour, and before long Will found he was having a thoroughly good time.

A thought occurred to him as Molyneux told a frankly libellous story about certain high-ranking Signals officers. "Here," he said once he'd stopped laughing. "I don't suppose you and Cheveley were together? He was Signals as well."

"Johnnie? I only know him socially."

"I believe he'll be working with Phoebe and Ma—Marguerite, on her father's behalf."

"Yes, he's Waring's chap, isn't he? Not sure why he's inserting himself into this; it's not his world." Molyneux's working eye flicked down the table, in Phoebe's direction. "If I were Johnnie, I'd leave it to Phoebe. She knows her stuff, everyone likes her, and it's a business where women have a voice, not to say the whip hand. The Victorian style of masterly man won't do these days. Is he coming to Paris with them?"

"Not that I know of."

Molyneux nodded. He didn't speak, but Will got a strong impression of, *Good*.

The rest of the dinner passed swiftly in general conversation, and it only dawned on him that this might not have been the most useful way to take up Molyneux's time as the party broke up. He caught Kim's eye guiltily and got a brow-twitch in return.

"It was delightful meeting you," Molyneux told him. "I do hope Miss Zie will come to rue Royale to see me. I like her style very much—it has great flair, and what one might call a measured eye, daring without recklessness—and I should be pleased to talk further. Er, are she and you...?"

"Friends, that's all."

Molyneux smiled, a little slower. "In that case, I should be delighted to see you too."

Kim ushered Will and the women into a taxi for a drink at his place, where he set about cocktails. Maisie and Phoebe sat together on the sofa, eyes bright; Will lounged by the cocktail cabinet watching Kim's mixology.

Kim gave him the ladies' drinks—sidecars, apparently—to pass on. "That was a success, I think. Except Bubby. What in God's name possessed you to invite him, Phoebe?"

"I invited him before all that, with Adela," Phoebe protested. "I got Elizabeth Ponsonby to ask him on a spree tonight to get him out of the way, but he must have changed his mind."

"Does he have one?"

"Don't be unkind. And I'm awfully sorry he turned up, but I can't be blamed because Will decided to thump him in a night-club."

Will held his hands up to that. Maisie said, "*Why* did you?"

"Don't ask," Kim said. "Were you pleased with tonight?"

"It was wonderful." Maisie's eyes were bright. "I can't thank you enough."

"Don't thank me at all. My reward was watching Will discuss signals intelligence with Teddy Molyneux."

"Oh, is *that* what you were discussing, darling?" Phoebe said. "I did wonder."

"As well you might, since Molyneux invited him to Paris. I am shocked, William."

"What?" Will said, startled and alarmed. "No, he didn't. I mean, he did, but—"

"Darling, we all know Teddy," Phoebe assured him. "You should be flattered: he's dreadfully handsome. And only just divorced, so you really might go and comfort him as a kindness." She gave him a mock-reproachful look before bursting into giggles. Maisie's eyes were wide.

"Yes, but he got married for comfort after that affair with Harold Nicolson," Kim pointed out. "And God knows who Nicolson was comforting him about, but it was probably some good-looking soldier, in which case we come full circle. He should stop for a minute and take stock."

"Not of me he shouldn't," Will said. "I mean, nice chap—"

"And *staggeringly* good-looking," Phoebe added.

"But not my sort," Will finished firmly, if not entirely accurately. Molyneux was a looker all right, and not greatly dissimilar to Kim: dark, fine features, clever mind, and given his war record he'd probably be a useful man in a tight corner. In fact, there was everything to like about him and Will did, but that space was filled.

"I feel awfully Bohemian," Maisie said, clutching her cocktail. "Goodness. Did he really invite you to Paris, Will?"

"Of course he didn't." Will reviewed the conversation. "Well, maybe a bit, but—"

"Ha," Kim said.

"But mostly he was inviting you, professionally," Will pressed on and repeated Molyneux's words.

Maisie squeaked. Phoebe said, "Teddy has a beautiful line, desperately clean. This is quite perfect. We really must go as soon as possible. Strike while the iron is hot, as they say, although I can't honestly see how that helps or what one is supposed to strike."

"Iron as in blacksmiths, not laundry maids," Kim said. "And you're quite right. London is too provincial, and Paris is delightful in the spring. Have you booked your passages?"

"I think we should do that tomorrow," Phoebe said. "Honestly, Maisie, we've so much to do."

Maisie shot Will a panicked look. He could guess at her thoughts: *But my sick auntie in Watford. But Paris is a long way from Cardiff. But people like me should know their place.*

"That lot tonight took you seriously," he said. "You should too."

"Will is quite right," Kim agreed. "Full many a flower is born to blush unseen and waste its sweetness on the desert air. Don't be afraid."

"I'm not afraid," Maisie said indignantly, drawing herself up with a decided shake of her shoulders that did remarkable if unintended things to her bosom in that dress. Will averted his eyes out of courtesy, which meant he saw Phoebe's blink. "I'm awfully excited and very grateful to you for that lovely dinner. It's just all happening a little bit *fast*."

"The best kind of happening," Kim said. "Tell me, what did we think of Adela Moran's frock? Because I bow to your expertise but I thought she looked like a Russian Futurist painting, and that's not a compliment."

"Perhaps not to you, darling. Adela would be delighted."

Maisie and Phoebe stayed a good hour for cocktails, slander, and gossip that made Will choke laughing before Maisie finally protested she had to work in the morning. Kim went downstairs to have the doorman hail them a taxi-cab, since Phoebe insisted they would share. She lived west and Maisie lived east, so that made limited sense to Will, but he'd had a few drinks and everyone seemed happy.

He waited for Kim to return, watching the fire.

"Hello," said his partner in crime, slipping back in. "That went well, I think. And you survived."

"It was a near thing. I can't believe you managed to distract Fanshawe."

"I've stubbed my toe on things with more intellectual heft than Bubby. How did you find Johnnie Cheveley?"

"He's an arsehole."

"Isn't he?"

"Molyneux didn't think much of him either."

"No, he wouldn't. Johnnie is not an admirer of the modern world. He has old-fashioned ideas on appropriate behaviour for men, women's place in the world, the superiority of the ruling classes, and so on."

"He can't think much about Phoebe working with Maisie, then."

"Indeed not. It's Waring's money, though, so Johnnie will have to live with it. Tell me, what was troubling you when you arrived?"

"What—oh, that," Will said. "I had a visit from Tommy Telford."

Kim's eyes snapped wide. "I beg your pardon?"

Will gave him the story. "Nasty bit of work. I was glad I had the Messer to hand."

"And it was a generalised message to keep your nose out? No specifics?"

Will shook his head. "It has to be about the High-Low, I suppose. Not sure why he came for me now rather than before, though, or why Fuller wouldn't do his own dirty work."

"That might have been a bit unsubtle, perhaps? Or not, given Mrs. Skyrme mentioned Telford to you. Hmm. Are you worried?"

Will shrugged. "If he'd meant to act, he'd have acted. He was there to intimidate me, and he can stick *that* where the sun doesn't shine."

"As night follows day," Kim murmured. "I'm surprised Zodiac haven't yet realised you don't take threats well. Though you will of course take care."

"Eh. Are you going to tell me what that was about tonight?"

"What part?"

"You making a fuss about Molyneux inviting me to Paris." In another man he might have assumed jealousy, but that didn't seem to be one of Kim's many faults, and he knew better than to take anything at face value by now.

"Ah, yes." Kim raised a brow. "I don't know how to break it to you, dear boy, but if Maisie pursues a career in fashion, she is likely to meet people of the homosexual or sapphic persuasions. Try not to be shocked."

"So?"

"So Phoebe thought she should learn to react in an environment where a misstep wouldn't hurt. As it turned out, she is sure-footed, and a quick study. I see why you both like her so much. I'd like to know her better myself."

"It went well, didn't it?"

"Extremely."

"I'm grateful," Will said. "Not that it's up to me to be grateful for her, but she's a damned good friend and I want her to have her chance."

"I feel the same. Phoebe is finding her vocation as a midwife to talent. I should very much like to see them both succeed."

Will nodded. "Something good would make a nice change. Uh. Were you serious about Molyneux, though?"

Kim's smile was wicked. "Why, are you interested?"

"No! Just, you know—"

"Flattered?"

"Oh, sod off," Will said, but he couldn't help a grin. "Just bear in mind I have options, next time you're thinking about being an arsehole."

"That you most certainly do; he was over you like a rash. I don't blame him: you're positively delicious in evening dress."

"I look ridiculous."

"You do not. You look sophisticatedly thuggish, and quite the most fascinating thing that's happened to the Criterion in a while. I'll be fielding enquiries for *weeks*."

"You posh lot really aren't like the rest of us, are you?"

It was meant to be a joke, but it didn't feel quite like one as he said it, and Kim's frown suggested he'd noticed. "Is there a problem?"

"Not a problem. It was just a bit peculiar tonight watching you being Lord Arthur. Condescending at people. Playing the marquess's son with people calling you my lord."

"Part of the game," Kim said. "It sugars the pill, not to call the lovely Maisie a pill. My value lies entirely in my birth, you understand. *We dined with Kim—Lord Arthur, but we all call him Kim, his people have a place in East Anglia.* It scarcely matters in fashionable circles that I am no more welcome to set foot in my ancestral home than they are; the point is to say they dined at Lord So-and-so's table, no matter who he is. That's what they want, so it's what I give them."

"You do it well," Will said. "I definitely felt like you were a lord."

"That wasn't my intention."

"It may not have been, but you are. Even if it's a courtesy title, you're still a lord."

"But Will," Kim said softly. "When have I ever asked you for courtesy?"

That was true enough, and Will had been pretty damn discourteous to him in here, several times, mostly on the sofa. "I know. I just hadn't seen the title in action before."

Kim's brows drew together. "I'd like to say it doesn't matter. It doesn't matter to me, but that's part of the privilege, isn't it? It didn't occur to me that it would bother you."

"I don't know if it bothered me exactly," Will began, and then, "No, it did. It made me think about Sir James back home. He owned the factory and most of the land, and all of us, boys and men, had to take our caps off when his carriage went by. I'm not saying you were doing that, but it's the way you weren't doing it, if that makes sense."

"My father's the same. He doesn't make his staff stand facing the wall when he passes but he's not far off. I don't choose to follow in his footsteps, but I suppose it's foolish of me to think others can ignore it."

He sounded bleak enough that Will gave himself an internal shake and said, "Well, I've ignored it before, and I dare say I will again. And if you think I'm taking my hat off to you, now or ever, forget it."

"I should be devastated if you did. My Lord Arthur performance is nothing but cheap tinsel, but I'm sorry it disturbed you. I have a bad habit of assuming your feet are so firmly planted on the ground that you can take whatever damned thing I throw at you."

"Who says I can't?"

"Not I." Kim's eyes glimmered. "I shouldn't dare."

"It's not like a title makes you better than me. You're still a bloody unreliable twisty liar."

"A dab hand with a cocktail shaker, though," Kim countered.

"A ruthless son of a bitch."

"It takes one to know one."

Will stepped forward, bringing them close, watching Kim's face. "And you'd still suck me off the minute I asked you to."

"Why would you have to ask?" Kim said, and dropped to his knees.

ELEVEN

I t was a late night, and Will awoke far too early the next morning to the insistent ringing of the telephone. He made his way downstairs, cursing the device, and answered without charm. "Darling's Used and Antiquarian. What?"

"It's Beaumont," said the hurried, tinny voice at the other end.

They were to meet him and the returning Mrs. Appleby this morning. Will said, "Everything all right?"

"No. We can't meet you."

"What? Why?"

"Because I'm afraid, that's bloody why! That brute Fuller has been shouting in all our faces since you pulled that stunt the other day. Those hostesses you were with have both been sacked —I hope you're proud of that—and I had Mrs. Skyrme interrogating me about you. She knew I'd had dinner with you, she wanted to know what we'd talked about—"

"What did you tell her?"

"I said we were in the show together, that's all, that I didn't know anything else. And she asked me if I was going to meet you again, and whether I'd bring my girl! What the hell is going on?"

It sounded like Mrs. Skyrme was abreast of Kim's interest in her activities. "She's got the wind up," Will said. "Good."

"*Good?*"

"Means we're on the right track. Still, we'd better not meet at my place—"

"We're not going to meet at all! Aren't you listening? I can't risk my job, and I can't risk her setting Fuller on me. Whatever Brabazon's problem is, it's his problem. Leave us alone."

"Don't be a damn fool," Will snapped. "It's your problem because your girl's in it up to her eyebrows. Mrs. Skyrme is afraid of being found out, and if I were Mrs. Appleby I'd be very worried about that. Or do you think Mrs. Skyrme will trust her not to talk?"

There was silence on the other end of the phone. Will pressed his advantage. "You've got two choices here. Let Mrs. Skyrme carry on doing as she pleases, or help Brabazon go after her. I hope you're not giving in."

"Don't be ridiculous," Beaumont snapped. "This isn't Flanders, and you should have kept your nose out of my business. Just leave us alone."

Will had walked back from Kim's at two in the morning through dark streets, and for all the afterglow of extreme discourtesy on the carpet, he'd been aware of every shadow and every footstep behind him. It was barely six now, his bare feet were freezing, and the kettle wasn't even on. "You turn up or I'll report her," he said flatly. "The police can find out what Mrs. Appleby's been smuggling, and deal with it. No skin off my nose."

"You wouldn't!"

"I'll find a place to meet that isn't here. Call me back at nine. If you're late, I'll ring the Old Bill."

They met in the private room of a small hotel, swiftly arranged by Kim.

Mrs. Appleby was a pretty woman in a fragile china-doll way, with big blue eyes that were swimming with tears before they'd even started. Beaumont was a sullen, resentful presence, his eyes ringed heavily with sleeplessness. They sat across a table from Kim; Will stood by the door and ignored Beaumont's looks of loathing.

"Thank you for coming," Kim said. "Mrs. Appleby, what do you know about the goods you've been smuggling for Mrs. Skyrme?"

"Nothing! It was only furs. Nothing important—the duty is iniquitous—Theresa made me—"

"Mrs. Skyrme has been using you." Kim infused his voice with sympathy. "Abusing you, even. I quite understand why you agreed to take the furs, but I believe you have unknowingly been carrying something else, which has put you in grave danger. Can I have the cigarettes and chocolates, please?"

She hesitated. "If Theresa finds out you've opened them, she'll be furious."

"I'll be very careful," Kim assured her. "She won't be able to tell."

She reluctantly passed over a shopping bag. Kim extracted two elaborately wrapped boxes of chocolates and a carton of cigarettes. He opened the latter first, rolling a couple of the cigarettes in his fingers, sniffing them, weighing up the box in his hand.

"Cigarettes," Beaumont said, with some sarcasm. "What were you expecting?"

"Have you opened these? Tampered with them? Replaced the original cigarettes with innocent ones?"

"We haven't done anything," Beaumont said.

"*I* haven't done anything." Mrs. Appleby's voice thickened. "All these accusations—these terrible things—"

"Darling, don't," Beaumont told her. "It will all be over very soon."

"It won't!" Mrs. Appleby said shrilly. "Theresa told me not to tell anyone. You don't know how frightening she can be, how ruthless."

"I do understand." Kim turned to the chocolate boxes and examined the ribbon, stiff and gold. He pulled one bow undone, very carefully, and eased the top off the box, instantly filling the room with the trapped scent of chocolate.

There were two layers. He lifted the top layer out, and picked up first one then another chocolate from the bottom layer, turning and weighing them. Will watched his hands. Beaumont's breathing was harsh.

Kim put a chocolate on the desk, and brought his palm down hard.

Mrs. Appleby shrieked. Kim lifted his hand revealing thick shards of chocolate and an oozing liquid with the cloying smell of Parma violets.

"What have you done? You said she wouldn't know!"

"And what have you achieved?" Beaumont demanded. "It's a chocolate! What the devil is wrong with that?"

Kim put the other chocolate on the desk and pushed the heel of his hand down, applying more force this time. When he lifted his hand, the sweetmeat was barely squashed. He picked it up, applying his nails, and broke off a chunk of chocolate, then another, revealing something dark.

"What the devil is that?" Will said, coming closer.

"Some sort of filling," Beaumont retorted. "What do you think it is?"

Kim rapped it on the desk with a sharp tap. "You'd break your teeth." He cracked off another piece of chocolate and turned what remained so it caught the light.

"Bloody hell!" Will said. "Excuse my French."

Kim was holding a faceted red stone the size of a thumbnail, smeared with brown grease. Beaumont's jaw dropped. Mrs. Appleby stared. "But—but—what is it?"

Kim picked out another couple of chocolates, assessed them, put one back, and broke chocolate off the other. This time, the stone was blue. Will picked it up. It was about the size of his little fingernail, cut to a roughly oval sort of shape. When he rubbed the chocolate off and held it to the light, it sparkled.

"Is this what I think it is?" he said.

"Those are jewels!" Mrs. Appleby said shrilly. "Are those jewels?"

"Russian, I expect," Kim said. "The Bolsheviks came up with this trick back in 1920. They had chocolatiers looking for work after the Romanovs fell, plenty of jewels lying around, and a powerful need for foreign currency. During the Revolution and then the civil war, Tsarist jewels were stolen by the sackload, stripped from their settings, washed clean of blood—metaphorically or literally—and brought out through Eastern Europe to be sold on. Stolen jewels, ripped from Russian throats and reset to decorate European or American ones, helped fund the Red Terror. It's no longer a State-run business to my knowledge, but there are several private enterprises still taking loot through Eastern Europe into the West. Hoarding jewels which were previously owned by the wealthy, which now should benefit the Russian people, and which certainly do not belong to Mrs. Skyrme."

He smiled mirthlessly at Mrs. Appleby. "Why, you're probably one of the nation's most lucrative smugglers. Four trips carrying two boxes of Tsarist loot each time?" He clicked his tongue. "You face a significant gaol sentence. Mr. Appleby will be dismissed in disgrace if he's lucky. I expect your personal affairs will be spread across the papers as well. And since any defence you make will incriminate Mrs. Skyrme, she will want to silence you before you can testify. You will be gaoled or dead within weeks."

"Stop it!" Mrs. Appleby almost screamed. "Stop! Michael!"

"You said you'd make sure this didn't touch her!" Beaumont said furiously.

"The man who came to ask you questions was an agent of the British security forces, Mrs. Appleby," Kim said. "You gave his name to Mrs. Skyrme and now he's dead." He picked up the chocolate-smeared ruby. "Over these."

She had gone fish-belly white. "I said, stop!" Beaumont shouted, leaping to his feet.

Will swung an arm across his chest. "Don't."

"You—"

"Enough," Kim said, so coldly authoritative that they all froze. "Luckily for you, Mrs. Appleby, I want Mrs. Skyrme more than I want to see you face the consequences of your actions. So you are going to make an appointment to see her at the High-Low under my direction. If you give me your fullest assistance, I will deal with her, I will not name you to any investigation, and if need be I will testify that you cooperated. With a bit of luck, you two can carry on with your lives and forget this ever happened."

There were tears running down Mrs. Appleby's face. "And without *luck*?" Beaumont demanded.

"Then she'll have to see whether the police catch up with her before Fuller and Skyrme do."

"Michael!" Mrs. Appleby whimpered, clinging to him.

"For God's sake, you damned swine!" Beaumont said. "Can't you see you're scaring her?"

"Good," Kim said. "Your best hope to avert all this is me. Cooperate or face the consequences. And don't even think of playing the fool. If—when—Mrs. Skyrme finds out that the cat's out of the bag, she will want you dead. Telling her what's going on would be digging your own grave."

"But if Flora helps you, Mrs. Skyrme will realise that anyway!"

"Indeed," Kim said. "So I suggest that as soon as Mrs. Appleby has made that telephone call, you leave. Don't pack, just go. Get on a train somewhere and stay away. It might save you from Mrs. Skyrme while the law catches up with her."

Mrs. Appleby's eyes rounded in shock. "Run away? Together? What about my divorce?"

"Not my problem," Kim said, with something of a snap.

"Darling, leave it to me," Beaumont told her. "This is the devil of a web that's been spun around you but I won't let it touch you." He turned on Will. "And you. I had your word. If you had left all this alone—"

"Mrs. Skyrme would have kept on using Mrs. Appleby and then got rid of her, probably for good," Kim finished. "Let's make that telephone call now."

"I suppose you had to put the frighteners on them," Will said once arrangements had been made and the miserable couple had left.

"They were more afraid of Skyrme than me. That had to be remedied."

Will picked up the ruby and turned it in his fingers. "They put in some real chocolates in case of inspection, I suppose. What do you think, half of these are jewels? More? What would you get in this lot?"

"Who knows. There's forty-eight chocolates. Thirty stones, perhaps? At this size, and depending on where you could sell them—I don't know. Six or eight thousand pounds?"

"Per box?"

"Maybe."

"That's enough to leg it to the south of France and live in luxury," Will said. "Not saying we should, of course."

"Just that we could? Tempting."

"Mrs. Appleby must be kicking herself she didn't help herself to a chocolate before. I should never have promised we'd try and get her off. If you think it's best to go to the police, or your Bureau, I'll understand."

Kim gave him a narrow look. "Is this some sort of coded message? Or have you got the real Will Darling stashed in a cupboard somewhere?"

"I'm serious. You were right: I oughtn't have promised Beaumont. I was trying to play your game my way, and that was stupid. There's a dead man and crimes to be accounted for here. I can't ask you to cover up for her."

"I don't give a damn for Mrs. Appleby, who I hope has learned her lesson, and I don't have to because I'm not in the police force. Cover-ups are what the Private Bureau *does*."

"Maybe they shouldn't."

"If we're to get at Zodiac, it won't be through the courts," Kim said. "This game is not played in front of an audience. Look, if you don't want to do the next part, I understand. It's tantamount to a declaration of war."

"Who'll be backing you up then? You can't go in alone and you're not telling the police. Will you bring in people from this Private Bureau?"

Kim hesitated. "I could, but I am taking it on myself to let Mrs. Appleby get away. I can't swear that DS would do the same."

Will stared at him. "You're going it alone because of my promise. You are, aren't you? Jesus, Kim. I—"

"Don't. For Christ's sake don't say anything," Kim said harshly. "It's absurd, considering how much I've done to you. And don't feel obliged to be involved. You really aren't."

Will still wanted to acknowledge this. He wanted to say *You're doing this for me because you care*, and for it to be true, and then...

Then what? He didn't know how to push beyond that, or where it might take them. He only knew that Kim was thinking of him in this damn fool dangerous business, and how much that mattered.

"Of course I'm coming," he said in lieu of the words Kim didn't want. "Wouldn't miss it. Shall we go?"

Kim checked his wristwatch. "I think so. Got your knife?"

Noon on a Sunday was a bloody stupid hour to have a confrontation with a criminal, in Will's view. There was a reason that people did these things under cover of night.

He made a remark to that effect. Kim countered that Fuller would be asleep, the club didn't open on Sunday evenings, Mrs. Skyrme was expecting the soggy Mrs. Appleby so would not be surrounded by support, and mainly, they would be best off not giving that lachrymose lady a chance to change her mind and betray them. Mrs. Appleby had choked out a description of how she met her nemesis to hand over the jewels in the empty surroundings of the High-Low. She'd also sobbed on the telephone while setting up the meeting, but hopefully Mrs. Skyrme would consider that normal behaviour.

Kim had given Beaumont forty pounds to cover the costs of vanishing with his lover. Will very much hoped they would be safe, and also that he wouldn't see them again.

It was a cold grey day. Kim held the bag with the boxes of chocolates—that was something, carrying five figures' worth of jewels around London—and made his way silently down the stairs to the club's basement area, Will at his heels. Even from outside it stank of cigarettes and stale alcohol. At least they weren't too exposed from the street, since they were below ground level, but Will still felt horrendously conspicuous.

Kim knocked on the door. They waited several moments, and then it opened.

"Good—" Mrs. Skyrme began, before her eyes caught up with her mouth.

"Good morning," Kim said.

The door began to slam shut, although it didn't get very far because Will had a grip on the handle. He yanked it back open. Kim said, urbanely, "I have your special delivery of chocolates."

"What chocolates?" Mrs. Skyrme demanded. "I didn't order any chocolates."

"That's odd, because I have a witness who'll state the opposite. I tried one, by the way, I hope you don't mind. Delicious, but the centres are a little hard."

There was a tiny silence.

"If you wish to speak to me, Lord Arthur, I must insist on you making an appointment," Mrs. Skyrme said. "Will you let go of this door or must I call a policeman?"

"You're welcome to call a policeman. Would you like to talk to him about Leinster, or about Mrs. Appleby?"

Her eyes narrowed. "What is it you want?"

"To talk. Let's do that now."

Will took that as a hint and put his weight into the door. Mrs. Skyrme stumbled back with a curse, and they were in, facing up in the dark interior of the empty night-club. She inhaled sharply.

"Don't shout," Kim said. "Don't shout *at all*. This is your last opportunity to have a conversation, rather than give a statement. If I were you, I wouldn't waste it."

"Empty threats, Lord Arthur." Mrs. Skyrme's eyes flicked to Will for a second, considered him dispassionately, and moved back to Kim. She was about five foot three, with overdone face-paint, a garish frock, and cheap bangles on her wrists, and Will had a sudden shuddering urge to draw the Messer because he could tell a danger when he saw one.

"Sadly, no," Kim said. "Sadly for you, that is. I've got the dates of Mrs. Appleby's trips, plus her signed statement and, of course, the chocolates. I can match some very large sums to Mrs. Appleby's confectionery deliveries and put you in the middle of it. I could have come here with a pack of police officers and had you nailed."

Mrs. Skyrme looked at him without emotion for a very long moment, and then she smiled. "So why didn't you?"

Kim smiled back. "Tell me something, Mrs. Skyrme. Let's say I had you arrested now, and you sat in a cell while men drilled your safe open—what might that take, a few hours? Half a day? And then all the papers would be ours, and you would need to decide whether to save yourself by giving up your Zodiac colleagues, particularly Capricorn."

"And you want to know what I'd choose?"

"I don't care what you'd choose," Kim said. "I want to know how long you think you'd live. Do you really believe he would risk you talking? I've got you, Mrs. Skyrme, and once Capricorn finds that out, you're a liability to him."

"If that's the case, it isn't you I should be scared of, is it?"

"Indeed not. The very opposite. I'm here for a friendly chat about what to do with these two boxes of delicious chocolates. Shall we go to your office?"

There was a long, considering silence, which Mrs. Skyrme broke. "This way."

Will followed them both up to the office, keeping a weather eye out for treachery, or movement. Their steps echoed in the vast space in a dead sort of way. The stairs were sticky underfoot.

Mrs. Skyrme went in and sat down at her desk. It was set against the back wall, facing out to the club. With the blinds up as they were now, she would have a view of the whole place, balconies and dancefloor alike. Kim helped himself to the other chair and sat opposite. Will leaned against the door.

Mrs. Skyrme gave him a cold look. "You caused a great deal of trouble the other night, Mr. Darling. I suppose you were up to something."

"Never mind him," Kim said. "Nice to speak to you face to face at last, Mrs. Skyrme."

"Likewise I'm sure, Lord Arthur."

She leaned back, hands going to her lap, which was to say,

under the level of the desk. Will said, "Hands where I can see them, please."

"Are you going to make me, Mr. Darling?"

"Yes."

She put her clasped hands on her desk. Kim took one of her hands and turned it, so the blue stain of a tattoo was visible through the bangles.

"Aquarius," he said. "Does Capricorn himself bear one of these highly incriminating little marks, or does he reserve them for his inferiors?"

"Ask him."

"I intend to. Let's not waste time, shall we? I have the entire story from Flora Appleby, and I also have two boxes of supposedly Hungarian chocolates with full provenance and very hard centres. Here." He put them on the desk. "I prefer the liqueur fillings, myself."

"Then you should buy your own."

"Very true," Kim said. "Flora Appleby is ready to testify about everything, including that she told you about Leinster's questions shortly before his 'accident'. You ought not to have threatened her divorce, you know; they do say about a woman scorned. I'm surprised you made that mistake."

Mrs. Skyrme's nostrils flared but she didn't speak. Kim went on, "I've a very good chance of getting a murder charge to stick on that alone. You're done for, I fear. Unless you cooperate."

"But as you say, cooperation would get me killed," Mrs. Skyrme said. "Whereas telling you that I don't know what you're talking about—that I've never heard of this Leinster, that Flora Appleby is a silly hysteric—would create plenty of time in which all sorts of things might happen. Why, you might even have an accident, just like Mr. Leinster."

"That wouldn't get you off the hook."

"It would make being on the hook more entertaining." Again

Mrs. Skyrme smiled; again Kim smiled back. Will looked between them and felt goosebumps rise on his neck.

Kim pulled the bow of one of the chocolate boxes and opened it. "Lucky dip?"

"I won't, thank you. Watching my waistline."

Kim took a chocolate, considered it, and bit it carefully. He made an annoyed noise and dropped it on the table with a little clunk. "Hard centre."

Another silence. Mrs. Skyrme and Kim watched each other. Will just stood there. At least in the trenches he'd known what war was being fought.

Kim spoke first. "Do you know, I think we could benefit from a frank discussion. Off the record, even. Will, would you excuse us?"

Will gave him a look, but Kim nodded, and he was the expert here. "All right. Just a second, though. Stand up please, Mrs. Skyrme." He came over to the desk, and pulled open each drawer in turn. There was a small handgun in one, loaded. He took out the bullets, dumped them in the wastebasket, and was about to drop the gun in when Kim said, "Wipe your fingerprints off it first, old chap. You never know what a nice lady like this might do with your fingerprints on a gun."

Mrs. Skyrme sniffed. Will did as bid. "Shout if you need me."

"Because Lord Arthur is in so very much danger from me," Mrs. Skyrme said sardonically.

Will ignored that and went out. He didn't know what Kim was up to, but he was welcome to deal with Mrs. Skyrme, with her cold, clever eyes. Will preferred the kind of trouble he was trained for.

He moved into the shadows outside the office, hearing the murmur of voices but no clear words, and surveyed the great main room as best he could given the bright light from the office spilling into the darkness before him. It felt cavernous, and horribly exposed. A sniper on the top balcony could control the entire room. Lucky there weren't any here, he reminded himself, and did not pull the Messer no matter how much he wanted a weapon in his hand.

And then he saw it. A vertical line of light, up at the far end of the higher balcony.

Had that been there before, or had it just come on? He wasn't sure. It was bright enough to be clearly visible in the dimness and there was a faint horizontal line meeting its top. The outline of a door. Was the light behind it that of daylight, or the yellow of electricity?

As he stared, it winked out. Well, that answered that.

Will started moving. He'd have liked to run, but not on a balcony which was probably not solid enough to muffle footsteps, and certainly not through a litter of chairs and tables, which he could only see in the spilled light from the office—

He stopped. He turned.

The bloody office blinds were bloody open. He hadn't thought to pull them, like the fool he was, so anyone looking from the top balcony would have a magnificent well-lit view of the office desk, and Mrs. Skyrme's face, and Kim's defenceless back.

Will swore under his breath, but if he shouted he'd give away his position, and if he went back to warn Kim now, he'd be in the wrong damn place. So he kept going, picking his way along the balcony to the spiral stairs with agonising slowness, worth it not to make a racket. He had his foot on the lowest step when he heard the soft whisper of a door opening above him.

He held his breath. Fuller—he had to assume it was him—wouldn't be able to see him from here, but if he came down the stairs...

Fuller didn't come down. He stood unmoving for a few very long seconds, and then started forward along the upper balcony. You wouldn't do that if you simply wanted to get to the office on the lower balcony. You'd do it if you had a gun, because a man with a gun half-way along the upper balcony would have a perfect line of sight on the office window. It was a fair distance for a shot, though: Mrs. Skyrme's little discarded pop-gun wouldn't be enough. He wondered what Fuller had.

Will went up the stairs as slowly as he dared, telling himself that Fuller couldn't see Kim's face and wouldn't recognise him from his back, not from this distance. Surely he wouldn't shoot without knowing what was going on. Unless Mrs. Skyrme had had some sort of bell-press installed that Will had missed...

Don't turn round, Kim. Don't move. Please.

He crawled onto the upper balcony, keeping low, peering through the legs of tables and chairs. The man was indeed Desmond Fuller, and Will recognised the shape of the weapon he held, the long, narrow barrel. A Webley service revolver. It was a good practical gun with plenty of accuracy over the distance, even better if Fuller went further along the upper balcony to get an angle on Kim that didn't risk Mrs. Skyrme. Which was what he was doing right now.

Will had strong views on bringing a knife to a gun fight, but needs must. He pulled the Messer and made his way forward.

Fuller didn't notice him. He was probably groggy from sleep, and focused on the office. Will kept going, moving softly and steadily, keeping in a low crouch. He'd done this closer to upright in the German trenches, which was easier on the thighs, but at least there wasn't any mud here.

Fuller made a little exhalation and raised his gun arm. Will tensed to leap, and just stopped himself as the arm kept rising and the man fired into the ceiling. The noise was shockingly loud. Fuller swung the gun down again, aimed towards the office and Kim, and roared, "Hands up! Hands up or I shoot!"

Will risked a glance at the office. He saw Kim's hands go up, and Mrs. Skyrme rise from her desk, raising her arm to point towards Will, and he went for Fuller as hard and fast as he could.

The man whipped round, too quick. Will grabbed at his gun hand, forcing it up, but Fuller had got hold of his knife wrist at the same time and was pushing it down. They struggled savagely, locked together, moving no more than inches back and forth with neither able to let go.

Will was pretty strong, but Fuller was bigger, and he could feel the pressure on both arms. If the trial of strength lasted minutes rather than seconds, bulk would win. Will shifted his weight, let Fuller come forward, and went for a knee in the balls. He made glancing contact only, and regretted the miss as Fuller gave a bellow of rage and pushed back so hard their grips broke. Will stumbled, tripped over a chair, and fell backward, the edge of a marble-topped table brushing through his hair as he went down.

The next second or so lasted an eternity. The gun barrel swung towards him, Fuller's finger tightening on the trigger; Will dropped the Messer, all but flinging it away in his haste, and pulled the heavy table above him sharply forward. There was an explosion far too close, and a bullet cracked into the tabletop, almost jarring it from his grip.

The fucker was trying to kill him.

Will scrambled to his feet in pure desperation as Fuller fired again. He lifted his impromptu shield and charged at the enemy, using the table as a battering ram. Fuller tried to dodge, but the heavy marble caught him square on. He span sideways and hit the banister rail hard.

That put him on the ropes, and Will didn't intend to let up. He barged the table into Fuller again with all his weight, and once more, needing him to lose his gun or his breath, but the surge of panic that had let him lift the table as if it were plywood was already dropping, and the sodding marble was too sodding heavy. Will made a last effort and half threw, half dropped the thing just as Fuller staggered forward. It landed edge down, right on the bastard's foot.

Fuller gave a howl of pain and fell backwards. There was a splintering crunch that sounded loud even through Will's still-ringing ears. Fuller's eyes widened, and the whole section of banister gave way.

Fuller's arms windmilled frantically in a desperate effort to defy gravity. His body bowed forwards, and it looked for just a second as if he was going to recover himself, then his feet went out from under him. Will lunged forward, hurling himself down, and just caught Fuller's disappearing hand as he hit the floor.

The shock damn near pulled his own arm out of its socket. He skidded forward, dragged by Fuller's dead weight, sliding fast to the gaping gap in the banisters, and the two-storey fall beyond.

Will flailed for something to hold on to, and found the nearest surviving baluster with his free hand, a table-leg with his feet. He gripped onto both for dear life, and his slide stopped with his head and shoulders hanging over the dark void below.

Fuller swung from his hand, yelling. He still held the Webley in his other hand.

"Drop the gun!" Will bellowed. "Drop it or I drop you! Now!"

Fuller let go of the Webley. It bounced off the lower balcony, and hit the floor a long way down.

"Pull me up!" Fuller flailed his free arm in a fruitless effort to reach the balcony edge. The movement pulled Will another inch closer to certain depth.

"Stop struggling!" he snarled. "You'll have us both off!"

"Pull me *up*!"

Will's muscles were screaming. Fuller was over six foot, well built, and hanging off an arm that hadn't enjoyed recent proceedings as it was. "Calm down. See if you can get your other hand up. Grab the edge."

Fuller tried, straining upwards. The effort dragged Will forward again. "Fuck! *Stop!*"

Running footsteps. "Will!" Kim shouted.

"Get up here and hold me down!"

He couldn't look round, couldn't afford to concentrate on anything but his feet, painfully flexed around the table-legs, and his hands, one on the baluster, one savagely gripped by Fuller's sweaty fingers, and on his breath. Breathe in, breathe out. One. Two. He could hold on till ten. Kim would be here by ten. Four. Five. He *would* get to ten breaths. Six.

He didn't even know why he was doing this for a man he'd been prepared to stab two minutes ago, except that it would have been inhuman to let him fall. He just held on, to the count of ten and then one more breath after that, and then there was a weight on his back and thighs straddling him, anchoring him to the floor.

"Hold on. Let me grab the banister." He felt Kim brace over him. "All right. I've got you."

"Fuller!" Will forced the word out through his tense throat. "Get ready to take my other hand."

He released his grip on the baluster and extended his newly free hand. Fuller reached up, the shift of weight putting enough strain on Will's shoulder that he had to bellow the pain out, and grabbed it.

Better. His overtaxed right shoulder was aflame and the left one wasn't liking this either, but at least the heavy bastard was more evenly distributed, albeit crushing his hands. "Get hold of my wrists. My wrists, damn you!"

"Get me up." Fuller was blotchy, sweaty-faced with fear, too afraid to shift his fingers. "Pull me up!"

"No," Kim said.

"What?" Will and Fuller said in chorus.

"Information first, rescue later. Who's Capricorn?"

"Pull me *up*!"

"Capricorn," Kim said implacably. "And talk fast. He can't hold you forever."

That was truly shitty, the sort of shitty you got from intelligence officers. If Kim hadn't been sitting on his back as ballast, Will would have consigned him to the devil and pulled Fuller up anyway. As it was, any sort of silly buggers would lead to one or both of them going over the drop. "Kim—" he snarled.

"Who is Capricorn?" Kim said again. "Quick."

"I don't know!"

"Drop him." Kim spoke with icy command.

"No!" Fuller thrashed like a fish, fingers digging into Will's hands. Will yelled aloud.

"Capricorn. A name."

"I don't know his name!"

"Then you're no use to me."

"*Kim!*" Will was damned if he was letting go, he would *not*, but his muscles were exhausted and in a few moments more he wouldn't have the choice.

"They'll kill me!" Fuller shrieked.

"So will the fall," Kim pointed out. "Do it my way and you can run with a head start. Name."

"I don't know!"

Fuller's sweaty fingers slipped a half-inch. Will forced his own grip tighter by sheer bloody-mindedness, defying the dreadful ache of failing strength. "Just tell him something, you arsehole!"

"*I shall!*" Fuller screamed, rushing the words out in panic. "I shall, I shall—"

Kim's thighs tightened on Will's waist. "Let's get him up."

It wasn't easy with Will's muscles turned to dead meat, but Kim put his back into it and they managed it together, dragging Fuller up until he could grip the edge of the balcony, heaving at his arms until his torso was safely on the floor and he could wriggle forward like a landed fish, breath sobbing out.

Kim rose and stepped away. Will pulled himself to a crouch, nursing the searing pain in his shoulders and arms for a miserable minute, then to a vaguely upright position so he could park his arse on a table. He'd have liked to pick up the Messer but his arms weren't having any of it. He kicked it out of the way instead, and concentrated on breathing the burn down.

Fuller lay on the balcony floor, gasping. After a few moments he struggled to his knees, then straightened, wiping sweat from his face. He took a few more painful breaths, turned to look down at the office, and froze.

Will couldn't help looking. Mrs. Skyrme was on her way down the spiral stairs to the ground floor, in coat and hat, holding a pair of bags.

"Theresa?" Fuller said, almost to himself, then screamed it. "*Theresa!*"

Mrs. Skyrme looked up. She didn't call out to him. She didn't wave or blow a kiss, or explain why she'd been packing up her things as he hung inches from death. She simply contemplated her guard dog trapped and trembling above her for a long expressionless second, then turned and carried on down the stairs. Walking away.

Fuller stood rigid, mouth slightly open, mouthing her name. Kim said, "Oh, dear." And Will returned his attention to Fuller very nearly too late.

He'd got a hand under his coat already. Now as he turned, he pulled out a second gun, and his arm swung to Kim, point blank.

Will was already moving, launching a solid, savage boot to the groin. Fuller went backwards, arms flailing wildly, so that the bullet went up to the ceiling instead of into Kim, and he had nothing to grab on to as his foot slipped off the balcony edge.

There was no saving him this time. Not that Will tried.

Fuller's scream was cut off by an extremely final thud. Will went to look over the edge and saw the body splayed in a dark pool of blood that would doubtless get bigger. The angle of his neck told its own story.

"Silly bastard," he said.

Kim looked down too, then nodded. "I'm going after her. Wipe your fingerprints."

He set off downstairs. Will managed to fish out a handkerchief and rubbed, clumsy and weak, at the baluster they'd both held and the table he'd used. Once he'd finished, he retrieved the Messer with sausage fingers and went down to the office.

The safe stood wide, the chocolate boxes empty. It looked like Mrs. Skyrme had taken the chocolates, the gun in the waste-paper bin, and the cartridges. He hoped Kim would be careful.

His partner returned a couple of minutes later, unharmed and alone. "She'd locked the door on her way out. By the time I got it open, she'd long gone. All right, I'm going to clear the safe. Put that bloody knife away."

Will's arms were starting to feel more like they belonged to him. He sheathed the Messer, then rubbed down the drawer-handles and anything else he could remember touching while Kim stuffed papers into his satchel. "That'll do. Come on."

They hurried downstairs, Will very aware of the body on the floor. Kim grabbed his arm as they approached the back door and pulled him round to scrutinise his appearance. "Stop looking like you're at war."

Will had no idea what that meant, but he breathed out hard, trying to smooth his features. Kim reached out to straighten his clothing with quick, impersonal tweaks, hesitated, then ran his hand through Will's hair, finger-combing it to order. Will let him, resisting the urge to push his head into the touch of his hand.

"Better," Kim said at last. "I'll go first. Give me a minute, then head home."

"Where are you going?"

"To get this lot to the office. It'll be a race against time once Zodiac hear about this."

"Are you calling the police?"

"Christ, no," Kim said. "Go home, pretend it didn't happen, and I'll catch up with you as soon as I can. If you get in any trouble, contact me. If I'm not there, tell Peacock it's urgent and he'll reach me. Are you all right?"

"Just the arms. It'll be fine."

"I meant, are you all right what with having killed him?"

Will shrugged, for lack of anything useful to say. Kim gave him a sort of half smile. "You do realise you saved my life?"

"Get going."

Kim slipped out of the back door. Will gave it a few moments before he followed, emerging into the grey watery daylight. There was nobody in the street above and if anyone had heard the racket from the High-Low, they were clearly unconcerned.

He set off down the street, hands in his pockets because they'd started shaking.

TWELVE

Will didn't have a marvellous day after that. He didn't regret Fuller's death as such: he would have preferred a different outcome, but the silly sod had pulled a gun on Kim. All the same, he didn't feel much like explaining his part in the whole thing to the police. Kim had better be right about his shadowy organisation's powers.

It seemed he was, because after three days, nobody had come to ask Will questions, and he hadn't seen anything in the papers. He'd bought the Standard and Evening Standard daily, and seen nothing about 'Shocking Discovery In Night-Club'. That meant he felt less like he was about to be arrested, which was nice, but increasingly in the dark as to what the hell was going on. He wanted to know what happened now, what Mrs. Skyrme was likely to be up to, and what was in those account books and papers Kim had taken.

But he wasn't finding out, because along with the rest of the silence, there hadn't been a peep from Kim.

Not a call. Not a visit. The nerves receded, the time passed, the hours mounted up without communication, and Will discovered he was furious.

He had killed a man, *another* man, to save the bastard's life. He'd trusted Kim enough to put himself at risk of a prison sentence, and Kim couldn't take three minutes to say, *By the way, what's happening is...* He must have found out plenty by now from the contents of Mrs. Skyrme's safe; he'd had a private conversation with her that had clearly ended in some sort of deal, given she'd left the safe open. A private conversation Kim hadn't wanted Will to hear.

There was something else, too. He'd lied to Mrs. Skyrme about having Flora Appleby ready as a witness, which was fine—Will had no problem with him lying to other people—but it was also, very clearly, what he should actually have done, which raised the question of why he hadn't. Will had been all too ready to believe that Kim had respected his promise to Beaumont. Now, as the silence ticked on, he had a growing, sick, feeling that he'd fooled himself again.

He didn't want to believe that. He didn't want to believe that Kim would spoil everything that had grown between them. But here he sat with another body added to his tally and the dead man's fingermarks dark on his wrists, and didn't hear a bloody word.

He'd thought things were changing. He'd truly thought Kim was letting him inside in a way that mattered, and he'd been wrong. The barriers had come crashing down again and he was sick of it. Sick of being dragged into messes not of his making (he was aware he'd signed up eagerly, that wasn't the point), sick of being used for dirty work, and thoroughly, deep-down heartsick of feeling like he was good enough for fighting or fucking, even for Kim to vent his feelings on much as Beaumont had, but no more. Not a partner. Not an equal. Not included.

He called Maisie to see if she'd have dinner with him, but she declined. "I can't. Will, we're going down to Lord Waring's house on Saturday, to stay! He told Phoebe yesterday to bring me so he can meet me properly in a comfortable setting, and he's even sending his chauffeur to drive us. Can you imagine?" Her voice thrummed with excitement. "So kind—and I've got such a lot of work to do before we go to Paris, Phoebe is having dozens of ideas and there's no time at all to prepare. I'll tell you all about it later. I've got to go."

She hung up, which was him told. Will glared at the phone. He didn't have Phoebe's number since she always called him, but he had a copy of Kelly's London Royal Blue Book. He looked up Viscount Waring, found the address in Grosvenor Square, and asked the operator to put him through.

A plummy voice answered the telephone. "The Waring residence."

"Is Miss Stephens-Prince in?" Will had a sudden, random urge to call her Lady Phoebe, just to balance out the poshness. "It's William Darling."

After a lengthy pause, Phoebe came on the line. "Will, darling? Oh, it is you, how lovely."

"I wondered if I could take you to dinner. If you're not busy."

"Dinner tonight? I can't do that, but have you had lunch yet? No? Wonderful. I can be with you in two shakes of a lamb's thingy. Oh, not *that* thingy, how awful. I shall meet you in our usual place at one."

That was fine, Will decided. And he'd go to the cinema in the evening, and generally get himself out and about. If he sat around here thinking about Kim any longer, he'd break something.

He picked up a paper to read since Phoebe was reliably fifteen minutes late, and was embarrassed to arrive at the restaurant at five to one to find her already there.

"Hello, darling," she said, kissing him on both cheeks. "Marvellous to see you, and thank you so much for calling. I was quite desperate to leave the house."

She spoke lightly, as she always did, but there was a look in her eyes that made him say, "Is something wrong?"

"Oh, not *wrong*, not to complain about. My mother is endlessly wearing. Well, she would be, of course."

"Sorry?"

"Lady Waring. Kim always says he doesn't know if it's a title or a description."

"Ouch."

"Never mind. She is herself, and she *will* say things, and she's dreadfully annoyed by my plans with Maisie. Well, life is full of disappointments. Hers certainly is." She smiled dazzlingly at the waiter who handed her a menu, but didn't open it.

"Because you're working?" Will guessed. "Or because it's with Maisie specifically?"

"They haven't met; I wouldn't inflict Mother on her. Honestly, it's mostly because Daddy supports me. I do wish they'd divorce. Still, I'll be away soon."

"Maisie said you're off to your place in the country."

"To meet Daddy, yes. He's being awfully good. I dare say Johnnie will be there too, but never mind. Have you decided?"

The waiter was hovering. Will hadn't even looked at the menu. He asked for the pâté and boeuf bourguignon—French for stew—adding a carafe of wine. Phoebe ordered something involving salad, and glowed at the waiter again. "You were heroic at the dinner, by the way. Teddy really was struck by you." She gurgled with laughter. "So was Bubby, of course, just differently. Poor Will, what an awful time Kim gives you. It was terribly nice of you to support Maisie through it."

"I can't see what good I did."

"Oh, just being there, darling. You're a desperately comforting presence, you know. Safe. Not that you're safe yourself, but one feels that nothing can go terribly wrong if you're about."

"That's not true, I'm afraid."

"Well, of course not, but one still *feels* it. I feel better now just talking to you. I really don't know why I let Mother bother me so. And to be fair to her, she sent Johnnie Cheveley packing. He came for her blessing to court me, would you believe? As if he could charm her into forgetting he's Daddy's man, no matter how much she dislikes Kim. I'm not sure I could bear it if she was on at me to marry Johnnie on top of the rest of it. I can't wait to go to Paris."

"I bet you can't," Will said, watching her eyes. "Look, if you want someone to have a word with Cheveley, I'm happy to. He can't carry on at you like this."

"You're sweet to offer, darling, but you can't punch *everyone* in the face."

"I don't mind trying."

Phoebe's mouth moved in the sort of smile that might go into laughter or tears. She squeezed his hand. "Thank you, Will. You are kind. I shall carry a mental picture of you giving Johnnie what-for in my heart, and that will sustain me."

"Up to you. Why doesn't your mother like Kim?"

"Well, so few people do. He was always the black sheep, long before the War, and he's always taken my side, which she dislikes. You might think that she would have been grateful he swooped in to rescue me, but no. Do you know the most absurd thing, though? She objects to me marrying him, *and* to the long engagement. She actually said, 'Don't marry him, but if you must, do it at once.' Have you ever heard anything so silly? It's like that joke about the bad restaurant—'Such terrible food! And such small portions!' Oh, not you, darling," she added swiftly to the waiter, who had arrived with their first course at that inopportune moment. "This looks wonderful."

Will managed to hold back his laugh until the waiter departed. Phoebe made a comically embarrassed face. "Well, that serves me right. Anyway, you didn't want to hear me rattle on about Mother. How are you? What's happened with the High-Low?"

Will lifted a hand, not dramatically, but enough that she stopped at once, eyes widening. "Oh. Is it hush-hush?"

"Well, you know. Kim business."

She pressed her lips together, smiling. "Naturally. Talking of whom, where on earth is he? I haven't heard from him in days."

"Nor have I." Will wasn't sure if it helped that Kim hadn't been chatting to Phoebe. It didn't make things worse, but that was a pretty low bar. "He's vanished again."

Her eyes narrowed. "Is he being Kimmish?"

"Yes. Yes, he blasted well is."

"Oh, darling. I did think—not that it's my business."

"Does he trust you, Fee?" The words spilled out without him quite meaning to speak them. "Sorry. That's not *my* business."

"It's a fair question," Phoebe said. "Does he? As far as it goes. He trusts me with some things, but not everything by a very long way. He loves me, but he doesn't tell me about what matters most. He holds onto things that hurt as if it would be cheating to let anyone help."

"He told me some things," Will said, leaning forward a little as if the very mention was secret. "About what happened with his brother. I thought he was talking to me. And now he's gone again, and I think he's hiding something. Again."

"Something he ought to share." Phoebe was watching his face. "Personal or professional?"

"Professional, but—well, it *is* personal. If he asks me to do things and then slams the door in my face, it's personal."

"Yes," Phoebe said. "It is. And he ought to know better, and he does know better, and he ought to *do* better. I couldn't agree more."

It was just words, just a bit of sympathy and understanding. There was no reason for Will to feel a hard lump in his throat. "Yes, he ought. Thanks, Phoebe. I'm sorry, I brought you here just to moan at you."

"We clearly both needed a moan. It's a very good thing you called or we'd have ruined two other people's lunches instead. I am sorry, Will. I wish I could help."

"You have," Will said sincerely. "If I make you feel safe, you make me feel better."

"I'm glad of that." She forked up a bit of salad. "I suppose one needn't consider that we're the people Kim wants around him."

"Or the people he pushes away."

"Yes," she said slowly. "He does, doesn't he."

"He does something bad, one of those his-own-worst-enemy things, and he makes sure not to let anybody forgive him for it, still less tell him not to be such a, a—" He couldn't think of a term fit for a lady's ears.

"Prima donna," Phoebe said. "Oooh, for once *I* knew what *you* meant, that's new. And you're quite right. He's never happier than when he's making himself miserable. Why now, though? I *know* you and he were getting on better. What changed?"

Their visit to the High-Low had changed things, but Will couldn't talk about that. He gave an awkward shrug. She looked at him with uncomfortable shrewdness, then shook her head. "Honestly. The bloody man."

Will blinked. Phoebe raised her wineglass with a wry smile, and he clinked it. "Bloody man."

Time with Phoebe made him feel better for a while, as did a trip to the cinema so that he wasn't sitting around waiting, but as Thursday passed without a word, it took the remnants of his patience with it. He went to the pub on Thursday night, threw his darts rather too hard for accuracy, and returned home around eleven to see electric light from upstairs illuminating the stairwell.

He couldn't even be bothered with subtlety. "Get your arse down here so I can kick it!"

"Are you talking to a burglar, or to me?" Kim called down.

"Either," Will snapped, and stamped up the stairs.

Kim was in his armchair again. He looked shocking.

"Jesus," Will said. "Have you not slept?"

"Slept? Yes, I'm sure I did that." He was grey, his eyes dark slits, like a bad black-and-white cartoon of himself. "Not for a while, but I'm sure I did at some point."

"Feeling guilty, are we?"

"Oooh. Temper."

"I bloody killed someone on Sunday, Kim. During the commission of a felony. A word would have been nice, along the lines of *all hushed up, don't worry about it*."

"That's a sentence," Kim said enragingly. "But it's hushed. Believe me, it's hushed. The body's gone, the club is closed, and Mrs. Skyrme took the boat from Dover with a bagful of chocolates and hasn't been seen since."

"She's gone? Why didn't you have the ports watched?"

"Because I made a deal. She opened the safe for me, and I let her clear off with the loot. Admittedly she left before we'd entirely finished our conversation, but she did her part. Not one of the true-believer idiots, Mrs. Skyrme, she got when the going was good. When the getting was good? When the going had got good, by God."

"You're drunk," Will said, noticing.

"I'm not fucking drunk. I'm *drinking*. So would you be."

There was an empty bottle by the chair which had been half full of cheap Scotch this morning. If Kim had put that away voluntarily, they were probably in big trouble.

"Why did you let her go?" Will demanded. "What was the deal?"

Kim shrugged. "Didn't want her. I wanted Capricorn. A big pile of lovely incriminating undeniable evidence all about Capricorn. That's what I asked for."

"And did you get it?"

"I got lots of stuff. Lots and lots. Codenames, references.

Financial johnny piecing it together as we speak, page after page. Sodding marvellous."

"You never gave a damn for Skyrme," Will said. "You never meant to arrest her for what she did. You meant to get at Capricorn all along, and you leant on Mrs. Appleby so you could lean on Skyrme." He looked at Kim's face, the empty bottle. "And you haven't got him. Have you?"

Kim met his eyes, murder in his dark gaze. They stared at each other for a couple of seconds that made Will's knife hand itch, and then Kim looked away. "He isn't in the stuff from the High-Low. She told me he wouldn't be. 'You won't find him here,' she said, and we haven't and won't. And she's fucked off and Fuller's dead, and there's still no bloody evidence, which means I still can't pass the cup and say, *This is Capricorn. Deal with him,* so it's still down to me. I don't know why I ever thought it wouldn't be."

It took a second for Will to grasp the implication. He stared at Kim, the words slotting into place. "You know. You do, don't you? Jesus Christ. You know who Capricorn is!"

"Of course I do," Kim said. "If I'm honest, I've known for a while. 'If I'm honest'." He gave a little giggle. "That's rich."

Will had so many things to say to that, he could barely speak. He went for the least of them. "Then why don't you bloody arrest him?"

"On what grounds? I've got a lot of nothing. Straws in the wind, and fears, and the words of the dead. The case needs to be iron-clad, and mine is wet tissue paper. I need objective proof. Not objective. What does Othello say? Ocular proof. Villain, be sure thou prove my love a whore, be sure of it. Give me the ocular proof."

"Steady on."

"Othello's wrong anyway. Lear would be better."

"I'm sure." There was no point venting his feelings with Kim in this state—Will wanted him to remember what he said—and he might even be drunk enough to tell the truth, if pumped. That was doubtless a shabby, deceitful way to go on, but Will had learned from a master. "If you know who he is, we can get him. Tell me about it. We'll make a plan."

"If I could get him, I'd have sodding got him." Kim's control of his speech was slipping now, the words slurring. Will wondered just how fast he'd put away the Scotch. "You think I've been sitting around doing nothing?"

"Of course not."

"You should. I might as well have been. This is a fucking nightmare and it doesn't stop. It's never going to stop. I thought I knew best in 1914 and I'm going to pay for it the rest of my life. And I wouldn't mind that, not really, it's only fair. *This* isn't fair."

"What isn't?"

"Any of it. Shit. I'm drunk."

"I know."

"You should throw me out."

"I don't need telling. How much have you had?"

"About…I don't know. I finished the brandy. That's a civilised drink, not like this muck." He picked up the bottle on the second try and contemplated it as if wondering where the whisky had gone.

"Sorry my booze isn't up to your standards." Will wondered if it would help to march him downstairs and find a water-butt to stick his head in. It would certainly relieve his own feelings. He tried again. "Look, why don't you tell me about it? You'll feel better."

Kim blinked. "Want to lie down."

Will had plenty of experience with the incapacitatingly drunk. He persuaded Kim to use the chamber pot he kept under the bed for emergencies before he collapsed, and took his shoes off after. He went downstairs to get water and check Kim hadn't done too much damage on his way in through the window. By the time he returned, his unwanted guest was snoring, fully clothed, on top of the covers.

It was a big bed, but Will had no intention of sharing it with him. He found a blanket to put over Kim and another for himself, left a mug of water on the table, rescued his pyjamas, turned off the lights, and went downstairs to sleep on the bloody rickety camp bed again.

THIRTEEN

W ill woke up to the sound of mortars far too close to the trench, a noise that sent him from deep sleep to sitting upright in a dizzying movement. Nausea sloshed through him as his brain caught up with his body and the bombardment—

No. No explosions, no trench, no war. He was in the shop, someone was banging at the door, and it was the middle of the bloody night.

He dragged himself to his feet. It wouldn't be Zodiac—they usually just broke in—so he probably didn't need the Messer. He fumbled for his dressing gown, realised everything would be easier if he put the lights on, did so, then spent the next seconds blinking painfully. The banging was shaking the room.

"All right!" he bellowed, and stormed through the shop to the door.

It was the police.

Will stared through the glass. Three uniformed men, two constables, one whose hat suggested a more senior position. They were here for him. Someone had found Fuller's body, or worked out what had happened, and they were here to arrest him, and he was fucked because Kim hadn't hushed it up after all.

Turn and run? But he was barefoot, the back door locked, and the front easily smashed in. He couldn't do anything but brazen this out.

He unlocked the door. "Officers? What's all this about?"

"William Darling?"

"Yes."

"We're here on information received. May we come in?" The sergeant walked in, without waiting for reply, forcing Will back. "Upstairs."

"What information? What are they doing? Hey!" The two constables were disappearing upstairs. "What's going on? Do you have a warrant for this?"

"If I were you, sir, I'd cooperate," the officer said with a sneer. "You're in enough trouble as it is."

"What trouble?" Will demanded, sticking to the principle of *Deny everything*. "What are you talking about?"

A constable appeared at the top of the stairs. "Well?" the officer said.

"There is a gentleman up here, sir," the constable began, a little awkwardly.

"Right. Come down and keep hold of this one in case he makes a run for it."

"What the—? What do you mean, make a run for it?"

"No, but Sarge," the constable on the stairs said. "He's fully clothed and out like a light. Fast asleep. Stinks of booze."

"Is that illegal now? It's..." Will looked at the clock. "It's four in the morning! Why wouldn't he be asleep?"

"May I ask who the gentleman upstairs is, sir, and what precisely he's doing here?"

"He's Lord Arthur Secretan," Will said, aware he was deploying the title as a shield and resenting it as he did it. "And he's sleeping off a heavy one, just like your man said. What's it to you?"

"What it is to me, sir, is that we received a complaint of gross indecency at this address."

Gross indecency. Not manslaughter, or murder. Will felt a dizzying wave of relief, which was almost immediately swamped by a second of alarm, and a third of pure boiling rage.

"A complaint of *what*?" he demanded. "On what grounds?"

"I beg your pardon?"

"Grounds. You know, reasonable suspicion? Evidence? Something that would give you a justification for banging on my door at four in the morning?" The officer hesitated. Will pressed his point. "Whose complaint was it? Based on what? What the hell are you playing at? Do you even have a warrant?"

"We asked your permission to enter, sir."

"And you didn't wait for it," Will said. "You forced your way in here while I was half asleep on the basis of what, precisely? What the devil is going on here?"

The officer shot a look at the constable on the stairs, who said apologetically, "No sign of anything untoward, sir."

"Of course there bloody isn't! I've been asleep down here. My bed will still be warm. In there. Go and check. Go and check right now!"

One of the constables started a salute. He caught himself almost immediately and went off, meeting Will's eye as he passed with an apologetic look. Will waited, fuming, until he came back out. "Camp bed, sir, been slept in."

"Right," Will said. "*Thank* you. Now, am I not allowed to let a pie-eyed mate sleep it off in my own home? Is there something wrong with that?"

"I'll ask the questions, sir," the sergeant said. "How is Lord Arthur Secretan your 'mate'?"

"Tell you what, why don't you ask him that? I expect he'll be pretty keen to talk to you tomorrow. In fact, I expect he'll bring the sort of lawyer his type can afford to ask why you were hammering on my door in the middle of the night like the bloody Cheka, making slanderous accusations. What's your name and what's your station?"

"I'd like to know your relationship with Lord Arthur, sir."

"Have you seen any evidence of anything unlawful here? *Have* you?"

"Sir—"

"Don't give me 'sir'." Will was fizzing with rage, and had a strong feeling he knew what was going on. "Answer my question. Evidence of any offence whatsoever. Any grounds for barging in here. Well?"

"No, sir," one of the constables put in. The officer shot him a glare.

"No. And since that's what you're here to harass me about at four o'clock in the morning, I don't think I need to stand here any longer. So you can all three give me your names, numbers, and stations for the complaint I'll be making tomorrow, and get off my property."

He wrote down the details, saw the sergeant and his discomfited flunkies out, and bolted the door in a thoroughly bad mood.

Kim crawled downstairs at about ten the next day. It was lucky the shop was empty.

"You look like a tramp," Will said, in lieu of greeting.

"That's surprisingly positive, since I feel like a corpse. I imagine I have a fair bit to apologise for."

"You have no idea how much. Get cleaned up, get some food and coffee into yourself, and then get back here. And don't piss me about, Kim. If you disappear on me now, you don't ever show your face again."

"Worse than I thought, then."

"You've got half an hour. Try not to let me down, for once."

Kim was back within the allotted time, which was mildly impressive since he looked as if it hurt to move. Will doubted he'd eaten anything.

"Tea?" he said, because the kettle was on and he was furious but not a monster.

"God, yes."

Will locked the door, switched the sign to Closed, and led the way into the back room. Kim shot a glance at the camp bed. "I take it I stole your bed last night. Sorry."

"Don't be. If I'd been in it with you, we'd have been up a gum tree when the police came round."

"*What?*"

Will gave him a brief summary. "I'm no expert, but I don't think the rozzers generally bang on the doors of private homes at four in the morning to check whose beds people are in. The chap in charge was a Sergeant Spencer Thomas at Vine Street station, which isn't the local nick, but is the station that covers the High-Low. I suppose that was Mrs. Skyrme's parting shot at us."

"Spencer Thomas," Kim repeated.

Will passed him the sheet with the sergeant's details. "He knew you were here, and exactly what he was looking to find. So we have to assume Zodiac know about you and me."

"Balls." Kim shut his eyes. "I'm extremely sorry."

"I told Thomas that you'd be round with a lawyer in the morning."

"Consider it done. Anything else I need to clean up?"

"You owe me a new bottle of Scotch, since you drank all mine."

"Christ, did I? No wonder my head hurts."

"And just one more thing," Will said. "You admitted last night that you know who Capricorn is, and have for a while. So do you want to tell me what the fuck you're playing at?"

Kim's face froze. Will said, "If you give me any flannel now, I will kick you down the street. I'm not in the mood. I've been kidnapped, I've had guns pointed at me, I've killed people and mixed up Maisie in this and pissed off the War Office, and now I've got the police sniffing around me, all because of Zodiac, and you knew who Capricorn was all along? And you didn't trust me to tell me so?"

"On the contrary," Kim said. "I clearly did trust you once I was sufficiently plastered. In vino veritas. Give me a moment."

"To come up with a lie?"

"Jesus, Will, let me think! Are you under the impression I'm doing this for fun?"

That sounded raw enough that it might even be true. Plus the tea was well brewed by now. Will poured it out, waiting.

"All right," Kim said at last. "I have no idea what I said last night, but it is not correct to say I have known who Capricorn is all along. I had a suspicion at the end of last year, which has since become what you might call a moral certainty, unsupported by evidence. I've been looking for proof since. My belief was confirmed on Sunday at the High-Low. And there is absolutely damn all I can do about it."

"Why not?"

"He's covered his tracks all the way, been incredibly careful about who knows his identity, and to make them fear revealing it. Skyrme wouldn't stick around to testify at any price; she's not stupid. We've found a lot in her papers, but she told me at the time we wouldn't get Capricorn in them, and I don't think we will. It's been like that all the way. I can't make a case that I can pass over to DS, still less the police."

"Who is he?"

"I can't tell you."

Will put his mug down hard enough to splash tea over his fingers. Kim flinched at his expression, but he said, doggedly, "I *can't*, Will, do you think I'm trying to annoy you? I cannot share this."

"Why the hell not?"

"I can't tell you that either. I realise that's tiresome."

"Tiresome?" Will repeated, at a volume that made Kim wince. "*Tiresome?* What's tiresome here is that you demand my time and work when it suits you and leave me in the bloody dark! What's tiresome is that when you have a use for me you'll talk for all the world as if I matter to you, but the second it's not convenient, it turns out I don't mean a thing!"

"I know. I *know*."

"Then why don't you stop?" Will shouted. "You choose to do this! You choose to make everyone around you miserable and shut out the people who give a damn for you—not just shut us out, insult us. Do you think Phoebe doesn't see how you ignore her when it suits you? Do you think I've nothing better to do than wait for you?"

"I never asked you to wait," Kim said, white-lipped.

"That's always your excuse, isn't it? *I never asked.* You bloody did, Kim. Just because it's not in words doesn't mean you never asked, or promised, or made people hope. If you don't want lovers or friends, stop fucking making them!"

"Your expectations are your responsibility."

"Right, it's my fault for asking too much, so now I'm embarrassed to tell you what a shit you are. Christ, the state of you. You're so busy torturing yourself for your sins, you don't even notice how much you're hurting other people."

Kim had gone entirely white. "You have no idea what you're talking about."

"Why, because I'm not as refined as you? I could hang, Kim, do you understand that? Never mind two years for gross indecency: I killed a man!"

"It was an accident."

"It bloody wasn't," Will said impatiently. "I kicked him off a two-storey drop so he didn't shoot you. You said yourself I saved your life, and if you say 'I didn't ask you to', so help me God I will break your jaw. I'm not asking for thanks, but for Christ's sake, I'm not your fucking hired killer! I helped you because—"

"Because you wanted to," Kim said. "You're bored out of your mind and you wanted adventure. Let's not pretend I forced you into this. I told you it would be dirty."

"I didn't think you meant you'd do the dirty on me!"

"Then more fool you, because you've plenty of experience to suggest exactly that."

"Don't you dare blame me for this. And horseshit," Will said. "You know bloody well it's been different between us."

Kim's eyes were weary, and desperately miserable. "I know."

"I don't understand why you'd build all that up just to smash it down again."

"You would if you listened. I literally cannot tell you about Capricorn. I'm not doing this because I like hurting you. I'm *stuck*."

"Then get unstuck. Do something. Don't just hide in a bottle of whisky like a coward."

"You have no idea what I've done," Kim snapped.

"No, because you won't tell me! I thought—"

I thought we were in step. I thought you knew I'd stand by you if you only let me, but you won't.

"I thought we were together," he said inadequately. "I really thought we were. And you've been lying to me every second of the day."

Kim's face was painfully drawn. "I don't know what I can say. You're asking for more than I can give."

"Well, that's me told. I thought we were both grown men and equals. I forgot I should be coming cap in hand to your lordship. My mistake."

"Oh, go to hell. That's not what I meant."

"You dole out information like Lady bloody Bountiful at the village tea. Everything we do is on your timetable, your decision, and if I don't like it I can leave."

"Yes. You can."

"That's not a relationship!" Will shouted. "That's not how you treat a friend or a lover or a partner, or any damn thing! 'Take it or leave it' is for customers, not people you care about. You're meant to compromise, and find a way through, not just say *this is how it is* because you don't have the guts to face up to things. You're meant to give a damn when you hurt people!"

"Will—"

"I told you not to use me, Kim. You know what I feel about that, and you did it anyway, and—oh, the hell with this. We're finished. I'm done. Get out."

Kim couldn't have been surprised to hear it and yet his face twitched, a single tiny flinch that made Will even angrier because he had no right in the world to be upset.

"Go on, go," he said. "Don't come back. Keep your precious secrets if that's all you care about, and leave me alone. This isn't forgivable."

Kim went. He didn't even have the decency to give Will a fight or slink out shamefacedly; he just picked up his coat and hat and left. The door closed behind him, setting the bell jangling.

Will stared at where he'd been, breathing hard, then kicked his chair across the room.

The rest of Friday was, frankly, trying. He cleaned the shop with vindictive vigour, boiling with anger and going over the whole sorry business in his head, plus all the things he should have added while kicking Kim out.

Bastard. Absolute bastard.

He kept the shop open all the same, and sold a few books without breaking bits off his customers, for which he probably deserved another medal. He went along to a gymnasium that evening and pummelled a punchbag till his arms hurt. He slept in sheets that smelled of whisky and Kim, and ended up sitting on the side of the bed with his face in his hands at five a.m.

The fact was, he had only himself to blame. *Fool me once, shame on you…*

He didn't think Kim had been lying throughout. That was the worst part. He knew that Kim's desires matched his, that their growing intimacy had been real. It wouldn't have hurt so much if it wasn't real, because that way Kim would have discarded something of no value. Instead he'd looked at everything he and Will might have meant to one another—the truths, the secrets, the care—put it all in the balance, and decided it still wasn't enough.

Will didn't give a damn if Capricorn was the Prime Minister himself. What difference could it possibly make for Kim to tell him? He wouldn't have run to the bloody papers. If Kim was sitting on a major problem, why wouldn't he let a trusted friend and ally help him with it?

The only possible answer was, he didn't want to. For all they'd been through and shared and done, he would always put his secrets first. Maybe Phoebe could love a man who hid everything that mattered and could only be known through the things he didn't say, but Will wasn't that generous-hearted, or that clever. And he really wasn't in the market to play the enlisted man to a posh bloke's officer. He'd done four years of that.

To hell with Kim Secretan. If he wanted to be a lone wolf, he doubtless knew where the Russian steppes were. Will had more self-respect than to trail after him any more.

FOURTEEN

Will put in a hard morning's work with book catalogues on Saturday. He usually closed at noon on Saturdays, but he stayed open till past one as penance, then went to the cafe down the road to treat himself to a pie and mash lunch. He was sick of the sight of books.

They usually had the papers, but he was late enough that all the copies were taken. He picked up a stray copy of *London Life* instead. It was all pictures of Bright Young Wankers, men in tuxedos photographed mid-bray, women in drapes and dresses sitting improbably on furniture. There was plenty of puffery about clothes and couturiers, including a piece on Molyneux's salon in Paris. Maybe Maisie would be in these pages one day. Maybe he should drop in on Molyneux when he visited her, try out what it would be like with a man who wasn't a bloody liar.

He flicked through for anything readable. There was an entire page of guff about parties people were going to. Did ordinary people really pay money to read about events they'd never be invited to?

He forked pie into his mouth as he scanned the page, and an image caught his eye.

Miss Phoebe Stephens-Prince with Edward Molyneux, Adela Moran, Johnnie Cheveley, and rising designer Marguerite Zie, at the Criterion for a dinner given by Lord Arthur Secretan. Inset: Miss Stephens-Prince and Gloria Glade at Lord Waring's Hertfordshire residence, Etchil.

He'd seen the photographers at the party, not that any of them had wanted to photograph him. Phoebe doubtless had a press-agent who fed this guff to the papers. It was what people did in her world, the Lord Arthur world. He hated it.

He hoped Maisie didn't hate it. He hoped she was a success, and that Phoebe would launch her into a new and exciting life. He wasn't the kind of arsehole who'd be bitter about his friend's happiness just because his own brush with high life had brought him nothing but misery, hurt, and legal peril. He told himself that very strongly indeed.

The next page held a piece entitled 'What's Next For The Cloche Hat?' Will couldn't imagine. He finished his meal without enthusiasm and went back to the bookshop.

He needed to go back to his own sort, that was what it came down to. He had plenty of casual friends down the pub but he needed to put more effort in. Join a football team, perhaps. Spend time with people like himself, not starlight people. Maisie might be turning into one of them but Will's feet would always be clay, and nothing but misery came of mixing with those who, in the end, didn't see you as their equal.

Maybe he should get stuck into politics. Labour's stint in government had had a shaky start: they probably needed more support on the ground. He didn't have much appetite for the Communists after what he'd heard from Kim, but then again if they weren't worth Kim's time and nor was he, maybe he should take that as a hint. Obviously he should be with people who wanted to bring down barriers of class and privilege, rather than sitting in whatever Phoebe's ancestral home was called again, surrounded by bloody toffs.

Homes with names. He resented that to an irrational degree.

Numbers were good enough for most people, or descriptive names like Bluebell Cottage or what-have-you, but of course the posh lot needed houses with their own identity, ones so big they were marked on maps. Wankers.

Maisie had sounded so thrilled at her visit. She'd be able to swank now, like those people Kim had mentioned: *Oh, I took a bolt down to Etchil for the grouse shooting, la di da.* Will tried to imagine himself visiting whatever Kim's family estate was called. The idea was laughable.

The Kelly's Blue Book on his desk had a list of the aristocracy. He turned the pages in a scab-picking sort of way, and found Kim's family right there. The Marquess of Flitby, family name Secretan, heir Earl of Chingford, London address Belgrave Square, family seat Holmclere. All those names and places, belonging to just one man. But then, their sort had to own everything.

Phoebe's father was in there too. The Viscount Waring, family name Stephens-Prince, family seat Etchil, pronounced Eye-shull because obviously it was. No name for an heir since there was no son.

Will slammed the book shut. He was not going to sit here any longer, brooding over things he couldn't have like an idiot. He'd pursue things he could have instead, starting with a cup of tea.

He got up, went to the back room, and was half way through putting the kettle on when the penny dropped.

He didn't drop the kettle along with it, though he might have. He stood still, holding it in mid-air, then he put it down very carefully, turned off the gas, and said, "Gas is off," aloud in case he couldn't remember later. Then he went back to his desk, sat down, and opened the Blue Book again.

Viscount Waring, family name Stephens-Prince, family seat Etchil. Pronounced Eye-shull.

"Fuck," Will said aloud. The word had a dead sound in the empty, book-lined room.

Kim had demanded Capricorn's name of Fuller and he'd screamed what Will had taken for agreement to speak, because it hadn't meant anything else. *I shall!* And Kim hadn't waited for him to say more. Will had assumed he'd noticed it was inhuman to let the man swing there, as if being inhuman had stopped Kim before.

Christ, he'd even said it. *The words of the dead.* Will had assumed that was Leinster. Kim had meant Fuller.

And Kim wouldn't, couldn't tell him who Capricorn was, not at any price.

And Maisie was down at Eye-shull, Etchil, now.

"Fuck!" Will said again, louder this time, and lunged for the telephone.

He barked Kim's number at the operator. The phone rang and rang and rang. He was on the verge of giving up and going over to kick the door down when there was a click and a near-snarl of, "Secretan."

"It's Will."

"Oh God," Kim said, sounding exhausted. "I don't—"

"Shut up. Phoebe's father's house. How do you say its name?"

Silence. Long, damning silence.

"How do you say it?"

"Right," Kim said, very calmly. "Listen—"

"Maisie is there!"

"What?"

"Phoebe's taken her to this Etchil place. Lord Waring wanted her there badly enough to send a car. They're there right now. And we just pissed Zodiac off badly, and they know all about me —I even took her to the fucking High-Low Club—"

"Will—"

"Is she safe, damn you? *Is she safe?*"

"Stop!" Kim shouted down the line. "Let me think."

Will forced himself to be silent. The line hung empty in space for perhaps thirty seconds, then Kim spoke, more calmly. "Get over here. Come round to the mews entrance, I'll order the car. But, and listen to me: shave first, change into something decent, pack your evening clothes. Do it carefully, don't rush. And come armed."

It took Will about twenty-five minutes to get himself together, and an irritating twenty more on the tram to Holborn with his bag, telling himself it would not be quicker to walk. He more or less ran to the mews, where Kim was waiting with the Daimler. The last time Will had ridden in that, he'd been escaping from imprisonment at the hands of Zodiac.

"In you get," Kim said. "I've called Etchil to let them know there'll be extra guests."

"I suppose you know what you're doing. Why are we going as guests?"

"Because that's how this is played." Kim nosed the Daimler into traffic. "Waring pretends to welcome me as his future son-in-law, I pretend to think he's a genial sort of chap, and we both pretend everything is normal. It's why he's going to win."

"What?"

"When this blows up, he will not hesitate to use Phoebe as a weapon. I will hesitate, because I don't want to hurt her, and he knows it. So I'm going to lose."

Will needed to say it out loud, no possibility of misunderstanding. "Etchil is Lord Waring's house. He's Capricorn. Phoebe's father is Capricorn."

"Yes."

"Does she know?"

"No."

"You're sure?"

"Yes."

"Jesus Christ, Kim." Will couldn't begin to imagine what that meant. "Jesus. You must have been living in hell."

There was a long silence. Will watched his profile. He could see the shimmer of his eyes, the tension of his lips, set hard against collapse.

"Yes," he said at last. "I have."

Will didn't want to imagine it. He felt sick thinking about how it must have been: the growing fear, the knowledge that he might —would—hurt Phoebe, who Kim loved most in the world.

"Oh, hell," he said. "I'm sorry about yesterday."

"Don't apologise," Kim said harshly. "Please don't. You were absolutely right. I deserved everything you said, and I've screwed you around far too much to merit any faith. I just—I didn't do it to hurt you, Will. I was truly trying to do better."

"I know."

Kim grimaced. "Do you?"

"That's why it hurt. You've made a flaming mess of things, yes, but I don't know if I could have said anything either, in your shoes. Christ alive, what a business."

"You're not wrong."

"Why, though?" Will demanded. "Capricorn, Waring. He's a viscount. Why would he do that?"

"Why not? He's clever, persuasive, charming, and utterly without morals or scruples. I dare say a psychoanalyst would have a word for him. It's not that he's particularly cruel, though he is cruel, and he knows right from wrong very well: he just doesn't care. It's a game of chess to him. The only genuine emotion I have ever known him display is resentment."

"Of what?"

"That he's only a viscount, for a start." Kim's lips twisted. "There's simply too many people in the world who have more than him. More important titles, more extensive lands, bigger houses. Happier marriages. Phoebe's mother is profoundly unlikeable, but she knows bloody well there's something wrong with her husband. She won't be in the same room with him by choice, and she's done her best to steer Phoebe away from him and get her married off. All she's achieved is to drive her closer to the man, but it's the thought that counts."

"Phoebe said her mother didn't want her to marry you—"

"But if she had to, to get on with it. She wants Phoebe away from Waring at any price, and she's right to. Phoebe's the only child, you know. Another resentment of Waring's: he lost his son while other men still have theirs. Really, he is abused by Fate. It's only reasonable he should take this course." Kim whipped past a roundabout without slowing. "The engagement happened when I was already working for the Private Bureau. DS recruited me to cause trouble for Zodiac and I'd had my first direct tangle with them, which resulted in the previous Libra getting shoved off this mortal coil. I felt almost as if my existence might have a point. And then Phoebe got in trouble, and it seemed obvious to offer her my name, antiquated though that sounds. I really believed I was doing some good, making restitution. Look at me, the hero."

"You don't have to feel guilty about wanting to help."

"But I can feel stupid for believing I could do so," Kim said. "God knows what Waring thought was going on. He certainly encouraged the long engagement, which suited me very well. And he watched, and it must have dawned on him that I had no idea. DS hadn't picked me because of my connection to Phoebe's family, but simply because I was lost and potentially useful. I hadn't proposed to Phoebe to get close to Waring, because I didn't have a clue. God, he must have laughed."

The Daimler was purring through Islington now, heading west. Kim kept talking, apparently desperate to get the words out.

"He used to ask me what I was up to, I think to amuse himself, and he tried to use Phoebe to spy on me. That was what gave me the first hint, in fact. He gravely underestimates her, since she's female and talks nonsense, and she thought he was being odd and spoke to me about it. There were other things, too. A paper I saw at Christmas that he ought not have had; his name coming up on lists of people who'd bought or sold stocks for companies that took unexpected dips or jumps. Some things were literally staring me in the face. It was nothing that couldn't have been coincidence, but there were enough straws in the wind that the thought came to my mind. And once it was there, I started to see more and more. I felt morally certain by the start of this year. But I still don't have solid proof."

"Can you not take this to your chief, this DS?"

"I hoped to find hard evidence that I could hand over along with my resignation," Kim said. "I can't give him a tissue of suspicions and coincidences and unsupported accusations. DS would tell me to go off and find out more, and what would I say? *Sorry, that's my future father-in-law, no can do?*"

"Yes? Surely he'd put someone else on it?"

"No. He'd tell me I was perfectly placed to do the job, and he'd be absolutely right. Cornering Capricorn isn't going to be done from a distance, which is what I've been trying to do. It'll be up close and personal, and it will be nasty. And he is Phoebe's father, and she will know what I've done."

"She won't side with him. Not when she knows what *he's* done."

"Of course not. She'll turn her back on the parent who doesn't constantly tell her she's a painful disappointment without a second thought. I'm sure she'll get over it very quickly."

Will didn't reply: the ugly sound in Kim's voice didn't brook answers. After a minute Kim said, "Sorry. It's new to you. I've thought about very little else for months."

"It's all right."

"It truly isn't. I might have gone mad without you."

Will had to turn and look. Kim had his eyes on the road, but the tension in his face suggested that was a truth.

"I could think about you," Kim went on. "I could remember

something better, something clean and decent. I decided to stay away from you at the start of the year because I'd realised what Waring was, and I feared him knowing that I knew. I couldn't risk him targeting you because of me. And he would: Waring would destroy you without compunction if it seemed expedient. We hadn't known each other long, so I hoped, if I stayed away, that Zodiac would decide you weren't of interest to me. That would have been something, if I could keep you safe. But the High-Low business put the wind up me. I thought you must have been entrapped into it—they are very good at making unwitting recruits; look at Mrs. Appleby—and I couldn't let them use you. That wouldn't have ended well."

Will let a long breath out, and something hard and painful with it. "You should have told me. I don't need—" He was going to say *your protection* but that wasn't quite true. Kim had kept the law off him twice in a week, where he'd have been helpless. "I don't need coddling. I'd rather have known the truth. I could have helped."

"You have no idea how much I wanted your help," Kim said. "I thought about hurling myself on your shoulders on a near-daily basis, but..."

He paused there so long, Will wasn't sure there would be a conclusion. He still waited, because he wanted one. "But?" he said eventually.

"I don't know. *But* I hoped I could keep you out of it. *But* this is my burden to carry. *But* I didn't trust myself to make a sensible, unselfish decision, and rightly so. I couldn't have handled any of this worse. I should have handed Appleby over to DS and got Skyrme arrested, and let the whole business play out, no matter how much pain and humiliation it would cause Phoebe and her mother. I knew that, but I couldn't do it. I told myself I was respecting your promise to Beaumont, but that was a lie."

"I know."

"I'd have liked it to be true. I owed you that much, and it

sounds better than admitting I lack the courage of my convictions. I wanted to find some irrefutable proof to hand DS so he could force Waring's submission and keep the business hushed up. A bad habit of the Private Bureau, I fear."

"Of course you don't want it in the papers," Will said. "But what's the alternative? Give the man a bottle of whisky and a revolver?"

"Maybe. But it would require cast-iron proof to force his hand, and I don't have that. He's got significantly more on me than I do on him."

"That hasn't worked out well," Will agreed. "How come he hasn't used it before?"

"I honestly can't say. Possibly he's amusing himself watching me flail around. Possibly he wants me to make his daughter a marchioness."

"Could you?"

"Certainly, if my brother Chingford were removed from this mortal coil."

"You don't seriously think Waring would have your brother killed. Do you?"

Kim shrugged. "Are you familiar with Charles the First's belief in the Divine Right of Kings? Lord Waring is much that way for his own benefit. There is nothing to which he does not believe himself entitled."

"Charles the First got his head cut off," Will pointed out. "I'm on the Cromwell side myself."

A smile flitted over Kim's face, there and gone. "Glad to hear it. Thank you, Will. And I'm so sorry for all of this, I truly am. I've brought you nothing but trouble, and I realise how shitty it was not to say anything for so long, but I couldn't—I *couldn't*—"

"I know."

He wished they could pull over somewhere secluded, but they were on the outskirts of Metroland now, new red brick houses carpeting the land as the city grew like a tumour. There was no seclusion to be had.

"You haven't told Phoebe any of this?"

"No."

"I'm not sure you've a right to keep it from her. I know you're trying to protect her—"

"Don't be absurd," Kim said. "I'm protecting myself. Of course I should have told her, though damned if I know exactly when, since there was never a single point when I tipped from ignorance to certainty. I simply haven't had the guts."

"You're afraid of how she'll react?"

"I'm afraid she'll hate me. I'm afraid she won't believe me, or that she'll choose her father over me, or worst of all, that she'll forgive me. I'm afraid it will knock the joy out of her. Her life is going to be divided into Before and After by this, whatever happens, and I wanted to make Before as long as possible because After will not be good. You needn't tell me I'm a coward. I already know."

"I wasn't planning to," Will said. "I'm sorry for the things I said before."

"Why? You were right. I've treated you abominably."

"You have, yes. And you drank my Scotch."

"That carried its own punishment."

"But I don't know what else you could have done, except bring your own booze. This is the stuff of nightmares. I'd have done no better in your place, and probably worse. And it is going to end horribly because there's no way for it to end well, but I'm telling you now, that won't be your fault."

"Of course it will."

"You need to stop that," Will said. "Right now. You've got plenty to feel guilty about, but if learning her old man is a criminal mastermind hurts Phoebe, that's his fault. What are you going to do, let him carry on regardless? Zodiac have killed people, blackmailed people, tortured people. They chained me up in a room for six days and for all I know I'd be there now if you hadn't come to get me. Mrs. Appleby's a harmless woman who's been turned into a criminal. Leinster's dead. If you can stop Capricorn, the only thing you should feel guilty for would be turning your back on what needs doing."

"Ah, yes. One must always sacrifice love on the altar of duty." Kim's jaw was tense. "Because only duty matters. *Dulce et decorum est pro patria mori*."

"Beaumont loves Mrs. Appleby. Someone probably loved Leinster."

"But I don't care about them. I'm sure I should, but I don't. I'm going to put out the light in Phoebe's eyes, and no matter whose fault it is, I'll extinguish my own soul doing it."

The Daimler purred on.

"Here's the thing, though," Will said after a while. "I told you Maisie was at Etchil an hour or two ago, and we're in the car now, and you're driving pretty fast. Why's that?"

"Because I do not want a woman Waring doesn't value in an isolated house with him as he works out how to best use her against me or you."

"Right. And that's not 'duty', that's doing the right thing to stop an innocent woman getting hurt. Two innocent women, because do you think Phoebe would forgive herself if something happened to Maisie?"

"I know she wouldn't. I know you're right. I *know*."

"You want to stop him. You're doing your best. So how about you don't hand him yet another weapon by loading yourself with so much guilt you can't move under it? Bloody hell, Kim, I've killed more men than you ever will, and I'm not wandering about repenting at people. Do your damned job."

There was a short silence.

"You really do have a way with words," Kim said at last.

"Be dramatic on your day off. We've got to stop Waring doing anything to Maisie, and while we're there we might as well find the evidence he's Capricorn, right?"

"Easy as that?"

Will shrugged. "You seem to be pretty good at locks these days. Get into his study. Or tell him lies, that's your area. Tell him you got more from Mrs. Skyrme than you did. *Something*."

They drove in silence for a while. Will thought about the situation, going over what he knew, what he could do, what their chances were. It wasn't pretty.

Kim pulled off the main road at Berkhampstead and onto a smaller road through fields, lined overhead with skeletal branches and the odd burst of pink blossom.

"Questions," Will said. "First, are we going to have more trouble with that policeman?"

"No. I put my lawyers abreast of it, and more to the point told DS everything. This is very much the Private Bureau's area of expertise."

"Everything?" Will repeated. "You don't mean us?"

"He doesn't like not knowing things. Don't worry about it." Kim glanced over at what must have been a dumbfounded expression. "I didn't tell him anything he didn't already know or couldn't have found out. The pressing issue here is a policeman on the Zodiac payroll, and Sergeant Thomas is currently being skinned like a rabbit. Don't give it another thought. And the same for Fuller, by the way. It's dealt with."

That was something. "Thanks," Will said. "Second, then: what are we going to do when we get there? Do I tell Maisie what's going on? Get her out of there?"

"That is indeed the question. I was inclined to say we remove her from the situation at once, but I doubt that would go down well. All Waring has to do to make us look like fools is nothing, but if he chooses to hurt her, we'll be heavily outnumbered. We're on the back foot here."

"That's a good place to throw a punch from. How

outnumbered?"

"I have to assume he'll have staff in the know, ready to follow orders, but I don't know how many. And there's always Johnnie Cheveley."

"Phoebe said he'd be there. You don't think—"

"Oh, yes I do," Kim said grimly. "He's deep in Waring's business and trying very hard to marry his daughter. If I were Waring, I wouldn't have someone that close that I couldn't trust."

"Isn't he meant to be a gentleman?"

"Heavens, yes. His father was an earl. Really, it seems *noblesse* doesn't *oblige* anyone any more." Kim gave a mirthless smile. "Cheveley's family was cut off at the knees by death duties during the war, leaving him, as the youngest son, with nothing. He harbours a great deal of resentment about it. I have often wondered if Waring picked him up because they have such similar characters, actually. Entitlement, arrogance, and a sense of superiority that takes anything less than full submission as a personal affront."

"He doesn't have a tattoo."

"No. Maybe he hasn't been admitted to the inner circle, or maybe Waring is grooming him for the leadership in the future, although that argues a willingness to give away power that I don't associate with him. Maybe upper-class members aren't required to bear the brand. Or maybe I'm wrong, but I doubt it. We should consider him hostile until proven otherwise."

"No problem there," Will said. "All right, third question: what's your aim for Waring? Arrest? A trial? Nasty accident?"

There was a long silence. Kim turned the car down a narrower lane.

"I don't know," he said at last. "Even if I had irrefutable evidence, he's got the funds and the network to bribe and blackmail his way out of trouble. It would be extraordinarily difficult to make a case stick. This is why the Private Bureau is the one taking Zodiac on."

"Because you don't do things the legal way."

"In a word."

"Do you want him dead?" Will said bluntly. "I need to know."

Kim grimaced. "Not at your hands. He's Phoebe's father and a viscount, and this is Hertfordshire, not the Wild West."

"It feels like the Wild West."

"The rules are certainly flexible from here on in. We're going to have to improvise."

"We did that before. We've done it a few times. I don't know anyone I'd rather have in a tight spot than you."

"That wasn't the impression I had yesterday." Kim spoke as if it were a joke, and maybe another time it could have been.

"All right, stop the car," Will said. "Stop it."

Kim brought the Daimler to a halt. Will glanced around. They were in a country lane, trees on either side, nobody in sight. He reached to cup Kim's face, felt him tense.

"Listen. We've given each other a bit of a kicking over the last few months. You've been pretty foul to me sometimes, and I've said things that weren't fair along with some that were. But I wouldn't have bothered with any of it, wouldn't have given a tinker's curse, if you weren't…" He wished he had words for what Kim was, the aching pain and the starlight, the beauty and the ugliness. "Do you know *Lepanto*?"

"The Chesterton poem?"

"There was a bit I was trying to remember it when I was chained up in that bloody room. I looked it up afterwards. 'Dim drums throbbing in the hills half heard, Where only on a name-less throne a crownless prince has stirred, Where risen from a doubtful seat and half-attainted stall, The last knight of Europe takes weapons from the wall.'"

Kim's lips parted. Will held his eyes, willing him to believe. "That's you."

"It truly isn't."

"The last knight. He's got a bad reputation and maybe he

deserves it, but he's still taking up arms, fighting the battles other people don't want because somebody's got to do it. That's what you make me think of—sometimes, anyway. That's what I see, and I reckon it's what Lord Waring is scared of."

"You think he is?"

"If he's not, he's going to find out his mistake. I'm with you, Kim. I'm in this. Let's get a war on."

Kim stared at him, eyes wide, and Will didn't even think. He just kissed him, hard, and felt Kim's mouth responding desperately, hands clutching his shoulders, hanging on for dear life. Kissing in the open because nothing at all mattered at this moment but to know they were together. The rest could wait for later, if there was a later.

"Will," Kim whispered at last, against his lips. "I don't want to do this."

"I know."

"You're with me?"

Will reached up for one of his hands and gripped it. "Right here. Not going anywhere."

Kim's shoulders heaved. "Thank you."

They held on for a few silent seconds, drawing strength. "Come on, Lord Arthur," Will said at last. "We've a battle to fight."

Kim took a deep breath, straightening his back. "If I'm a knight, does that make you my squire?"

"Sod off."

"Yeoman, then. You look like a yeoman."

"I don't even know what that is."

"A horny-handed son of toil."

"Did you say horny-handed?"

"I know your hands. If the cap fits…"

Will told him to sod off again. Kim started the car. They drove on, towards a reckoning.

FIFTEEN

Etchil wasn't a palace along the lines of Althorp or Deene Park or suchlike, but it was impressive all the same. It was an old mansion in red brick with a lot of chimneys and windows, and they'd driven for a couple of minutes on a winding road through open grounds to get there. Nice for some.

Kim brought the Daimler to a halt and checked his wristwatch, which Will still found a rather silly affectation in a civilian. "Quarter past five. We're here in time for cocktails, although it's always time for cocktails. Hello, there." He swung out of the car to greet a distinguished man in tails who had come to greet him. "How are you? I hope that trick elbow's better. Sorry to spring extra guests on you at no notice."

"It is of no import at all, Lord Arthur. My elbow is quite comfortable, thank you."

"Glad to hear it. My pal, Will Darling."

This must be his host. Will wasn't entirely sure how to greet a viscount at all, let alone one who he knew to be a criminal. He extended a hand, and snatched it back when the man bowed instead, doing a good impression of not having seen it. "Welcome to Etchil, Mr. Darling. My name is Benson. Don't hesitate to mention anything we can do to make you comfortable."

Will shot a glance at Kim, who said, "Thank you, Benson. Where's Phoebe?"

"In the Italian garden, I believe, Lord Arthur."

"We'll go through."

He sauntered into the house. Will followed at his heels. "Who was that?" he muttered.

"Butler."

"What about our bags?"

"They'll be brought in."

"They won't unpack them, will they? I've got my—you know, in there."

Kim swung on his heel to a man in livery who had apparently materialised out of nowhere to bring their luggage in. "By the way, just leave Darling's bag in his room, will you? Thanks."

Will would have added an excuse. Kim simply turned back and walked on. Clearly being a lord meant not having to justify yourself. That explained a lot.

The interior of the house was quite something. The great hall was stone-flagged and wood-panelled, with a gigantic fireplace topped with a stuffed stag's head and a pair of muskets. There was a magnificent oak flight of stairs that plucked at Will's long-dormant joinery experience, huge furniture, a big painting of a battle scene from the Napoleonic wars, all frothing horses and gunsmoke, some full-length portraits of people in olden-days clothes, and a lot of weaponry. There were no fewer than six sets of crossed swords, spears, and sabres on the walls, plus some tattered and faded military flags. Will attempted not to look like a day-tripper, gawping at the museum around him.

Kim led the way at a brisk trot through a panelled room that was mostly book-lined and another that was all cream wallpaper and paintings of horses, and into an airy sitting room with a glass-panelled door out to the gardens.

"Here we go," he said, and opened the door.

He strode out. Will tagged along, shivering at the cold and wondering why anyone would stand around outside in a British mid-March. The answer came as Kim turned down a gravel path through a gate in an ivy-covered wall and into a walled garden that was about five degrees warmer thanks to a brazier. There were carved stone Roman masks on the pale yellow stone walls, a grapevine on wires overhead, and enough bushes and statues scattered around to give Will an idea of what this must be like in summer. He bet it would be beautiful.

The party seemed to be here: Maisie, Phoebe, Johnnie Cheveley, and a distinguished-looking older man, in tweed with a bit of a paunch. They all held champagne glasses and cigarettes.

"Hello, Fee," Kim said.

Phoebe turned with a shriek that set the other heads turning. Maisie nearly dropped her glass.

"Kim? Dearest, what on earth are you doing here? This is so utterly typical." Phoebe gave him her gloved hands as she spoke. Kim kissed them both like a film actor. "And Will! How absolutely lovely. Was I expecting you both?"

"You were not," Kim said. "But I got your father's message." He turned to the older man with a smile.

"Arthur, my boy." Lord Waring held out a hand. "Good to see you."

Kim shook the hand. "And this is my friend William Darling. Will, Lord Waring."

Lord Waring turned and looked Will in the eyes.

He wasn't sure what he expected. Something snakey, some reptilian air of cruelty or menacing look, something to advertise that this man was behind kidnapping, extortion, murder. What he got was a direct gaze of slow, deliberate assessment, and then a society smile. "Welcome to Etchil, Mr. Darling. A pleasure to have you here, having heard so much of you."

"What message did you send Kim, Daddy?" Phoebe asked. There was a tiny line between her eyebrows.

"Why, I thought it would be pleasant to make a party of things, since we have Miss Jones," Waring said. "And I have very much wanted a chat with Arthur. Come and see me once you've had a drink and a chance to dress, will you? A small thing to discuss before dinner. Bring your friend."

"Certainly, sir."

"Excellent. John, give our guests a drink."

Waring turned and strode off to the house. Cheveley said, "Good to meet you again, Darling. Bubbles?"

Will took the proffered champagne with a word of thanks and sipped it. The taste was far drier than he'd expected, almost biscuitty, and delicious. He had another sip.

"Lord Waring does us well with his cellar," Cheveley remarked. "Don't miss the brandy later. I think this is your first visit? You'll find the house rather impressive, I suspect. Do ask the staff if you get lost."

There was no sneer in his voice, just a warm, friendly effort to put Will at ease. It might have been the most patronising thing he'd ever heard. "Thanks," he said. "Hey, Maisie, I fancy stretching my legs after that ride in the motor. Show me the grounds?"

She took his arm and steered him out to walk along a path. The wind bit. "God, it's cold," Will muttered.

"Never mind that," Maisie said. "What on earth are you doing here?"

"Long story. Is everything all right?"

"Well, it depends if you count me staying in a lord's house being treated like a lady. Good heavens, Will, this place! So many bedrooms, and mine's a lovely one, and these grounds! My ma won't believe it when I tell her. And Lord Waring has been so welcoming. He says he wants a private conversation with me later."

"Right," Will said. "Yes. Lord Waring. What's he like?"

Maisie stopped dead, turned, and narrowed her eyes. "All right, what's going on?"

"What do you mean?" Will said, a reflex he instantly regretted.

"Don't give me that, Will Darling. You've turned up here when I know very well you weren't invited, you were making me nervous earlier just by the way you stood there, and now you're asking questions in that voice."

"What voice?"

"The one when it's all going wrong, that's what voice. I can tell there's something up, so don't treat me as if I'm stupid."

"I'm not. It's just—Has Lord Waring been odd, at all? Asking funny questions?" He had to say it. "Do you feel safe?"

Maisie took a long, slow breath. "Are you saying I shouldn't?"

"I don't know."

"I want to know what is going on. Now."

"Look, Maisie—"

"No, you look," Maisie said, sounding extremely Welsh. "Phoebe is helping me. We have *plans*. She's done so much work to have me here with all sorts of useful people, and Lord Waring's her father. If there's something wrong, I need to know what it is."

"I don't know what I can say." Kim's anguish at Phoebe's future pain was too raw in his mind. "It's not something I can share. You know I would if I could."

"I don't know that at all, and I tell you what, you're letting that Kim Secretan go to your head."

"I am not!"

"Oh yes you are, running round hitting people and making cryptic remarks like him out of *The 39 Steps*. You own a bookshop! What are you up to?"

Will braced himself. "I think it might not be a good idea to trust Waring."

"Me? Or Phoebe?"

"Anyone. I'm going off what Kim's said."

"And he's messed you around often enough," Maisie pointed out swiftly.

"And *you* haven't told me what a nice old man Waring is, even though you've had plenty of chances."

Maisie walked on in silence for a few steps. At last she said, "He isn't a nice old man. Of course not, he's a viscount. He's very charming and well-mannered and hospitable."

"You don't like him."

Her nostrils flared. "I didn't say that, and it's not up to me to like him. He's very courteous." She took a couple more steps. "And now you're making me doubt myself, because I thought that he smiled with his mouth and not his eyes, and I decided he just doesn't know me yet."

"You once told me that girls should never ignore their feelings about men."

"Don't you quote me against myself. Will, what's happening? You've got me worried."

"So am I. Would you go home?"

"I can't do that! Phoebe's done so much, she's putting up with Johnnie Cheveley for us, and Lord Waring's giving us the money. I can't just walk out because I've got a funny feeling. About her dad, too!"

"I wish you'd both go. Could we fake a message from your sick auntie and ask Phoebe to come with you?"

"No," Maisie said comprehensively. "And I don't know where you've got this taste for lying from—well, I do, but it needs to stop, and you need to *talk* to me. I'm not throwing away everything Phoebe's done for me because of a few cryptic comments."

This felt like some sort of cosmic punishment for shouting at Kim. Will fervently wished he hadn't raised the subject. "Maisie, I *can't*, not yet. All I can say is, I think Waring's bad news. Really bad news."

"But you aren't telling me why. You can't do this to me, Will. It isn't fair."

"It wouldn't exactly be fair to Phoebe if I told you a lot of things about her father that she didn't know!"

"Things Kim knows."

"Yes."

"And hasn't told her."

"Uh—"

"I'm not having this," Maisie said flatly. "You don't treat friends this way, or people you love, and you know that yourself, Will Darling. I expect better from you than this cloak and dagger nonsense. And your Kim needs to think very hard about what matters, because Phoebe's kept him on his feet long enough and he won't even be honest with her, and now you're playing his game too? Have some respect."

She stalked back towards the house. Will trailed after her.

Kim was talking to Cheveley when he returned to the garden, looking particularly saturnine. "Will. Let me show you your room, and then we'll have that little chat with the viscount."

He led the way inside, up the grand oak stairs and along a series of elegantly wallpapered corridors. "It's just down here. You're in Borodino and I'm in the Pyramids."

"Sorry?"

"All the bedrooms are named for Napoleonic battles. Lord Waring is a great admirer of Napoleon. Phoebe sleeps in Corunna. The master bedroom is of course Austerlitz."

"Is that right," Will said. "Does he have a Waterloo?"

Kim's eyes met his as he stopped by a door that bore a sign reading *Borodino*. "Not yet."

He opened the door and gestured Will in, then stepped in after him.

It was a very nice room, with a single bed, a dresser with a mirror, a vase of fresh flowers. Will's bag was on a chair, apparently unopened. He checked inside and found the Messer.

"Lovely," Kim said. "So pleased you've brought a murder weapon to a house party."

"You said to come armed. Are you going to tell me what's going on?"

"Not a clue." Kim sounded almost cheerful. "I expect we'll get a hint from Waring shortly. You probably don't need to go armed to that meeting unless it makes you feel better. Did you have a set-to with Maisie?"

"I was trying to warn her about Waring and see if she'd go home. But I couldn't say why, so it didn't go well. Actually, I did about as badly as was humanly possible."

"At least we're consistent," Kim said. "This is the hell of it. Prepare to feel like the villain of the piece to Maisie, to Phoebe, to whatever audience Waring decides to perform in front of, and primarily to yourself as you wonder if, after all, you are quite rational and have not been deceived, or deceived yourself. I spent a long time persuading myself I was wrong."

"I heard Fuller say Etchil."

"Keep that in mind. It isn't going to make things easier with Maisie, though, right or not. I'm sorry about that."

"She doesn't like Waring," Will said. "Can't put her finger on why."

"I expect because she is used to moving defensively through life. When people are obliged to keep an eye out for threats, their eyes tend to be sharp. That's what women's intuition means, if you ask me: being unconsciously alert for dangerous men. Let's dress before we descend, shall we? I for one feel better when I look the part."

Will readied himself accordingly, though he did not feel in any way better for wearing evening dress. He felt, and looked, like an idiot.

Kim knocked on the door while Will was attempting to control his unruly hair. He looked superb, as usual, born to the clothing, with crisp shirt front and gleaming white cuffs, not to mention glittering amethyst cufflinks.

"Fancy," Will said.

"You scrub up nicely yourself."

"Mutton dressed as lamb," Will muttered. "Or something like that."

"Nothing like that," Kim said. "I said 'sophisticatedly thuggish' before, and I meant it. Smooth outside, hard centre. The effect is mouthwatering, trust me."

He might even mean it, from the look in his eyes. That was a little bit heartening. "If you say so."

"I do, I truly do. Let me adjust that tie a fraction."

This apparently meant retying it. Will didn't object to that either. He'd done it badly, and anyway it put Kim in front of him, dark eyes intent and body close.

Kim's hands moved gently at his neck. Will watched his face, noting the lines of strain around his eyes and the bruised-looking skin under them that betrayed exhaustion. Those were the only giveaways: the rest of his face was still, the way he liked to keep it when he had something to hide.

"Kim?"

"Mmm?"

"I don't know how much this is hurting you," Will said. "I don't know how scared you are. But I'm here if you need to stop pretending for a bit. You're not alone, all right?"

Kim's eyes were on his, very wide. His lips parted, but he didn't speak. Will wasn't sure what to add, or if there was anything else to say at all. They simply looked at one another, silent but for the whisper of breath, the gentle thud of pulses.

"I," Kim began at last, and had to try again. "I would like to be —not alone."

"Shoulders right here. Suitable for leaning on, crying on, or standing at for the purposes of a fight."

Kim's mouth moved in something that ended up as a smile.

"They are magnificent shoulders and I shall take you up on it. Though in a fight I shall doubtless be cowering behind you."

"Nice try, but I've seen you with a knife," Will reminded him. "Are we going to do this?"

"Yes. It's going to be ghastly."

"We've both had worse."

"Have we? Well, you have."

Will took Kim's slim forearm and ran his thumb over the black cloth that covered the old scars. "Pretty sure you have too."

Kim paused on that. "Perhaps. I don't know. Shall we go and find out?"

Will cupped the back of his head and kissed him. Kim's hands came to his shoulders, gripping them, opening his mouth to Will and pulling him in. They kissed deeply for just a moment, a snatched few seconds in a world that gave no space, and pulled apart by what felt like mutual decision.

"Right," Will said. "*Now* let's go."

Lord Waring's study was the sort of room Will might have expected—more oak panels, lots of books, an oil painting of a dignified man with a moustache, a watercolour of Phoebe, a big desk. There was an ornate fireplace with beautiful carving and a painted coat of arms at its centre. A large filing cabinet struck a rather ugly note of modernity.

Lord Waring was standing at the desk. "Ah, Arthur. And Mr. Darling. Shut the door."

Kim did so, then came to stand by Will. "Well. What did you want to talk about, sir?"

"Oh, nothing formal. Just a little chat." Lord Waring's voice was genial. "I wondered what you've been up to in the past—oh, week or so. Since last Sunday, say."

"This and that." Kim smiled back at him. "Pootling about, don't you know."

Waring's smile didn't falter. "And you, Mr. Darling? I understand you're a bookseller."

"That's right."

"A delightful occupation. How do you come to be acquainted with Arthur?"

"He dropped into my shop last winter, and we got talking. Struck up a friendship."

"Of course Arthur is a great bibliophile. Well, that explains it. What's the phrase? Business makes strange bedfellows. Is that a fair description? Strange bedfellows?"

This would doubtless be what Kim had meant: veiled threats, verbal games, generally playing silly buggers. Will had known a couple of officers like that. "As you say, sir."

"Oh, harsh," Kim said. "I may be considered a queer fish by some, but Darling's quite the petit bourgeois. The exemplar of Napoleon's dictum that the English are a nation of shopkeepers." He smiled back at Waring. "Which is perhaps a *little* dismissive on the great man's part. After all, the shopkeepers won."

"Hm. And how is business, Mr. Darling? Thriving, I hope? Your generation faces so many challenges. The struggling economy, the precarious nature of prosperity. It takes very little to make a small business fail these days. Could you survive if you were forced to close your doors?"

"Why would I have to close my doors?"

"So many things can happen." Lord Waring's eyes glinted. "Some misfortune to your shop, or yourself. Slipping and falling on a train platform, say. Accidents happen so easily, especially in wet weather."

Kim's nostrils flared, a tiny movement. "And it often rains in this country, doesn't it?"

"I don't know about that," Will said, meeting the viscount's eyes. Bugger not reacting: he wasn't going to stand here and be threatened. "Summer's coming."

"Not soon enough," Lord Waring said. "Not soon enough, I fear, for you."

Will shrugged. Possibly you weren't supposed to shrug at viscounts; he couldn't make himself care. "It rained a lot in Flanders. Sometimes seemed like it never stopped. I made it through all the same."

"Ah, but it's peacetime now," Lord Waring countered. "Quite different."

"The shop's a good way to remind me of that," Will said. "It keeps me busy. If I was forced to close my doors, it would be a lot harder to remember I'm not at war right now."

"Military Cross," Kim murmured. "Three bars."

"Admirable." Lord Waring was smiling still, face relaxed. "One can truly respect a man who did his part."

Kim's bland, blank expression suggested he'd expected the taunt. Will took a leaf out of his book, looking past Waring's ear rather than directly at his face, which meant he saw the coat of arms.

You have to be bloody joking, he thought.

"Something wrong, Mr. Darling?" enquired the viscount. "You look startled."

"Not at all, your lordship. I was just looking at your fireplace. Excellent workmanship."

"It's over four hundred years old, and considered one of the in situ masterpieces of Hertfordshire. I'm honoured it meets with your approval."

That was probably meant as a snub. "Well, I did a bit of joinery back in the day, so I can tell good stuff when I see it," Will said cheerily. "Is that your coat of arms? What do you call that creature?"

Lord Waring turned, as if he needed to look at it. The central shield held an aggressive-looking goat with cloven hooves and curling horns; from the midsection down it had an elaborately curved and scaled fish-tail.

"A sea-goat," he said. "Family legend holds that the first Viscount Waring was, before his ennoblement, a privateer."

"A pirate," Kim said. "One might even say, a murdering thief with a good press-agent." He gave a little laugh as if that was a joke, and Waring laughed too. All friends together.

"If you are interested in heraldry, I'm sure Arthur can inform you further," Lord Waring went on. "My daughter is less knowledgeable though she takes great pride in our name, as Arthur knows. That reminds me, Mr. Darling. I understand you're great friends with Miss Jones."

Will had almost started enjoying himself. Maisie's name acted like a bucket of cold water. "That's right."

"A remarkable young lady. So much ambition. Talent too, Phoebe tells me. With my daughter's help, I imagine she could achieve great things. I'm sure we all hope she finds her path clear in the future. It would be such a shame if she were forced to return home defeated and humiliated, with her hopes dashed and her prospects destroyed."

"She'd better not be," Will said, and he didn't even try to make that sound like chit-chat.

Waring's smile broadened. "It's the way of the world, Mr. Darling. Young women—especially of her class and race—are very vulnerable."

"And old houses are flammable," Will said through his teeth. "Just like old bones are breakable."

That got a reaction. It was contemptuous anger, but at least it was a reaction, not that punchably bland smile.

"The world is full of peril on all sides," Kim said, voice quelling. Will stepped back a fraction, calming himself down. "I take it you invited Maisie here to make that point, sir. Consider it made."

"But do you understand?" Waring said. "You see, Arthur, a

business in which I invest recently suffered a serious incident. It seems a member of my staff was killed while going about his duty. A very grave matter."

"Graves only be men's works," Kim murmured. Will knew that one: it was a line from *Timon of Athens* that had come up in the course of his first entanglement with Zodiac.

"It has caused me enormous inconvenience," Waring went on. "I consider it a direct attack. An unprovoked act of war, one might say, and as you remarked, Mr. Darling, one can so easily feel as if one is at war when one's business is threatened. I do not let injuries pass unavenged."

"Then avenge them on the right target," Will said. "Not on people who haven't done you any harm."

"It doesn't work that way, Mr. Darling. If you attack what is mine, then I shall retaliate against what is yours, do you see? I expect you would shrug off threats of personal injury or even real harm. I dare say you're very *brave*." He gave the word an insulting flick. "But if the punishment would be suffered, not by you, but by those for whom you care, I think you might be a little more circumspect. Arthur understands that, don't you, Arthur? You care very little for yourself; I imagine you would be eager to make some great dramatic sacrifice. But my daughter suffering distress, even by watching Miss Jones suffer—no, you wouldn't like to see that, would you?"

"I would not," Kim said. "I hope it will not arise."

"*I* shall decide what will arise," Waring said. "You have chosen to interfere in my business; you do not choose the consequences."

Kim took a deep breath. "Is there any room for negotiation?"

"Negotiation?" Waring's lips stretched. "No. No, I think not. There is only surrender—unconditional, absolute, abject surrender, and obedience thereafter. I will accept that, and nothing less." He looked between them, eyes hard. "I advise you throw yourselves on my mercy and pray that I show any, because the alternatives will be very unpleasant indeed for you and your friend. Consider well, Arthur, Mr. Darling. Consider well and quickly, because you have tried my patience too far."

"I believe I understand what you're asking." Kim's lips were white. "May I have time to think?"

"Do you need to?"

"I have loyalties, little though you may believe it. For God's sake, sir, this is an innocent girl. Let me at least have time to think!"

"You may have until the morning," Waring said. "Miss Jones will be quite safe until then, unless of course any of you attempt to leave my house. That would be a breach of my trust and a very bad mistake indeed. Make sure your obstinate friend here understands; I fear he may not have your moral flexibility. You may go. Oh," he added, as Kim began to turn, "by the way, until I have done with you, you will find your motor-car out of commission, and the telephone faulty. Now, why don't you pop off for a drink before dinner. A cocktail or whatever it is. I believe that's your main area of talent."

Kim took Will's arm and pulled hard. "Come on, Will. Let's go."

SIXTEEN

Will made sure they were well away before he let out a long breath. "Jesus Christ. He's mad as a hatter."

"Mad or bad. Certainly dangerous to know."

"I can't face the girls. Can we go outside?"

Kim led him into the gardens, away from the light of the house. It was very dark and bloody cold, but the air was clean. That made a change from Waring's study.

"I don't know how you've stood it so long," he said, keeping his voice low, just in case. This cloak and dagger stuff got on his last nerve. "I couldn't have."

"He usually hides it a great deal better. The gloves have well and truly come off."

"Hides it except for the bloody great sea-goat on his fireplace. That's a capricorn, isn't it?"

"Would you believe, I didn't notice it myself till my last visit. In fairness I'd seen the blasted thing so often it was invisible to me, but still."

"Bit risky to label himself so clearly."

"Well, he labels his people permanently," Kim pointed out. "He's dangerously arrogant. But you saw that."

"What leapt out at me is that he said it was an unprovoked attack. Unprovoked! Skyrme had Leinster killed, she set a black-mailer on you: what the devil did he expect you to do, thank him?"

"He'd consider it a gross injustice that he should face conse-quences for his actions," Kim said thoughtfully. "It is a bit much, though, isn't it?"

"It's all a bit bloody much. What does 'unconditional surren-der' mean?"

"I expect he'd like an informant in the Private Bureau. I'd be in a marvellous position to sabotage any investigation and let him know a lot of profitable secrets. Squeezed hard enough, I could probably make up for his losses on the High-Low. An attractive prospect for him, and one he won't let go easily."

Will was finding it rather hard to breathe. "He's going to hold Maisie and Phoebe over your head to make you—"

"I should think so, yes. And you, of course. I'm sure he'll find a use for you, if only for the satisfaction of making you jump through his hoops."

"Hell's teeth, Kim. Shit. What are we going to do?"

"A very good question. I don't know about you, but the posi-tion of hand puppet to Lord Waring does not appeal to me."

"Nor me. If I want someone sticking their hand up my arse—"

"Oh, do go on," Kim said, in a tone of great interest.

"I'm not going to be his hand puppet either, was what I meant."

"How disappointing. We'd better find another way out of this, then, hadn't we?"

"Sounds good," Will said. "Any bright ideas?"

"I'm working on it. We should go in, we've been out here too long."

Will didn't want to go in. He didn't want to play Waring's game, or pretend to behave normally, or lie by omission to Maisie and Phoebe. He didn't want to be in this filthy game where the threats and violence were coated in a layer of polite pretence; if there had to be blood, he didn't need it sugared. "All right."

"Will?"

Kim's fingers met his. Will wasn't sure why for a second, if he was being given a weapon or a warning, and then Kim's hand was palm to palm with his own, fingers entwined, and his breath caught.

"I would much, much rather we had taken those chocolates and gone to the South of France," Kim said softly.

"Me too."

"Sun. Sea. Sand. You in one of those delightful striped jerseys the fishermen wear over there, which are positively designed to flatter good shoulders. Long warm nights. No fighting, no scheming, nothing but lounging from beach to bed and back again."

"Bed, eh?"

"A *lot* of bed. It's rather more relaxed down there. Infinitely better food, too, not to mention the wine. Nothing to do all day but drink, swim, and fuck."

"Sounds better than the last time I was on the Continent."

"I'll tell Peacock to pack my blazer." Kim's fingers tightened. "I'm damned glad you're with me. I would not be doing well alone."

"You'd be fine."

"Then I'm glad I don't have to find out. Come on, I'm freezing."

Kim lit a cigarette as they walked towards the house, puffed quickly on it as they approached, and threw it away just before they came into the light that pooled on the paving-stones outside. "Sorry, darling," he told Phoebe as they rejoined the party in a well-lit drawing room. "Will and I nipped out for a smoke."

Something flickered in her eyes, but her voice was quite normal as she said, "Of course. Do make a drink now, won't you?"

What followed was the most excruciating evening Will could imagine, and made the Criterion dinner feel a happy memory.

Johnnie Cheveley was in the room, removing any chance of speaking frankly. He smiled too warmly at Phoebe and called her 'my love', and when he turned his smile on Maisie all the warmth drained away. You couldn't fault his manners or words, but his feelings shone clear through them, and Will could see Maisie's growing discomfort.

It seemed this was new, because Phoebe looked equally unsettled. Her eyes flicked between Cheveley and Maisie, and occasionally to Kim as if seeking help, but Kim didn't say a thing. He emptied his cocktail glass in short order, and returned to the table to mix himself another.

"What will you be wearing for Adela Moran's fancy-dress party, my love?" Cheveley asked Phoebe at one point. "The theme is Novels, I believe? I hear Dickie Plunket Greene intends to go as *Great Expectations*. The mind boggles."

"I shan't be there," Phoebe said. "We'll be in Paris by then. You do know that, Johnnie."

"Darling, Adela is one of your oldest friends, and it's her birthday," Cheveley said, with a touch of loving rebuke in his voice. "I'm sure you're excited about your new hobby, but we can't cast out everything old for the sake of novelty."

"I don't think Adela would appreciate being defined as the old," Phoebe said lightly. "She'll understand."

"It's always lovely to see your new enthusiasms burn bright, but they do burn out." Cheveley's eyes flicked to Maisie. "I think it's important to value what's most important. What you'll always come back to."

"Thank you for your advice." Phoebe's voice was chilly. "Talking of value, Will, darling, weren't you telling me about some positively wonderful book you found in your uncle's collection?"

Will had done nothing of the kind, but he could tell an appeal when he heard one, so he launched into an account of the rare-books pile he'd come across while going through the upstairs room, and the difficulties of identifying, pricing, and selling to the appropriate buyer. He was not a loquacious man except on the subject of football, but he dug in with all the obstinacy he could muster—a lot—and talked books non-stop in the teeth of Cheveley's clear irritation and everyone else's disinterest for a good six or seven minutes until the dinner-gong went.

And then it was even worse, because Lord Waring was at the head of the dinner table, smiling like a crocodile.

He talked easily, of various titled people and political matters. Will didn't want to eat his food, sit at his table, or listen to his voice. He kept his head down, thinking he'd done his bit, while Cheveley, Phoebe, and her father carried the conversation, and concentrated on the excellent dinner in front of him until something caught his attention.

"...the outside of enough," Lord Waring said. "The lack of respect is intolerable."

"I rather agree, sir," Cheveley said. "The younger set think of our generation as rotten war bores, and themselves as somehow hard-done-by because they didn't go, as if we—or most of us—had any choice about it. We did our duty. I'd like to believe that if the positions were reversed they would have done the same but I look at young men like Tennant or Fanshawe or Plunket Greene, and I must say I wonder. Then again, we had our own shirkers." He flickered a glance at Kim.

"Very true," Waring said with just a hint of relish.

"I don't think that's fair," Phoebe said. "It's not right to treat a whole lot of young people as a poor second best to a golden generation, and criticise them for not fighting a war when there isn't a war to fight in, which is frankly something we ought to be pleased about."

"That's very sweetly said, my love," Cheveley told her with a kind smile. "And I admit the war has set an impossible standard, not just for the younger people, but for all us who came through unscathed. My mother frequently informs me that 'Thomas would never have done this or that,' when we all know he would have done as he pleased after the war just as he did before it. But because he didn't come home, we've all to pretend he's a saint."

That last sentence had a resentful force to it that sounded like truth. Phoebe said, "Of course that's not fair either, just as it's not fair for the parents who lost sons. I think we should all have a little more understanding of one another."

"Perhaps, my dear," Waring said. "But I still should like to see those who did not go to the war show a little more respect and appreciation, a little less self-indulgence in the way of cocktails and fast cars. I grant it must be trying to see one's elder brother idolised for war heroism that one couldn't match oneself." He paused. "Or even one's younger brother."

"Daddy," Phoebe said sharply.

"Why not say what you mean, sir?" Kim enquired. His wine glass was empty for at least the second time, his voice a little slurred. "We all know what you're implying. Why not damned well say it?"

"Language, Arthur. I will speak as I choose, and you will not argue with me," Waring said softly. "We discussed this, did we not? The attitude that I expect from you? It begins here."

There was a short, nasty silence, then Kim said, "Sir."

Waring smiled with a triumphant contempt that made Will's fists curl. "Now, Miss Jones, why don't you tell us more about yourself?"

Will restrained himself from throwing his plate at his host and sat through the rest of the meal, listening to the two women's strained voices, and Waring and Cheveley's smug satisfaction as they carried on talking and talking. Saying whatever the hell they wanted, because they could. Because they saw from Kim's demeanour that they'd win, again, as they always did.

As they ate the sweet course, Phoebe's head came up. "Is that a motor coming up the drive? Who could that be?"

"You have good hearing my dear," Waring said. "No doubt it is a man I called earlier to do some work for me. He will wait."

They finished the cheesecake, Waring eating with particular slowness as if he wanted to drag this out. Will ate all his because the food was good even if everything else was awful; so did Maisie. Like Kim, Phoebe left her sweet untouched, and there were red spots on her cheekbones when her father finally put down his fork.

"Coffee?" he said.

"I won't, thank you, Daddy. We would rather have another drink and play some gramophone records."

"If you care to, my dear. You will have coffee, Arthur, Mr. Darling."

"We need them to dance with," Phoebe said with a bright smile. "Johnnie will have coffee with you. Come on, everyone."

Will rose, following her and Maisie out. They got into the corridor; Phoebe said, flatly, "A word, please," and walked away with Kim. That left Will and Maisie looking at each other.

She jerked her head in the direction of the drawing-room. Will accompanied her there. They both sat down on the sofa, and Maisie said, "Well, that was fun."

"God," Will said. "*Blimey.*"

"I want three things. I want to go home, but I suppose it's too late, and I want a drink please, and I want to know what's going on. All of it."

"I'll tell you," Will said. "But tell me something first, before I forget. The customer who gave you the champagne voucher, for the High-Low. What was her name?"

"You're asking me that *now*?"

"I should probably have asked before."

Maisie shook her head. "Her name was Mrs. Galloway. About thirty, perhaps a bit older, very fashionable. A lot more so than we usually get in the shop. She told me she wanted a hat for her grandmother's birthday. We had a bit of a laugh while she tried things on, and she gave me the voucher as a thank-you because she took so long about it."

"Is that usual for your customers?"

"Heavens, no. Half the time they barely speak to me. Does that help?"

Will had no idea if it would help, but he bet he knew a man who did. He handed her a gin and tonic—he was sticking to soda water—and sat on the sofa. "All right, here it is. You know those people I got mixed up with last year, who kidnapped me?"

She rolled her eyes. "No, I'd forgotten all about that."

"Lord Waring's their boss."

"*What?*"

He told her the lot. Their suspicions of Waring and of Cheveley, the whole High-Low business, Waring's threats. She finished her G&T on that, and held out the empty glass wordlessly. Will mixed her another.

"Question," she said when he sat down again. "You said a copper tried to accuse you of indecent behaviour. How was that going to work? You can't just turn up at someone's house and *expect* them to be behaving indecently."

"Right, no." Will took a deep breath. "Thing is, they probably did expect it."

Maisie's mouth dropped open. He added hastily, "Phoebe knows, all right? Kim isn't—*I'm* not—going behind her back."

"I know about Kim. We've talked about that. But I thought you liked girls."

"I do," Will said, with a sudden dread she might think he'd been playing the fool with her. "Really. It's just, uh—"

"*Oh*, like Edward Molyneux," Maisie said, with the satisfaction of one solving a crossword clue. "Phoebe says he's always falling in love and it doesn't matter who with. Well, it matters to him, but you know what I mean. There's a word for it. Ambidextrous? Something like that."

"I wouldn't know. You, uh, don't seem surprised?"

Maisie considered. "I'm a bit surprised. But maybe not that surprised, because you do talk about him an awful lot. Oh, and *that's* why Phoebe's been on at me for ages about understanding people in couture, so I wouldn't be shocked about this. Well, that was nice of her. I suppose." She rolled her eyes. "As if we never heard of it in Cardiff. Honestly, they don't half think they invented everything, the smart lot, do they? Always out in front of us provincials. 'No, no, nobody at home has ever noticed my uncle Dave living with his pal the schoolteacher for the last fifteen years.' Can I ask something?"

"If you like," Will said with a little trepidation.

"Are you happy?"

That was a hell of a question. "Right now, not at all. In general? I...don't know. I could be."

"Only I didn't think you were getting on with him very much."

"Sometimes I don't," Will said. "When I do, though— It's like the poem, honestly. When it's good, it's very, very good, and when it's bad, it's horrid."

"He needs to work on the bad parts, then," Maisie said with a snap. "You're a good man, Will Darling, and you deserve to be happy."

"I don't know what that looks like," Will said. "I mean I do, but not—not in this situation. I don't know what I'm doing, Maise. I'm not sure he does either."

"Then you need to talk about it, don't you? With him, I mean, but you can to talk to me too, if you want. Talk to *someone*, instead of storming round kicking furniture."

"Who says I did that?" Will demanded, uncomfortably aware of a chair in the bookshop that needed mending.

She grinned at him. "I can read you like a book, Will Darling. Daft ha'porth."

He'd wanted to talk to her so much; more than he'd let himself realise, because he'd been so sure he couldn't. He needed a moment to take this in. "God. Thanks, Maisie. Thank you."

She took his hand and squeezed it. "And to think I left home because I wanted excitement. That'll teach me. How long have you known about Lord Waring?"

"Kim's known for a while. I found out…God, it was this afternoon. Feels like about a month ago."

"And he hasn't spoken to Phoebe."

"He knows he should."

"Yes, he really should. I can see why he doesn't want to, but it's not fair." Maisie's mouth tightened briefly. "What happens now?"

"Lord knows. Waring talked about getting at you and Phoebe to punish me and Kim. I don't suppose he'd physically hurt Phoebe but—"

"You can't say the same for me," she said, with impressive calm. "Can we just go?"

"Waring told Kim his car's out of action. He said if we tried to leave the house there'd be consequences. I think we need to take that seriously."

Maisie's lips, normally a dusky pink, were rather pale. "I don't like this, Will. If—if he isn't even pretending to be nice any more—"

"I'm not leaving you alone. I'm staying with you, including in your room if that's all right."

"Yes, and never mind what my ma would say about it. Don't tell her, though," she added hastily.

"If they want to get at you, they'll have to come through me. We'll get out of this, Maise. It'll be all right." He hoped that was true.

"Will we? Where's Kim? What's he even doing now? He was putting away the booze—"

"He *might* be drunk and crying on Phoebe's shoulder because Lord Waring was mean to him," Will said. "But I wouldn't put money on that, myself."

Maisie looked at him. Then she went over to the chair where Kim had sat earlier, and felt the seat. "The side of the cushion's wet and sticky. Like someone spilled a cocktail down it."

"He's pretty quick with his hands. I think he wanted them to assume he was giving in."

"All right, I like him a bit more," Maisie said. "What's he up to, then?"

"Don't ask me, I just work here. Look, I want to get my knife."

"Your—"

"The big one."

"You did not bring that to a house party."

"No manners. Come up with me?"

Maisie nodded, but as she rose, the door opened and Kim and Phoebe entered. Kim seemed calm enough. Phoebe looked as close to furious as Will had seen, mouth tight and eyes stormy.

"Ah, Will," Kim said. "Just the man. Can I have a word?"

"I need to get something from my room. Can I leave you two down here?" Will asked.

"You go," Maisie said. "We'll be fine."

"Very much so," Phoebe added rather sharply.

Will hurried upstairs, alongside Kim, straight to Will's room. He looked into his bag and snorted. "Someone's been through this, and they haven't tried to hide it. All my things are turned up."

"Shit," Kim said. "They took the knife?"

"Don't know." Will reached under the bedside table, and found the Messer where he'd taped it earlier. "No, here we are."

"Your suspicious nature is occasionally a very attractive quality. Did you speak to Maisie?"

"Told her everything. I had to. Kim, listen, I thought of something. I said before that it was Skyrme's fault you got interested in the High-Low because she sent that blackmailer after you, right? Well, suppose it wasn't her who sent him?"

If he'd hoped for a reaction he was disappointed. Kim was nodding. "The same thing occurred to me, forcibly. I think something else is going on, and if I wasn't a bloody idiot in a flat panic, I'd have seen it days ago. None of this adds up. My intervention has led to a significant loss for Zodiac, which Waring clearly doesn't appreciate. Mrs. Skyrme didn't want me or you or Leinster looking into her business. And come to that I'm not convinced it was her who set the police on us. When she departed the club, she took her bankbook to the nearest branch, emptied the account, and got on a train to Dover without troubling to pack. Why would she waste time and money on that parting shot?"

"Waring might have. That remark about strange bedfellows. Wanker."

"Indeed, but it has not previously been in his interest to expose my peccadillos. He likes having that in his back pocket, and if he'd done it at all, I think he'd have done it properly. I think someone else is at work, not operating under Waring's instructions. The question is who."

"That's what I thought. And then I thought about what you said—that you came back because I went to the High-Low, and you were afraid I was involved. And it seemed to me that someone who knew about us might have known they could drag you into it that way."

Kim's eyes sharpened. "You said you'd gone there by chance. Maisie's pick."

"I thought I had, but the thing is, Maisie was given a voucher for free champagne from a customer at her work. That doesn't usually happen."

"I wish you'd mentioned that earlier," Kim said. "Any idea—"

"A woman called Mrs. Galloway. I just asked."

Kim's face set. "Galloway. You're sure?"

"That's what she said."

"Right. Right. The thing is, Will, Hetta Galloway is John Cheveley's mistress."

Will took that in. "Cheveley? Jesus."

"Quite."

"Bit ripe, proposing to Phoebe five times if he's got a mistress."

"So? Phoebe has a fiancé and Hetta Galloway has a husband. God, you're bourgeois."

"One day I will thump you," Will promised. "So, what, he wanted to be rid of Mrs. Skyrme? Does he want to be Aquarius instead?"

"To eliminate her as a rival in Zodiac. Let's say he sent the blackmailer to me—of course he'd know what to do there. Maybe he discovered that Beaumont was in the same regiment as you and that gave him the idea to drag you in, as a second means of keeping my attention on the High-Low? Either way, he pulled me in and the dominoes started to fall. Which got rid of Mrs. Skyrme very effectively, but has also destroyed a very profitable operation. If I were Johnnie, I'd very much hope Waring didn't find out about that."

"Hold on, though. He couldn't have known you'd get rid of Skyrme for him. She might have had you shoved under a train as well, or I might not have got to Fuller in time before he shot you. Jesus, Kim, was he trying to get rid of you?"

Kim sat on the bed. "Yes, that does seem plausible, doesn't it? Me—no, both. That's it. He wanted both her and me gone, and he let us do the work. Set your enemies against each other and sit back while they halve their number."

Will looked down at him on the bed, the tension in his face, the slim wrists. Young Kim had been careful to keep the scars under his sleeves, as of course he would be. Always hiding, always hurting. A quivering, sensitive mass of nerve endings, clever and sensitive and stupid and unique, and that smug smooth-faced domineering bastard Cheveley had wanted to wipe him out as though he were nothing.

"Will?"

"I'm just working out how I'm going to kill the fucker," Will said. "Don't mind me. Why is Cheveley trying to get rid of you?"

"The obvious answer is because he wants to secure Phoebe's hand, and it's still wearing my ring."

Will shook his head. "She's told him no a few times now. Why would he think she'd say yes?"

"Ah," Kim said. "Well. Did she ever tell you the events that led to our engagement?"

"I got the gist."

"I am going to give you more than the gist, in faith that you will not judge or condemn. Don't let me down."

Will would normally have said *Coming from you!* but Kim's eyes were as serious as he'd ever seen them. "Go on."

"You know that Phoebe required a husband sharpish. That or to be packed off to an aunt for a year to get rid of the evidence. Cheveley accepted his responsibility for her situation—"

"Was he responsible? I thought she said he wasn't interested."

"He didn't love her, but since when has that been a precondition for fucking? As I say, he accepted responsibility, on conditions. A substantial settlement on marriage, with the promise of inheriting Waring's fortune. In addition, Waring would attempt to amend the letters patent of his viscountcy to allow inheritance down the female line. That would let Phoebe become Viscountess Waring in due course, and make any son of Cheveley's the next viscount."

"Cushy for him," Will said. "What happened to marrying the girl you got in trouble because it's the right thing to do?"

"Idealist. Anyway, Cheveley was willing to accept his responsibility on those terms, until Phoebe told him that it wasn't necessarily his. There was another possible candidate." He shrugged at Will's blink. "Wild times. Phoebe hadn't betrayed any understanding between them, since there was none. She told him the paternity was uncertain because she has never been less than honest and true, and he might have appreciated that. He did not." Kim's dark eyes were hard. "She never told me the whole of it, only that he slapped her, spoke to her in words that no decent man would use, and told her parents in detail why he declined to proceed with the marriage. She miscarried a fortnight later, and that was that."

"Right," Will said. "Is there a reason you haven't done something about this turd before?"

"She told me not to, and she had lost enough control. If I had gone after Cheveley I would have been one more person running her life against her wishes."

Will wasn't sure he'd have thought that way. That said something about himself, and for Kim. "You're all right sometimes, you know that? I'm bloody glad Phoebe had you. All the same—"

"Let's disembowel him."

"Just checking. So why's he changed his mind, and why does he think getting you out of the way will help?"

"The latter, because he lacks any respect for her," Kim said. "He believes she'll do what a strong man tells her, and will be helpless once she doesn't have me to lean on. I suspect he thinks she regards having any man as better than no man. He is quite hilariously wrong, but Johnnie didn't get where he is by considering other people."

"Twat," Will muttered.

"Indeed. As to why now, that is the question, and the shape of the question suggests the answer." He grinned at Will's expression. "Does it not strike you that Cheveley seems to be in one hell of a rush?"

"Well, I suppose— Did you hear that?"

Kim rose, face sharp. Will pulled the door open, and heard the noise again—faint, muffled by distance, but unquestionably a female scream. He grabbed the Messer from the bedside table, tossed the sheath away, and ran like hell.

SEVENTEEN

Running with a bare eight-inch razor-edged blade was not a practice Will would generally recommend, but caution didn't come into it. He took the great oak staircase three at a time, skidded round the corner at a speed that would have caused severe if very short-term problems to anyone he'd bumped into, and hit the door of the drawing room with a solid thump.

There was a crash from inside. He rattled the door handle.

"Locked?" demanded Kim, arriving breathlessly behind him. "I can—"

Will took two paces back, and gave the door—panelled oak, beautiful workmanship, a good four hundred years old—an almighty kick. The oak held but a second boot split the lock out of the frame with a horrendous splintering noise, and Will was in.

Maisie was backed up against the wall, and there was a man in there, one Will didn't recognise. He'd turned from her to the door, and he was bleeding heavily from the nose. That would just be the start of his troubles, if Will had anything to say to it.

The man thrust out an arm menacingly, showing a clasp-knife with a wicked little two-inch blade. Will extended the Messer in silent reply, took a moment to enjoy the enemy's expression, and went for him.

The man leapt away. Will assumed Kim was blocking the door, so he feinted with the Messer, driving the man back. His eyes flicked frantically around for escape.

"Drop the knife, put your hands up," Will said. "Or don't and I'll gut you. As you like."

The man retreated another step. It was the last one he took, because Maisie was behind him by then, with feet planted wide, a militant expression, and an elaborate gilt candlestick that she brought around in a two-handed swing reminiscent of WG Grace batting at Lord's.

The heavy base connected squarely, sending the man's head sideways in an arc that was perfectly designed to meet Will's left hook coming the other way. Blood sprayed from his mouth, a tooth flew, he went down like the dead, and Will said, "Fuck!"

"Excuse me!" Maisie said. "There's no—are you all right?"

"Broke my bloody knuckle," Will said through his teeth.

"Oh, *no*. Are you sure?"

Regrettably, he was. He'd done it before, and the internal crunch and dull hot pain were all too familiar. "I didn't realise how fast he was moving. You caught him a cracking one."

Maisie looked at the candlestick she held. "Good manufacture, this. Solid. The factory stuff breaks when you look at it, still less when you hit people with it, I suppose, not that I usually—I'm going to sit down." She did so, on a chair, heavily. "Oh God. Do you know who he is?"

"His name is Anton," Kim said. "He's Waring's chauffeur. Are you all right, Maisie?"

"No, I am not. He drove us here. He was very polite. He opened the door and called me miss."

"Did he hurt you?"

"He was going to," she said thinly. "He told me so."

"Maisie!" It was a shriek, as Phoebe ran in. "Darling, what happened? I heard a scream—the door—Is that Anton? *Will?*"

Will was standing over a prone man, holding a massive knife. It probably didn't look marvellous. "I didn't stab him," he said, then realised he could have made that clearer. "That is—"

"We left Maisie with you," Kim said. "Where did you go?"

Phoebe had flown over to embrace Maisie, but that made her look round. "Are you blaming *me* because Anton went mad?"

"I want to know where you were," Kim said.

"Johnnie wanted to talk to me. Why—"

"I asked Phoebe for a private conversation," Cheveley said, stepping in, Lord Waring behind him. "We had things to discuss. Dear me. Oh, dear."

"What has happened here?" Waring demanded, pushing past him. "What the devil? Anton?"

Maisie gave her eyes an angry wipe. "He attacked me. He came in—he locked the door and said— I hit out at him, and I screamed. And then Will came in and scared him, and I hit him with a candlestick."

"Oh, well *done*, darling," Phoebe said.

"Anton—attacked—you," Waring repeated, enunciating each word.

Maisie turned on him ferociously. "Are you calling me a liar, Lord Waring?"

"In fact, I don't think he is," Kim said. "I think he's probably surprised. You wouldn't have expected your man to behave like that, would you, sir?"

"I would not," Cheveley said. "And I don't believe he did. I'm afraid this story doesn't hold water."

"Oh, it does, and enough for you to drown in," Kim said. "What's the plan, Johnnie? Get Anton to attack Maisie, force me and Will into direct conflict with Lord Waring? Another round of Last Man Standing, since the last one did for Mrs. Skyrme so nicely?"

Cheveley looked at him with disgust. "I don't know what you're babbling about, Secretan. This poor fellow has been brutally attacked on the flimsiest of excuses—"

"He attacked me!" Maisie said.

"Be quiet, Johnnie," Phoebe snapped. "Go and 'phone for a doctor if you want to be useful."

"My love—"

"And stop calling me that!"

Cheveley's face went rigid, nose flaring. "You don't see the situation, Phoebe. I do You've been dragged into a pretty murky business by these people, and it's time it was dealt with. I'm sorry you've trusted the wrong people, and I'm afraid you've been lied to a great deal, but it's over now. I'll see to it they won't hurt you any more. Please, darling, go to bed and let me deal with it."

There was a brief silence. Then Maisie said, "*Excuse* me?"

Phoebe's face was a picture, and not one from *Smart Set*. She stood, tall and outraged. "Have you gone quite mad, Johnnie?"

"Gone? No," Kim said. "But it would be an excellent idea for you and Maisie to go upstairs now, Fee."

"So that you can talk without me?" she flashed.

"With Maisie, Fee," Kim said, voice very gentle. "Please. She's had a bad shock and you need to look after her."

"I'm afraid that Miss Jones is not the innocent you pretend," Cheveley said.

"Do you like your teeth where they are, mate?" Will asked. "Because we can change that."

"Silence, all of you," Waring said, in a tone that brooked no denial. He looked around the room, expression unwavering as he contemplated each of them. Will felt like a medical specimen as Waring's merciless gaze swept over him. "This is indeed a peculiar and unfortunate situation, and one I shall lose no time in resolving. Phoebe, go upstairs. I shall deal with this."

"Certainly not," Phoebe said. "Really, Daddy—"

"Take her upstairs, John."

Cheveley grasped Phoebe's wrist. She looked down at it with a bewildered expression, looked up, and cracked her free hand across his face so hard that Cheveley's head snapped back. He turned on her, raising his arm.

Will moved but Kim got there first, grabbing Cheveley's wrist. "Oh, no. No you do not."

Cheveley snarled and wrenched his arm free. Will took a meaningful step forward, Messer in hand, and Waring said, "Telford."

Will turned to the door, and there he was, the bland, blank man he'd met outside the shop. This time, the gun in his hand was visible.

Phoebe gave a shrill gasp, reaching out a groping hand to Maisie, who grabbed it. "Daddy!"

"This man works for me. You need not be afraid of him."

"He has a gun!"

"Arthur's friend has a knife," Waring said. "Telford is here to protect my family and property. Either he will take you upstairs or John will."

Phoebe looked between them all; Kim gave her a swift nod. "Very well. Then Maisie is coming with me."

"No," Cheveley said.

"You do not give the orders in this house," Phoebe told him. "Maisie and I will go upstairs without supervision. I think I ought to be able to manage that, but I dare say she will help me if I get lost."

She stalked out on that bitter sarcasm, arm round Maisie's shoulders. Telford stood aside to let them go, then gave Waring a questioning look.

"Your gun." The viscount took the revolver, weighed it in his hand, and pointed it at Will. "Follow them up and lock them in, without fuss. Fetch my shotgun as you return. You, Mr. Darling. Drop the knife and kick it over to the wall."

Will did so, but kicked it at Cheveley's feet, hard enough that the man had to leap in the air to avoid it as it skittered by. Waring said, "Childish."

"But funny," Kim said.

"Shut up, Secretan." Cheveley's cheek was still red where Phoebe had slapped him. "Sir, do you want me to take that for you?" He indicated the gun.

Waring glanced at him. "No. No, I don't think I do, thank you."

"I wouldn't either," Kim agreed. "He is, after all, actively undermining you. I'm quite sure you told him we'd agreed a truce until the morning, so why did he order Anton to attack Maisie now?"

"He misunderstood his orders," Cheveley said. "I told him to do it later."

Will jerked forward. "You told—"

"Don't move, Mr. Darling," Lord Waring said, levelling the revolver at him. "Sit on the floor, both of you. Hands behind your head. I will not hesitate to shoot. After all, you have brought a lethal weapon into my house and injured my chauffeur, perhaps fatally."

"Yes," Kim said. "Perhaps you should consider calling a doctor."

"Sit."

He gestured with the gun. Will glanced at Kim, who nodded, and sat. It was something of a relief to put his hands up, as his left was throbbing ferociously now.

Unarmed, one-handed, outnumbered, and facing a professional killer. Will had to admit he wasn't feeling optimistic.

Cheveley strolled up to Waring and looked down at them with a grim smile. "Let's see. Anton was hit from behind. I dare say Secretan did that—a coward's blow. Indecent advances, perhaps, leading to a lover's tiff between Darling and Secretan that leaves one or both dead—I think this could wrap up very neatly, sir."

"Extremely," Kim said. "Except for Maisie and Phoebe, who

can state it's a lie, and the fact that it leaves Lord Waring with a traitor at his right hand. Otherwise, perfect."

Telford came back into the room with an expensive-looking shotgun. He and Waring exchanged weapons, Waring taking the shotgun with casual familiarity. Doubtless he'd shot a lot of pheasants or whatever, but he wouldn't have to be good with it. A weapon like that, loaded with shot, could blow a man's chest open at this distance.

"Very well," Waring said, settling the shotgun on his arm. "Now, John, you were saying—"

"Excuse me. I hate to interrupt," Kim began.

"Then do not," Lord Waring said, lifting the shotgun a fraction.

"You can't shoot me in this position," Kim pointed out. "It'll ruin your story, and talking of stories, don't you want to hear one about The Right-Hand Man Who Sabotaged Your Smuggling Operation?"

Cheveley started to speak. Lord Waring lifted his hand in a jerk of command. "If you are hoping to persuade me you're playing for time, Arthur, don't bother. The night is young, and no rescue is coming. We both know that you have not had the courage to speak to your master."

"You have a subtle brain, sir," Kim said. "I'm not that subtle and nor is Cheveley. He's been trying to force us into conflict, the very conflict that you rightly note I have made vast efforts to avoid."

Cheveley scoffed. "Bluffing, Secretan? You're not in a position to do that."

"You sent me a blackmailer, and used your mistress to get Will to the High-Low. You wanted me there; you deliberately set me against Mrs. Skyrme. Last man standing. You decided to get rid of her, even if it cost Zodiac the High-Low Club and an incredibly lucrative smuggling route; now you've done that you're trying to get rid of me. All in two months." He paused, letting two silent seconds tick by, and smiled. "What's the hurry, Johnnie?"

Lord Waring's face froze, in a way that reminded Will disturbingly of Kim. Cheveley said, "Sir, must we listen to this? He's trying to talk his way out of trouble."

"Let him talk," Waring said.

"I don't—"

Waring turned, bringing the shotgun round so that, just for a second, it pointed at Cheveley. Will tensed for an opportunity, but Telford, whose blank face suggested he wasn't listening, still had the revolver levelled on him. "I said, he can talk."

"Thank you. Where was I?" Kim's long legs were stretched in front of him. He crossed them at the ankle in a manner so casual, anyone would want to clobber him. "Oh yes. Johnnie needed both me and Mrs. Skyrme out of the way, just as he needed Maisie Jones dealt with before she could take Phoebe to Paris and out of his reach. You and I have been on course for a reckoning for a long time, Lord Waring, but it's Johnnie who's forced both of our hands. He wanted to clear his path as your successor and son-in-law, and he wanted to do it fast. I hope it isn't in poor taste to say he has a deadline."

Cheveley's face was twitching. "I don't know what he's talking about, sir."

"Oh, you do. Edward Leinster, my colleague, received a tip-off about the High-Low and Zodiac. Who from? Hetta Galloway, your mistress, gave Maisie Jones a voucher for the High-Low Club. Why would she do that except to bring Will Darling there? You used me to see off Mrs. Skyrme, then you used her departure as cover to set the police on my personal life, which might well have put paid to my engagement. If you could secure Phoebe, you'd be looking at inheriting Waring's legitimate property and the leadership of Zodiac. Maybe Waring might even revive that old promise about the letters patent and make your future son a viscount. That would be one in the eye for your brother Alan, squatting on his baronetcy and all your family money, wouldn't it? You'd eliminate your rivals, secure Phoebe, and claim the kingdom."

Cheveley's nostrils were white. "May I make the obvious point? Lord Waring is a picture of health. We may expect him to live another thirty years, God willing, and there's six months for Phoebe to see sense before your farce of a wedding. Why would I manoeuvre in this frantic manner you describe, risking my position and my neck? It makes no sense at all."

"Nor to me," Will said. "But I can tell a man protesting too much when I hear one, mate."

"Shut up when your betters are speaking," Cheveley snarled.

"Temper," Kim said. "Any thoughts on why Johnnie might be in such a hurry, Lord Waring? Perhaps to do with your trips to Harley Street in December?"

Waring's eyes flicked from Cheveley to Kim, and Will wasn't sure he'd seen an expression like that in a man's eyes through four years of war. There was a long, silent moment, and then the older man laughed, a genial, amused chuckle that suited the civilised host he looked, apart from the shotgun.

"I suppose you had that out of Phoebe. I must say, Arthur, I'm impressed. You've played a poor hand well. It won't help you, not at all, but you could scarcely have done more."

"Satisfy my curiosity," Kim said. "Not cancer, surely? You look hale enough."

"Thank you. No, nothing of the kind. An abdominal aortic aneurysm, I believe the term is. I had the best man in England open me up, for all the good it did. He claimed there was nothing to be done, the damned worthless quack."

"Aneurysm. That's a weakness in a blood vessel, yes?"

"Indeed. It could burst any time, he informed me, and gave me six months." He turned to Cheveley. "A prognosis he stated in the letter he sent me around Christmas, John, when, as Arthur observes, you renewed your courtship of my daughter. The letter that I kept in my personal, private correspondence."

"Uh," Cheveley said.

Lord Waring's smile was cold as charity. "I'm sorry to say, my boy, that you must have missed my other letters on the subject. I've an American surgeon sailing over even now to repair it, the best in his field. They have a lot more—I believe they call it *hustle,* over there, and of course they're rather more advanced, at least in New York. I shall be around for many a long year, I'm afraid, and some of that time will now be taken up in finding a new Aquarius as competent as Theresa Skyrme. I am not pleased by that, John. Not at all."

Cheveley had a rather patchy look to his skin. "Sir—"

"No," Lord Waring said. The shotgun rested loosely in his hand, but not that loosely. "I expect manoeuvres; I don't expect to be undermined. Theresa's business was worth thousands a year to me, and her ingenuity even more. You should have understood that, John. I am very disappointed in you."

Cheveley's face didn't move, but something shuddered in his eyes. Waring contemplated him for a second, then turned his attention back to Kim. "But if you imagine this will make the slightest difference to you now, Arthur, I must correct you. You and Mr. Darling have made yourselves an intolerable irritation, and you have now forced me to deal with you. I believe John's suggestion will do, with a few minor alterations. Let us say, John, that a brawl erupted subsequent to Anton's attack on Miss Jones, between you and Arthur and his proletarian lover. I will be happy to assure the jury that you were forced to fire on Mr. Darling in self-defence. I dare say that even bare-handed he will be able to inflict some convincing injuries on you, to help your case. Of course you will bear responsibility for the death of Flitby's son, which may be embarrassing, and certainly it will be impossible for you to marry my daughter having killed her fiancé. But you didn't expect to get off scot-free, did you?"

"Sir," Cheveley said. "You can't—"

"Oh, I can, John. I want Arthur out of my way, for which I need a scapegoat, and I see no reason my daughter should not indulge her hobby with Miss Jones unmolested. You will do me this service as recompense for the inconvenience you have caused. I think that will suit very well."

"Really? I have several objections," Kim said.

"You don't have a vote." Lord Waring's eyes were hard and dead as pebbles. "You have been, variously, an amusement, a convenience, and a nuisance to me. The nuisance now outweighs the rest and I will be rid of you."

"The nuisance will remain. Even the great British bobby will ask questions about two men shot while sitting on the floor—which is where we're staying, Will."

"Are you really telling me *You won't get away with this*, Arthur?" Waring asked. "I think I will. And the matter of your position when shot can be very easily remedied. Your Patroclus is straining at the leash; I'm quite sure such a brutish creature can be provoked to assault." His cold eyes rested on Will's face. "Especially when the alternative to your cooperation is to silence Miss Jones. Your choice, Mr. Darling. She can go to Paris with Phoebe for their little adventure, or—not."

The blood was scorching as it pumped through Will's damaged hand, a dragon's heartbeat. He was having a certain amount of trouble breathing. "How can I trust you to keep to that?"

"You will have to," Waring said. "But if you choose not to cooperate, I shall have Telford deal with her as he thinks best, and he will do it in front of you. I dare say you have done such things before, Telford."

Telford's blank eyes reacted to that, with a spark that looked like anticipation. "Yes, Lord Waring."

"A very reliable man," Waring said. "Now stand up. You have a brawl with John to execute, as it were."

Kim sucked in a sharp breath. Will rose, bracing himself on his right hand in as casual a way as he could. He didn't delude himself this would end well, with Telford and Waring both armed, but he could at least give Cheveley a hard time on his way out. He'd lived through the war and had seven years on top: plenty of men had deserved more and got less.

"Will," Kim said softly and urgently.

Will wanted to say something to him, something about having had a good innings, but they hadn't. They'd barely started. Fuck this.

"Hand him his knife, John," Waring said.

"Sir!" Cheveley yelped.

"You can have the gun, in due course. But we must give the fellow a chance first. It's only sporting."

Waring's smile looked very real, almost hungry. Cheveley said, "Telford!"

"Oh, no, no. Telford works for me. I fear he won't help—" Lord Waring began, and Telford wrenched the shotgun from his grasp, and drove the butt into his stomach.

EIGHTEEN

L ord Waring doubled over with an airless scream. Telford rammed the shotgun into his belly again, and brought it up smoothly, one-handed, and about an inch from Will's stomach, which stopped his movement dead.

There was a frozen silence. Lord Waring was on his knees, making unpleasant sucking noises.

"Heavens," Kim said. "Congratulations, Cheveley. You did your staffwork well."

Cheveley ignored him. "Gun."

He strode over. Telford passed him the revolver and adjusted his grip on the shotgun, and they both stepped back, levelling the weapons on Will and Kim.

Lord Waring had his arms wrapped round his gut. He croaked, "Help me."

"Want them dead?" Telford asked.

"We've got to do it right," Cheveley said, ignoring the viscount's groan. "Keep Phoebe quiet. Suppose—yes, suppose one or the other of them killed Waring and they ran away together and had an accident. Secretan always drives too fast. That's it. Crash his Daimler. Make it a fire."

"Fire doesn't hide bullets," Kim said. "Which means you can't risk shooting us. Actually you can't do that anyway if you don't want to upset Phoebe, but I have to point out that she won't marry you at any price, you flaccid, contemptible little shit."

"You think she'll have a choice?" Cheveley said. "You know, Secretan—"

Telford held up a hand. "What's that?"

"What?"

"Car."

Will could hear it too now, wheels on gravel. "Cars."

"Ah, yes," Kim said, "That'll be DS and the Private Bureau. You know, the rescue Waring thought wasn't coming? He was wrong about quite a lot."

Cheveley's jaw dropped. Will turned to look at Kim, and got a wink. "Surprised, Will? You should know how much you can trust me by now."

"Two cars," Telford said. "Could be eight men. Too many."

"Get these two into the cellar," Cheveley said. "Don't kill them unless you have to. Stay in there with them." He glared at Kim, still sitting on the floor. "Get up!"

"Come on, Will." Kim rose. "Do what they say. Don't provoke them."

The two armed men urged them out, down the corridor and to the great hall, leaving Lord Waring alone on the floor with the unconscious chauffeur. There was a sound of car doors slamming, and faint voices.

"Get them into the cellar and keep them quiet," Cheveley ordered Telford. "I'll get rid of the visitors. And mark me, Darling, Secretan, you will cooperate or Miss Jones will pay the price. Do you understand me?"

The doorbell clanged noisily.

"Understood," Kim said. "We'll behave."

"I'm glad you have seen sense," Cheveley said. "Now, hurry—"

There was the sound of footsteps above. Cheveley looked up. "Phoebe? Get back to your room at once!"

Phoebe, clad in a frothy dressing-gown, was running down the stairs. Cheveley cursed and started up towards her; Phoebe swung onto the banister, slid down it in a flurry of sea-green material and bare calves, and leapt lightly off the end, as if she'd done it a hundred times. Cheveley doubled back, sprinting after her; Kim stuck out a foot, and he went flying. Telford moved towards him, and Will took his chance in that chaotic second and put a fist into the bastard's kidney as hard as he could.

Phoebe was at the door, pulling it open. There was a raucous chorus of shouts and squeals, and a cry of, "Surprise!"

Will was too busy to care. He grappled savagely with Telford for the shotgun, trying with all he had to wrench it away. Telford pulled back hard, his bland face now a mask of rage. Will had the barrel firmly in his right hand, but he couldn't break the bastard's grip.

Well, fuck. He tensed everything he had against what he was going to do, stiffened the fingers of his left hand, and drove it into the middle of Telford's swollen biceps.

It was staggeringly painful as the impact shot up his broken knuckle, but it worked. Telford's fingers sprang open as he shouted with pain, and the shotgun dropped. Will slammed his left arm round Telford's neck while he had the chance, putting his strength into crooking his elbow because his whole left hand was on fire now, and vented his many feelings on the man, hammering his temple with short-range blows. He could hear Phoebe shouting, "The police, go and get the police!" and screams, and what sounded for all the world like Bubby Fanshawe bleating, "I say!"

For Christ's sake. He glanced up without stopping his work, and saw a group of gaping, shrieking Bright Young Things, all evening clothes and bottles of champagne. Fucking marvellous. All they needed now was a jazz band.

A scream from above cut through the chaos. He looked up the stairs. Maisie stood at the top, pointing down, to where Phoebe was facing Johnnie Cheveley.

She stood tall in the frothy dressing-gown and Cheveley had the revolver levelled at her point blank. There were a couple more screams as the Bright Young People caught up, and then a dreadful anticipatory silence fell.

With all eyes fixed on Cheveley and Phoebe, nobody was looking at Will, so he rabbit-punched Telford in the back of the neck with everything he had left, and let the body drop.

"What are you going to do, Johnnie?" Phoebe said into the silence. "Shoot me?"

"Don't be silly, darling," Cheveley said, lowering the gun, but not enough. "You're being hysterical. You're over-tired. Too much drink, too many late nights—"

"Liar," she said. "Why did Anton attack Maisie? Why did you tell lies about her, and protect him? Why didn't you call the police, or a doctor? Why didn't Daddy?" She paused. "Where is Daddy?"

Cheveley looked around at the large, rapt audience, down at Telford's unmoving body. Something ticked in his face, a man realising the odds had changed. "We must of course call the police but the telephones are out of order. Someone will have to drive to Berkhampstead in the morning."

"Stop it." Phoebe's voice was icy. "My father's chauffeur attempted to assault Maisie in a vile manner, and you tried to defend him. You've been scheming against her, against Kim—I don't know what else you've been doing, but I have had enough of you. And I want to know where my father is!"

"He's in the drawing-room," Kim said. "Cheveley ordered his man to assault him. It doesn't look good, Fee. Maisie, go with her."

Phoebe's eyes snapped wide. She stood for a frozen second and then ran, heedless of the revolver. Maisie hurried down the stairs. Cheveley shouted, "Stop!", raising the revolver, and Will scooped up the shotgun and said, "Don't."

Several of the Bright Young People shrieked. Cheveley sneered. "I don't think you'll find that's much use to you."

Will checked the safety was off. "We'll see."

Cheveley swung the revolver up at him and pulled the trigger. Will dropped amid the chorus of screams, rolled, and came up firing, or at least squeezing the trigger. The hammer clicked uselessly.

"As if Telford loaded it for the old man," Cheveley said. "You think we're fools?"

"You're a flaming lunatic, is what you are," Bubby Fanshawe said, from where he and Miss Moran cowered in the corner. "Put that gun down!"

"What's happening?" shrieked a woman.

"Cheveley's gone off his bally rocker!"

"Johnnie," Kim said. "You can't win this. There's a roomful of witnesses. Shoot anyone and you'll hang for murder. It's over."

Cheveley's eyes darted back and forth. Adela Moran said, "Oh, yes, *do* put the gun down, Johnnie. This is too panic-making."

"Shut up, you silly bitch," Cheveley said. "Did you drive here in your Hillman, Bubby?"

"Yes, of course. It's out the front."

"Does it have a door key?"

"Oh, yes, it's awfully—"

"Give it to Secretan."

"Eh? Why?" Fanshawe asked blankly.

"Because he's going to drive me wherever I choose. Aren't you, Secretan?"

"The hell he is," Will said.

The muzzle of the revolver swung to him, a gaping black hole. "He is if he doesn't want you dead. Get on your knees, hands on your head. Now!"

There were only a few yards between them. Too far for Will to catch him, too close for Cheveley to miss. Kim said, quietly, "Do it, Will. Please."

Will knelt. Cheveley said, "Right. Any funny business and I shoot him. Understand that, Secretan?"

"If you kill him in front of this crowd you'll swing. Do *you* understand that?"

"Give Secretan the keys, Bubby," Cheveley repeated. "Throw them to him."

"Yes, but, I say—"

"Do it now. Now, or I shoot! Where are you going, you moron?"

"To get the keys! They're in the jolly old car!" Fanshawe protested.

Cheveley said, "Jesus *Christ*." Will might have felt a moment's sympathy, except that he could imagine the sound of a shot on an isolated road, Kim's body left unmoving in the moonlight, Cheveley driving away alone.

Kim would not be getting in that motor-car, and that was all there was to it. His muscles tightened.

"Just try it, you jumped-up shopkeeper," Cheveley said softly. "I'll blow your head into red mist. All right, Secretan—"

The lights went off.

No expense had been spared in Etchil's electrification. The hall had a chandelier hanging from the ceiling and lights on the landing and more on the walls. They'd been beaming out this whole time and the darkness now was absolute. Several people screamed. Will hurled himself sideways as the revolver boomed out, and found himself sent rolling by a hard, painless impact on his left arm.

He knew *that* one. It was always painless at first.

The lights blazed on again, blinding. Will put his right hand to his left biceps, took it away, and stared at the wet red on his hand as pain began to sear through his arm. He looked up, at Cheveley's face, and the muzzle of the revolver swinging to him, and the Bright Young Idiots shrieking, and then Adela Moran screamed in real earnest, and Will turned and saw Kim.

He was running across the hall, with a cavalry sabre in his hand. Will stared, Cheveley simply gaped, and Kim swept the sword up like he'd done it all his life. The blade bit cleanly, deeply, and all but right through the outstretched arm.

Cheveley dropped the gun. Well, he would.

Everyone was screaming now. Kim dropped the sabre, eyes wide, as Cheveley folded at the knees and hit the floor. Blood sprayed.

"Get a tourniquet on him," Will snapped. "Quick!"

"Shit." Kim bent over Cheveley. "Hell. Are you all right, Will?"

"No. He fucking shot me."

"I saw," Kim said through his teeth. "But if one of you is going to bleed to death I'd rather it was him, so talk to me."

Will was bleeding a fair bit himself, now he looked, and starting to feel rather rough as the initial shock was replaced by the throbbing heat of a bullet wound. "Uh."

"Will!" That was Maisie, arriving in a flurry. "Oh God. We need cords, ties. Now!"

She got something from somewhere; Will wasn't paying attention. He heard her whispering unladylike language under her breath as she pulled a cord round his upper arm, painfully tight. "Ow."

"Is that too much?"

"Ignore him," Kim said. "He always complains when he's shot."

"Arsehole," Will managed. "Excuse my French, Maisie."

"Don't mind me," she said. "Hold on, I'm going to—"

Will knew what she was going to do—she had got a pencil in the loop, and she turned it now to tighten the tourniquet. He breathed out hard. "All right, that's slowed the bleeding," she said. "He needs a doctor quick."

"He's not the only one," Kim said. "Bubby, you useless sack of meat, get in the car and find a telephone. Doctors. Police. Now!"

Maisie brought a chair for Will to lean against. His arm was an unpleasant combination of the jabbing pain of the gunshot wound, the nauseous dull pain of his broken knuckle, and the outrage of nerves cut off by a ligature. He'd had significantly better evenings than this in the trenches.

"Cheveley?" he asked.

"Not so good," Kim said. He had stuffed his jacket over the man's wound, for what good that might do. Will let out a long breath, and waited in silence for the bleeding to stop.

NINETEEN

Things got a bit fuzzy after that. A doctor arrived eventually; Will tried to explain that he was probably the least in need of the various casualties but nobody listened, and then he got a needleful of something and went out like a light.

He woke up somewhere that, eventually, he identified as the room he'd been allocated. His entire left arm felt hot and resentful, his head was muggy, and he was painfully thirsty. There was a jug of water by his bedside, but it had been placed on the table to his left, which felt like a bigger obstacle than it should have. And there was nobody here. Not that he had any great expectation of a kindly nurse or trusty friend sitting by his bedside, because his experience to date had pretty much never included that, but it would have been nice.

He allowed just a moment for self-pity, then worked himself to sit upright. His hand had been strapped up and his upper arm was tightly bandaged. The bandages were stained, but not much, and the stain was dry which was presumably good. He got his feet to the floor so he could drink most of the jug of water more easily, and was contemplating lying down again when the door opened a crack and Kim peered in.

"Will? Good God, why are you up? Get back in bed."

"I'm fine."

"You're *shot*. The bullet was lodged a quarter of an inch off an artery, and don't talk to me about arteries. Lie down, damn you."

Words harsh, hands gentle as he helped ease Will back, and brushed the hair off his forehead. "God, you scared me. When he shot you—"

Will would have liked to hear about Kim being afraid for him, and then again, not. He didn't quite feel he could keep his equilibrium at this moment. "You scared me. What the hell was that, a sabre?"

"French, a relic of Waterloo. One of Waring's most prized possessions. If you had any better ideas, you were welcome to put them into action." Kim stroked his hair again. It felt good. "Oh, Will. Christ alive."

"What happened to Cheveley?"

"Bled out. I cut his arm damn near off. The doctors did their best—said I'd done *my* best to save him, and that he could probably have lived if we'd been in London to get him a transfusion. We weren't."

"Was that your first?"

"My first kill?" Kim's fingers moved through his hair. "Yes. Yes, it was. I've indirect death to my credit but I never..."

"He'd have killed me," Will said. "I saw it in his face." He couldn't swear to it, in truth; Cheveley had looked panicked and desperate, but you never knew what a panicked, desperate man would do. He might just as likely have run for the motor, or shot someone else, or himself. But Kim needed the reassurance, and the touch of fingers to his right hand suggested it was appreciated.

"Thank you," Kim said softly. "You know, the worst part is,

everyone keeps telling me that it's all right because I didn't mean it."

"Yes, you did. You don't slash at someone with a sodding sabre if you don't mean it."

"My aim was to make him drop the gun, but I had absolutely no interest in preserving his life, especially at your expense. I intended to hit him as hard as I could, and I did, and it killed him. I killed him."

Will squeezed his hand. "I owe you one. I don't know why the bastard had it in for me like that."

"I do," Kim said. "I wouldn't have stood a chance without you, and he knew it. And more than that—when he threatened you, he was watching my face. He'd have killed you to hurt me. I'm quite sure of that." His voice was strained.

"Then no guilt. Or I'll think you regret saving me, and that would hurt my feelings."

Kim bowed his head, brushing his lips over Will's fingers. "We couldn't have that. Thank you for the idea, by the way."

"What idea?"

"'The last knight of Europe takes weapons from the wall.' I've seen those swords so often; it hadn't previously occurred to me they had a use beyond decoration."

"It wouldn't have occurred to me that anyone covering their walls in blades would be fool enough to keep them sharp."

"Same," Kim said wholeheartedly. "I was expecting the bloody thing to be dull as a stick: that's why I hit him so hard. I wanted to knock the gun out of his hand."

"Well, it worked. Sort of."

Kim laughed at that, but it was the kind of laugh that hurt. Will disengaged his fingers in order to reach up, and get an arm round his neck, and hold on to him while his shoulders heaved.

"Sorry," Kim said after a while. He'd slid to his knees, leaning over the bed so his head was pillowed on Will's chest, and Will could stroke his hair. "Sorry."

"Nothing to apologise for. We've all been there. I threw up after my first."

"Done that. Twice."

"Well, then."

A moment slid by in silence. That was all right with Will, feeling Kim's warmth and weight. It was a better position than a lot of the ones they could have been in.

"What about the rest? Telford?" he asked.

"Well you may ask. What on earth did you do?"

"Rabbit punch. It's a blow to the back of the neck. They don't let you do it in boxing."

"I should hope not, since he's dead."

"Bugger."

"I wouldn't worry. He had a charge sheet as long as your arm; you saved the state some rope. As for Anton, the chauffeur, he seems to have got away."

"You're joking."

"No. Looks like he woke up, stole one of Waring's cars, and drove off. Not yet traced."

"He must have a hard head. And Waring?"

"Also dead," Kim said, his voice humming in Will's ribs. "When Telford struck him, it caused the wall of the aneurysm to split—I have the verbiage from the doctors. He bled out too, though internally, so at least he was less messy than Johnnie. He lasted about twenty minutes."

"Oh God," Will said. "How is Phoebe?"

"It's a lot for her to cope with."

That seemed to be all he had to say. Will didn't push it.

"We've got rid of the idiots," Kim went on. "Not to be ungracious, I know their arrival saved our bacon, but there is only so much I can take."

"Where in God's name did they spring from?"

"A Saturday spree. They drive around the countryside at random, thrusting themselves on households at ungodly hours and demanding 'drinkie-poos'," Kim said, handling the word as if it were contagious. "I find it deeply galling that I have to be grateful for that. Gratitude also goes to Maisie for turning off the lights at that moment."

"Oh, that was her? Is she all right?"

"Fine. More than fine. She's been a tower of strength for Phoebe."

Will nodded. "What does Phoebe know?"

"Most of it, now. It seems Maisie told her everything when they were sent upstairs."

That reminded Will. "How did they get out? I thought Telford locked them in."

"This is Phoebe's childhood home. She knows how to jimmy her own bedroom lock."

"So the final butcher's bill—"

"Three dead, one gone, you injured. DS is delighted, as you may imagine."

"DS? Your boss?"

"The Private Bureau is here en masse to clean up. Talking of which, I rescued your knife; it's in your bag. And I regret to report that DS wants a personal interview with you, so if I were you, I'd go back to sleep, and stay that way for the next six months."

Will was not inclined to do that. He did stay in bed long enough to eat a sandwich, drink a restorative few cups of beef broth, and have a mug of tea and several biscuits, all brought to him by a wide-eyed maid, and then he got up. He was bored.

His arm hurt a fair bit. He put his jacket over his right arm and managed to turn the empty left sleeve into a sort of makeshift sling, then headed downstairs.

The blood had been cleaned up from the hallway, which was good. Will followed voices, and found several men in the dining room going through piles of paper and ledgers spread out on the long table. One of them looked round. "Who are you?"

"Will Darling."

"Oh, yes." The man straightened, extending his hand, which Will shook. He had a serious sort of face, brown hair going grey, and ink on his fingers. "I'm a William myself—Merton of that ilk. Pleased to meet you. You've done your country a service." He slapped a ledger affectionately, much as one might pat the flank of a horse. "We're going to run what remains of Zodiac up a flagpole with this lot. Have you seen DS yet?"

"No."

"No time like the present. He's in the study. Good luck."

Will headed in that direction and knocked. The door opened, and Will found himself face to face with Kim, who was looking harried. "Will?"

"Ah, the famous Mr. Darling," came a voice from inside. "Our bellicose bookseller. Do come in."

Kim rolled his eyes and let Will in.

The study had been considerably disarranged, not to say ransacked, since Will had seen it last. The safe stood open, as did the filing cabinet, and there were piles of paper on the floor.

The man at the desk was a smooth-looking, handsome chap of Jewish looks, extremely dark of hair and eyes, but sufficiently into middle age that Will wasn't convinced the jet black hair was entirely due to nature. He wore natty horn-rimmed spectacles and a wearily sardonic expression.

"Sit down, both of you," he said. "You're Secretan's Darling, yes?"

That was a hell of a start to a conversation. "I'm Will Darling, yes."

"Delighted." The man smiled, though not in a reassuring way. "You may call me DS if you have to call me anything. Killed anyone interesting recently?"

"Uh—"

"Let me be frank, Mr. Darling," DS said. "I feel as though I have been clearing up after you for months. There was a smashed head in the North Wessex Downs last November, Price from the War Office to explain away, then Libra's mangled remains though I suppose you can't be blamed for that. Then that fellow off the balcony, which required mops, and now you've broken Tommy Telford's neck to go with Secretan's exsanguination of Sir Alan Cheveley's brother *and* the demise of Lord Waring. Are you two planning to stop leaving a trail of dead? Because I'm not your damned housemaid."

This felt rather harsh to Will. "Waring wasn't our fault. And Zodiac came at us first."

"'They started it' is an excuse that works on playgrounds," DS informed him. "All right, tell me about it."

"Which part?"

"All of it. Start with a shifty character walking into your bookshop last November. Not this one," he added, indicating Kim. "The other one."

It took a while. Will wasn't sure if it helped that DS already knew about him and Kim—it felt at this point as though everyone did, which was a whole pile of peculiarity he didn't have time to think about—but it was something of a relief not to have to watch his words too carefully. He told the truth, and felt Kim listening by him, and waited to find out what would happen.

What happened immediately was that DS steepled his fingers, leaned back in his chair, and said, "What was your rank in the Army, Mr. Darling?"

"Private."

"Really? If I were to classify you, I think I should take a leaf out of the insurance people's book and list you as an Act of God."

"Yes, all *right*," Kim said. "None of this is his fault."

"I'll be the judge of that." DS removed his spectacles, closed the arms, and set them down. "But in fact, I agree it isn't his fault. It's yours."

Kim's face didn't move exactly, but it set. Will said, "That's not fair."

"When I want you to speak, I'll let you know. You've made a damned mess of this, Secretan, and the only reason I'm not hanging you out to dry at this very moment is it would have been a damned mess anyway. I do wish rich men could content themselves with buying yachts or rolling around in heaps of gold, rather than this endless insatiable greed. Avarice, envy, pride: three fatal sparks have set the hearts of all on fire."

Will blinked. Kim said, "Dante," through rather white lips.

DS leaned forward, eyes hard. "You should have told me, Secretan. You should have told me as soon as you realised. That was your *job*. We could have taken Capricorn alive, and his lieutenant with him, got information and leverage instead of this charnel house."

"Leverage? What could you have threatened Waring with? To put him on trial in front of a jury and fill the newspapers with his crimes, and damn his daughter's name? I wasn't going to do that, sir. You may have my resignation when you please."

"You don't resign till I tell you to resign," DS said, and something in his voice went right down Will's spinal cord, making it straighten without his conscious intent. "How precisely did you intend to avoid blemishing his daughter's name?"

"*I* don't know!" Kim snarled. "I was hoping to squeeze him into it somehow."

"Happy with how that turned out?"

"I was overtaken by events. I didn't realise Cheveley was acting alone within Zodiac."

"That's quite understandable: it's hard to spot. After all, I didn't realise you were acting alone within the Bureau."

Kim winced at that, as well he might. DS let the silence spool out for a nasty minute.

"Well," he said finally. "Merton is rolling around in Waring's papers like a pig in—with great enthusiasm. We'll need to go in sideways to clean up the rest of Zodiac, but clean up we will, and if it has to be done under the table, that may yet pay off.

Meanwhile, as a matter of future public record, I think we can agree that Cheveley was embezzling from Lord Waring, having recruited Anton and Telford to assist him, that Waring confided in you, and that you brought your friend here to assist, while not expecting matters to turn as violent as they did. That should explain everything to the coroner's jury, which will be tomorrow."

"That's quick."

"I want it quick," DS said. "Go to the inquest, stick to the story. If the jury sees Cheveley as a thief trying to get away with his crimes, I dare say you'll leave without a stain on your character, or at least none that weren't already there. Then both of you go home and stay out of trouble, if that's possible."

"Thank you, sir," Will said.

"Go away. Oh, and Secretan?"

"Sir?"

DS glanced over his spectacles. "I'll have that resignation now. You can tidy up your own mess in future. Clear?"

Kim looked as if he'd been struck. Will said, "Crystal," and dragged him out of there.

And after that, they had to speak to Phoebe.

They went outside in silence, into the gardens where they could be sure of avoiding eavesdroppers. Phoebe's face was calm and remote but her eyes were red and she wore no powder or paint. Her face looked raw, almost ghostly, without the usual colour. Maisie stood protectively by her. Will hurt that Maisie felt protective; he didn't want to know how Kim felt about that.

He was white-faced, tense with misery. Neither he nor Phoebe looked inclined to start talking, which was some sort of record, but someone had to, so Will did.

"Phoebe," he said. "I'm so sorry. I truly am."

"You aren't, though," she said. "How could you be? Daddy tried to—to hurt you, all of you. My father."

"It's not your fault. You didn't know."

"I should have."

Maisie slipped an arm round her waist. Phoebe clutched her hand. Will wished he had a response to offer, but he didn't.

"I should have known, and I could have," Phoebe went on after a moment. "I could have expected this, if someone—if *you*, Kim, had told me the truth. I could have prepared, not lived in a fool's paradise where I thought he cared a little for me. I brought Maisie into danger because I didn't know. Because you didn't tell me."

"No," Kim said. "I didn't know how."

That was all he said, and perhaps it was all there was to say. Maisie met Will's eyes in a silent, urgent appeal: *What do we do?* He wished he had an answer.

They stood another moment in the bleak February afternoon, then Phoebe took the ring off her finger and held it out.

Kim took it back without comment. "What will you do?"

"It depends on Daddy's will. I dare say there will be things to sort out, lawyers to talk to. Mr. Merton said I should get a lawyer to help with all that. He advised me not to use Daddy's in case he was involved with—with Zodiac."

"I could find you—"

"I called Harry Mitra," Phoebe said over him. "He's on his way down now."

"Harry's a good man," Kim said. "He'll look out for your interests. Good. Good."

"We'll get it all sorted out, the inquest and the—the funeral and so on." She glanced down at Maisie. "And then, as soon as we can, we're going to Paris."

"Good," Kim said again. "If you need anything, any help—"

"I'll do it myself," Phoebe said.

And that was it. She and Maisie walked away. Kim stood unmoving, lips pressed together. Will extended a hand to his arm, and felt the fierce tension of the muscles under it. He put his hand on Kim's back, a careful touch as to a hurt dog that might bite, and Kim folded forward on to him and wept.

TWENTY

The three-part coroner's inquest the next day was about as much fun as Will expected. The Cheveley family attended, dressed in black that they presumably had lying around from the previous brother's death. Lady Waring, who Kim and Will had made strong efforts to avoid, was also in black; Phoebe wore a dove-grey dress and a black shawl. Kim had only the suit he'd driven down in, but he presented himself without any touches of colour and a suitably serious demeanour.

He unblushingly asserted that Lord Waring had told him Cheveley was stealing, leading to the late-night confrontation. Bubby Fanshawe and friends testified with great enthusiasm that Cheveley had been the aggressor, and that Kim had only attacked him in defence of another guest who he'd shot, and done his best to save him afterwards. Adela Moran recounted the events in the hall with suitable dramatic flourishes. Will watched Phoebe's face and thought that probably that friendship was over, but the jury seemed impressed.

Will kept his own testimony brief. It helped that Kim had sent urgently to London for his medals, which he wore pinned to his suit, and that the coroner, presumably primed, asked about his war record; it didn't hurt that he had his arm in a sling and his broken hand well wrapped up. A policeman from London gave details of Telford's character and career; several Bright Young People had seen Will fighting him for the shotgun; and while the medical expert was clear one of Will's blows had detached Telford's brainstem, he seemed to believe it might have happened by accident.

After a very long day, the coroner's jury found Lord Waring's death criminally attributable to Telford, and Telford's to Will in self defence. John Cheveley's demise was recorded as death by misadventure, and the jury asked to place on record their admiration for Lord Arthur's efforts to prevent further tragedy.

They filed out of the building into watery late afternoon sunshine. Phoebe and Maisie left with Lady Waring, without waiting for anyone. Johnnie Cheveley's mother walked up to Kim, looked him up and down, and slapped him full in the face. Kim rocked back on his heels, but didn't otherwise react.

Her surviving son hurried her away, making soothing noises. Will came up to Kim's shoulder, in case anyone who wasn't a bereaved old lady tried to have a go.

"All right?"

"Not really."

"Shall we get out of here?"

"Let's."

Kim had brought the Daimler to the inquest, with their luggage in the boot. That was possibly a hubristic way of going on since either or both of them could have been committed for trial, but it looked like they'd got away with it.

The motor purred along the country lanes, heading for London. It felt like a bloody long time since they'd come this way.

At last Will said, "Want to talk?"

"There's not a great deal to say."

"There's a fair bit. You've lost your job over this."

"My job, my fiancée, another chunk of my reputation. What a lovely week-end in the country."

"The jury commended you."

"The jury had the wool comprehensively pulled over its eyes, and I assure you that what my peers will recall of this is me murdering Johnnie Cheveley. Not some supposed act of heroism."

"Sod your peers. You saved my life. Saved me, cracked Zodiac wide open, stopped Maisie getting hurt—"

"But not Phoebe."

"That wasn't down to you," Will said. "Never was. What her old man did is his fault."

"But failing to speak to her was mine. You were right all along and the damned thing is, I knew it. Stupid, stupid. I couldn't bring myself to hurt her to her face, so I didn't, and thus hurt her far more."

"It wasn't the worst decision I've ever seen."

"Really?" Kim sounded sceptical.

"Well, I saw some incredibly bad ones in Flanders. Mostly decisions made when people had spent a lot too long with far more on their plates than anyone could handle, and they were terrified but afraid to tell anyone they were terrified, and the consequences were too big and awful to think about. You don't get good decisions that way."

"Very true. My only way out of that situation was to tell DS what was going on, and I couldn't bring myself to do that. Which is a magnificent irony, because none of the consequences I feared would have arisen, thanks to the aneurysm. If we'd known the bastard had six months to live, a trial wouldn't have been considered. If Waring had been open about his condition, Cheveley wouldn't have played his damn fool game. If, if, if."

"DS wasn't fair, if you ask me."

"I don't know. He doesn't like being kept in the dark, which I knew. And I've drawn rather too much attention to myself what with chopping Cheveley's arm off. You've probably seen the papers."

The front pages had gone to town. "Afraid so."

"What a pig's ear I have made of this," Kim said. "Thank God you had the sense to speak to Maisie, and she to Phoebe, or Christ knows where we'd be. But to put Phoebe through that, to have her learn about her father and lose him in the space of twenty minutes. My poor girl. She won't forgive me."

He sounded despairing. Will said, "Of course she will. Don't talk such rot."

"I assure you, easy forgiveness—from anyone—has not been my experience to date."

"Well, I've forgiven you, which is something considering what an arse you can be. Phoebe knows damn well you didn't tell her because you were afraid, and I doubt she ever thought you were perfect. She's got her own feelings to deal with. Give her time."

Kim was silent for a few moments as the hedges and trees whipped by. "I hope you're right. Christ, this is a business. If I feel this devastated by the end of an entirely meaningless faux engagement, I hope—"

"You hope what?" Will asked, when it became apparent that wasn't going anywhere.

"Nothing. I hope I never have worse."

"You could probably avoid worse by doing better."

Kim gave him a look of disgust. "You sound like my old nanny."

"She's got sense. You should listen to her more often."

Kim took the turn onto the main road to London at unnecessary speed. "And you? Are you all right?"

"Fine. Arm isn't infected, the quack said, and the hand will heal up soon enough. It's mostly a nuisance." It was rather more than a nuisance—the whole limb hurt—but he wasn't proposing to grumble about it now.

"And what about Maisie? She had a nasty experience at the start of all that and very little space to breathe after."

"She seems all right," Will said. "I think it helped that Phoebe needed her—you know, having something to do, keeping busy. And she's pleased with herself for crocking that chauffeur fellow."

"As she should be. An excellent shot."

"I told her, by the way."

"Told her?"

"About us. We had a proper talk, her and me, before it all kicked off."

"Did you. Was that all right?"

"It was fine," Will said. "Better than fine. Being able to talk properly about this stuff, about myself, with her—I needed that. I didn't know how much."

"I realise my limitations, Will, but I've been negotiating these waters for a while now. If you're struggling with your nature—"

"I can look after myself, thanks. The part I'm struggling with is a bit under six foot, and driving too fast."

A rueful grin twitched at Kim's lips, and he eased off the accelerator a touch. "Sorry."

"But," Will went on. "But then the thing was that she knew, and Waring and Cheveley knew, and DS knew, and it felt like everyone but Bubby Fanshawe knew. Like suddenly the whole world knows I'm—" He wasn't sure what to say. *Your boy friend. Fucking you.* Neither one sounded right.

"Ambisexual," Kim said, which didn't sound right either, or real.

"You what?"

"Ambisexual. Inclined to men and ladies alike."

"Oh, is that what Maisie meant? She said ambidextrous."

"That's a different state, probably one with more practical use."

"Speak for yourself," Will said, and won another smile. "Is that a word?"

"I fear so."

Will had never thought of himself as a person they had a word for. Then again, a word meant a thing was usual enough to need a word. He'd definitely want to think more about that. "Hmph. If you ask me, it sounds like a patent tandem."

"Oh, a hideous term. Mind you, there's people at this very moment trying to persuade homosexuals that we want to be called Uranians, as if I didn't have enough bloody stupid names to be getting on with."

"Stick to your guns," Will said. "Anyway, it was a bit odd to have half a dozen people talking about my personal business. But it did make me think about things."

"Such as?"

Maisie had said to talk, and she was right. Will steeled himself. "About you and me. What we want. What we want out of this, out of each other. We don't have to talk about it now, but we need to."

Kim's eyes were intent on the road. "You say you thought. Did you reach conclusions?"

He really didn't make this easy. "That depends on you as much as me. But I'd like there to be something between us. No: there *is* something, but the truth is I don't know what it, you and me, could look like. We're bloody good in bed, and not bad when we're facing guns, but the parts in between are a mess."

"We'd probably be better at those if you were able to trust me."

"I could trust you," Will said. "I truly could. Could you not let me down when I do?"

Kim breathed out. "I could try."

"That's what I want, then. To find out what we're doing, and to do it a bit better. What do you want?"

"I don't know," Kim said. "I don't say that lightly, Will: I have no idea. All my anchors have gone. Phoebe and the Private Bureau have given shape and meaning to my life for years, and I lost them both within an hour. I've got no idea what I'm going to do. And I shan't ask you to fill their place: that would be grossly unfair. I need to reshape my life myself." He swept round a slow-moving car with what seemed to Will insufficient caution. There was a blare of horns behind them. "But I would very much like the new shape, whatever it might be, to have you in it in some way. If you'd care to be there."

Will set his shoulders. "Yes."

"Fair warning: I don't know what that would look like any more than you do."

"You must have some idea. Like you said, you've had a lot more practice than me."

"Not at this, believe me. Not at having a lover."

The word gave Will an odd feeling, all at once overly intimate, and peculiarly transgressive, and right. Lover. Kim's lover. If he could make love to Kim now, if they could hold each other and rely on physical pleasure to bridge the gaps—

If he could, he'd be doing exactly that to avoid any more of this damn conversation, because it would be a lot easier and less frightening.

"Kim. Listen. Do you—" he began, and stalled there.

Kim's tongue darted out, moistening his lips. "Something you want to know?"

"Yes."

"But aren't asking. Should I take a guess?" He flicked over a glance. "I think—I flatter myself—that you want to know if I care for you. No: you must know that I do, so what you want is for me to say so, and I do, Will. I care for you far more than makes me feel safe. I want you, but you're well aware of that. I feel at peace with you, and I don't often feel at peace. And without excusing the trouble I have given you, it brings me to my knees that you're strong enough to bear it. I wish I were worth you, Will."

"Kim—"

"I'd like to be," Kim said. "I don't know if I can be, though you sometimes make me believe it possible. But I'll do my best to find out, if you're willing to give me the chance."

"We can just see how it goes," Will said, through a dry mouth. "Work it out along the way."

"You are ever practical. And talking of practicality, it does occur to me you could use some assistance in the shop while your arm is out of commission. Boxes and shelving and suchlike."

That thought had occurred forcibly to him. "I was thinking of getting someone in for a bit."

"Well, I'm unemployed." Kim had his eyes fixed on the road again. "I arrive on time and don't drink on the job. And I doubt any of the letters or telephone calls I'm likely to receive at the flat in the next days will be pleasant, so I'd rather like an excuse to be elsewhere."

Will suspected that was one hell of an understatement, and it made his chest hurt. "I've got space. Hole up as long as you like."

"I'll bring the whisky. For after hours, naturally."

"You owe me a bottle."

"I owe you more than that," Kim said softly. "A great deal more. I do know it, Will."

"Make it a really good bottle, and we'll call it a clean slate."

Kim's breath shuddered out. "You have no idea how much I would like a clean slate."

"You've got one now, don't you? All round."

"Hardly clean. Blank, perhaps. Ah, God, I don't know what I'm going to do. I always had a purpose, before, a job that had to be done, one way and another. And now—"

"You've been demobbed," Will said. "I know the feeling. And you want an answer right away, but that won't happen. It takes a while to get your head round, so give it time. Stay with me. Sort out the rare books: I need them priced up properly. And we can talk about whatever you want, important things or football—"

"No."

"—and you can have a few days with nobody expecting anything from you. Except getting the rare books right. I expect that."

"Low standards, that's your trouble."

"My standards are fine," Will said. "You just need to live up to them."

"And we'll see how it goes?"

The road ahead was reasonably clear, no bends or twists or obstructively slow traffic for a while at least. Will put a hand on Kim's leg for the warmth of contact, and met his eyes as he looked round. "We'll see how it goes."

Kim Secretan and Will Darling return in SUBTLE BLOOD.

THE WILL DARLING ADVENTURES

A m/m romance trilogy in the spirit of Golden Age pulp fiction. It's the 1920s and tensions are rising along with hemlines. Soldier-turned-bookseller Will Darling finds himself tangled up in spies and secret formulas, clubs and conspiracies, Bolsheviks, blackmail, and Bright Young Things. And dubious aristocrat Lord Arthur 'Kim' Secretan is right in the middle of it all: enigmatic, unreliable, and utterly irresistible.

Slippery Creatures
The Sugared Game
Subtle Blood

Slippery Creatures
(The Will Darling Adventures #1)

Will Darling came back from the Great War with a few scars, a lot of medals, and no idea what to do next. Inheriting his uncle's chaotic second-hand bookshop is a blessing...until strange visitors start making threats. First a criminal gang, then the War Office, both telling Will to give them the information they want, or else.

Will has no idea what that information is, and nobody to turn to, until Kim Secretan—charming, cultured, oddly attractive—steps in to offer help. As Kim and Will try to find answers and outrun trouble, mutual desire grows along with the danger.

And then Will discovers the truth about Kim. His identity, his past, his real intentions. Enraged and betrayed, Will never wants to see him again.

But Will possesses knowledge that could cost thousands of lives. Enemies are closing in on him from all sides—and Kim is the only man who can help.

"This romance has drama, intrigue, a thoroughly fed-up man who just wants to organise his bloody books, a secret plot, double-crossing, triple-crossing, knife fights, sexy looks of yearning, Noble Resistance to Physical Attraction, and excellent best friends. I could not recommend it more."— Talia Hibbert

Subtle Blood

(The Will Darling Adventures #3)

Will Darling is all right. His business is doing well, and so is his illicit relationship with Kim Secretan—disgraced aristocrat, sacked spy, amateur book-dealer. It's starting to feel like he's got his life under control.

And then a brutal murder in a gentleman's club plunges them back into the shadow world of crime, deception, and politics. Worse, it brings them up against Kim's noble, hostile family, and his upper-class life where Will can never belong.

With old and new enemies against them, and secrets on every side, Will and Kim have to fight for each other harder than ever—or be torn apart for good.

Coming soon…

ABOUT THE AUTHOR

KJ Charles lives in London with her husband, two kids, an out-of-control garden, and a cat with murder management issues.

KJ writes mostly historical romance, mostly queer, sometimes with fantasy or horror in there. She is represented by Courtney Miller-Callihan at Handspun Literary.

For all the KJC news and occasional freebies, get my (infrequent) newsletter at kjcharleswriter.com/newsletter.

Pick up free reads on my website: kjcharleswriter.com

Join my Facebook group, KJ Charles Chat, for book conversation, sneak peeks, and exclusive treats.

facebook.com/kj.charles.9
twitter.com/kj_charles

CPSIA information can be obtained
at www.ICGtesting.com
Printed in the USA
LVHW050553280122
709355LV00018B/2510

9 781912 688180